CW00663912

Children Of The Stars

Children Of The Stars, Volume 1

Houston Lee Andrews Jr

Published by Saint Andrews, 2023.

CHILDREN OF THE STARS

First edition. December 25, 2023.

Copyright © 2023 Houston Lee Andrews Jr.

ISBN: 979-8223664369

Written by Houston Lee Andrews Jr.

Also by Houston Lee Andrews Jr

Children Of The Stars
Children Of The Stars

Watch for more at https://www.facebook.com/cotsbooks.

In loving memory of my parents Houston Lee Sr and Gurtha Delois Andrews.

The Children Of The Stars
Book One: The Journey Begins
Written by Houston Lee Andrews Jr

"THERE ARE THOSE WHO are born whose destiny is written in the stars, and there are those who are the stars of destiny."
*   - Notsuoh, Son of Thoth, Keeper of the Mysteries and Guardian of the Halls of Amenti.*

Prologue

NIBIRU

Long ago, on a world called Nibiru, before the existence of mankind, a race of giants known as the Anunnaki searched for gold to save their dying world.

The king of Nibiru, Anu, had two sons, Enki and Enlil. One day, the wise men of Nibiru informed the king that their planet was headed towards destruction due to damage caused by unknown solar forces, namely the damaged atmosphere.

In response, the king ordered Nibiru's greatest savants and wise men to use their vast wisdom to find a solution and repair the planet's rapidly deteriorating atmosphere.

After many decades of experimentation, the savants finally informed the king that the planet's atmosphere could only be saved by using the precious element known as gold, transforming it into a vaporous dust cloud to mend the damaged hole in the sky.

Thus, by divine providence, before the first celestial cycle, Lord Enki and his half-brother Enlil, sons of Anu and Lord of the Command, were sent to the seventh planet in search of gold. They were tasked with mining the precious resource to restore the atmosphere and save their dying world.

However, as ages passed, the laborious task of mining the gold from deep within the Earth's core became too challenging. The Annunaki laborers rebelled against Enki and Enlil, refusing to work any longer.

To quell the uprising, it was decided that Enki would create a primitive worker using the indigenous beings they had encountered in the Apsu (South Africa). The Annunaki infused these beings with their own life essence or DNA, mixing it with their own genetic material.

And thus, it was the fate that man was created to serve the Annunaki as gods.

Initially, the primitive workers created by the Annunaki were hermaphrodites and unable to reproduce. To address this, Anunnaki females were chosen as surrogates. However, they soon grew weary of carrying the burden of bearing the primitive workers in their wombs.

In his wisdom, Enki ordered the Annunaki to create a female counterpart for the workers, allowing them to procreate. As a result, the children of men multiplied, leading to the development of various civilizations, each with their own gods whom they worshipped and served.

It came to pass that I, Lord Thoth of Udal, was chosen among the gods to keep a record and teach human beings to worship the Annunaki as gods. The children of men grew in knowledge and understanding. For those who proved themselves worthy, I, Lord Thoth, the Keeper of the Mysteries, initiated the twelve humans chosen to be my high priests into the secrets and knowledge of the gods.

Under my guidance, these twelve priests taught the children of men various skills such as agriculture, husbandry, weaving, marriage, and worshiping the gods. As time passed, the priesthood grew in power, ruling over the races of men and guarding their esoteric knowledge for a select few.

Through generations, the priests of Thoth passed down their occult knowledge to their descendants, preserving their sacred bloodlines and the secrets of the gods. For it was written: "The firstborn among them shall be chosen to safeguard the secret knowledge of the gods. And so it was written that the priest would safeguard this knowledge until the time of the new heaven and the new earth, even until the end of the age.

However, the progress of mankind did not please all of the Anunnaki gods. One in particular, Lord Enlil, grew weary of the existence of the children of men. Enlil considered the creation of human beings to be a violation of divine order, believing that the Annunaki had interfered with the natural evolution of primitive beings. In his eyes, man was an abomination that needed to be destroyed and wiped from the Earth.

Enraged by his discontent, Lord Enlil decreed a great deluge upon the surface of the Earth, intending to eradicate mankind once and for all. He commanded all the gods to vow to uphold his decree. However, Enki, in his cunning, deceived his brother Enlil and saved a remnant of the children of men from the flood by instructing them on how to build an ark that would preserve them.

Upon discovering Enki's betrayal, Enlil was overcome with anger and confronted his deceitful brother. A great and terrible war ensued between the two brothers and all the Anunnaki gods, spanning across the land, sea, sky, and even the heavens above the Earth.

Many gods perished in the fierce battles, while others were forced to flee the Earth, vowing never to return.

In the heat of his fury, Enlil unleashed the full force of his terror upon the earth, bringing death and destruction to Eden.

The aftermath of his wrath gave rise to an evil wind that drove the remaining gods back into the heavens. Alongside them, many of Earth's intelligent races and creatures were forced deep into the inner Earth, where they have remained hidden to this day.

After the war of the gods drew to a close, a new chapter unfolded amidst the chaos. The priests of Enlil descended upon the earth, forging a dark brotherhood known as the Shadow

Priests of Enlil, or perhaps more infamously, the Brotherhood of Darkness. This sinister order derived their power from the darkness that dwelled within the hearts of men and the unparalleled animosity Enlil bore towards humanity.

These malevolent priests propagated all sorts of wickedness and blasphemy among the children of men. They taught them to hate, steal, covet, lie, kill, and make war, plunging the world into a deeper abyss of depravity.

However, Enlil's reign of malevolence met its ultimate demise at the hands of his own brother, Lord Enki, and his loyal followers. In a climactic battle, Enlil was overthrown and imprisoned within the hallowed Halls of Amenti, where he remains tormented, yearning for the day he can exact his revenge.

Yet, within the annals of prophecy, it is foretold that a time will come when the Brotherhood of Darkness shall rise again, eagerly embracing their master's wicked plan to annihilate mankind once and for all.

"The Holy Scrolls of Sion"
-Lord Thoth

Chapter One

THE JOURNEY BEGINS
  White Plains, New York

Seth Strange sat silently in his room, gazing out of his bedroom window at the stars through his trusty telescope, a nightly ritual he cherished. The vastness of the night sky and the wonders held within it were his greatest fascination and source of joy.

As he twirled his fingers through his unruly red hair, Seth's gaze fixated on Saturn, the majestic planet adorned with its iconic rings. He recalled his mother once mentioning how Saturn ruled his natal chart, hinting that it could symbolize misfortune depending on the choices he made in life, in relation to other celestial aspects.

Unfortunately, Seth had experienced a series of unfortunate events in recent years, until this upcoming trip to Egypt came into the picture, offering a glimmer of hope.

Just like his mother, Seth fervently believed in astrology, finding the craft both captivating and remarkably accurate most of the time.

"I can't help but believe that there is life beyond our world, somewhere out there in this vast universe," he murmured to himself. "I wonder if they can catch a glimpse of me as I gaze up at them."

Yet, with the naked eye, Seth also beheld other celestial wonders. The constellation of Orion, with its magnificent bow and renowned belt of stars resembling the pyramids of Giza, adorned the night sky. And if he shifted his gaze just a few degrees, he could witness the grandiose horns of Taurus looming over the darkness.

Seth reluctantly tore his gaze away from the mesmerizing view through the telescope and checked his alarm clock. It read 3:30 am, and the realization hit him that he needed to start preparing for whatever lay ahead.

"I better get ready," Seth muttered to himself, feeling that going back to sleep was futile at this point. The recurring dream he had been experiencing surfaced in his mind once more, causing him to question its significance.

"It's strange how I keep having the same dream," he pondered aloud. "I wonder if that's normal?"

Curiosity prompted Seth to consider searching for answers on the matter. He reached for his trusty iPad, conveniently located on the dresser next to his bed. With Star Wars-themed decor adorning his room—from bed sheets to window curtains and even underwear—his deep fascination with the franchise was evident. Seth's passionate nature extended to many areas of interest, and Star Wars held a prominent place in his heart.

Ever since he was a young child, Seth had accompanied his father to Star Wars and UFO conventions, immersing himself in the vibrant universes of these beloved franchises. The conventions offered him a sense of belonging and excitement that fueled his dedication to all things science fiction.

Although the fatigue from the upcoming journey weighed on him, Seth deemed it wiser to remain awake. The last thing he wanted was to oversleep and risk missing out on what lay ahead. With determination in his eyes, he prepared himself for the journey that awaited him.

"I better get ready and pack the rest of my gear. Tomorrow is going to be so Sweet!" He said to himself. His ruddy face was covered from ear to ear with the biggest smile. He looked himself square in the mirror again and smiled even bigger!

Seth had every reason to smile. He had just won a place at this year's Young Archeologist Society International Summer Expedition. The trip of a lifetime to his most favorite place. He was going to Egypt, the Land of the Pharaohs.

Not to mention the Y.A.S is the top of the food chain for aspiring archeologists, the chance of a lifetime and an international honor.

Seth felt a sense of understandable pride knowing he had made the cut. He knew he deserved to go. He was good, and he knew his stuff.

"I am going to Egypt as the newest member of the Royal and Ancient Order of Young Archeologist Society". He thought to himself, He shook his fist in the air and grinned ear to ear. Seth couldn't remember a time when he was this excited about anything.

"I better get packed!" He said to himself.

Seth walked over to his dresser and put on his classic red wireless Beats headphones and cranked the volume all the way up and began cleaning up his room and packing for his trip.

After about 30 minutes of listening to his favorite playlist of hard head banging metal. Seth decided to take off the headset and looked around his room.

He turned his whole body around in every direction, nearly spinning on his toes again and again.

He stopped and looked around his room once more.

" So what am I forgetting? I don't want to forget anything I wanna bring!" He said quietly to himself.

"I know what it is... my game boy! I just had it a minute ago." He thought to himself.

Seth hastily tosses around a small stack of clothes he had just finished folding a few minutes ago.

"What the heck is the deal?" Seth thought to himself then he stood up straight and folded his arms across his chest and took a deep breath. His eyes wandered around the room from floor to desk, the dresser, then over to his bookcase and back to his bed.

His eyes were drawn across the bed to his pillow. Seth thought for a moment then flipped the pillow over it. "No way! How did it get over there?"

Seth decided he better scan through the list he made and check off each item. After he finished Seth sat down on the end of his bed and started to imagine the pyramids and Egypt, but suddenly he was startled by his now blaring radio alarm clock blasting "Master of the puppets" by his favorite band Metallica.

"Man that's totally too loud right now" Seth chuckled to himself and quickly reached over to turn the alarm off.

"Killer song though! It totally never gets old!" He thought to himself.

"Anyway, one more thing on my list." He said. He could be extremely ADHD and had a tendency to forget things unless he wrote them down.

Seth's heart skipped a beat as he picked up a small black velvet box from his computer desk. Opening it, he revealed a delicate gold necklace adorned with a silver and gold Ankh—the precious gift his mother had bestowed upon him before embarking on a tragic expedition that claimed her life. The memories flooded his mind, and he couldn't help but feel a pang of longing. "Mom, I miss you so much," he whispered, his voice filled with a mixture of sorrow and affection. Seth gently clasped the necklace, feeling its weight in his palm, before carefully placing it around his neck. As it settled against his skin, a warm sensation enveloped him, providing a sense of comfort and connection.

"Now I'm ready to go," Seth declared, determined to embark on this journey with his mother's spirit close to his heart. However, the deep longing for her presence lingered as he thought solemnly, "I wish mom was here to see me finally go to Egypt." Throughout his childhood, she had often spoken of their shared dream to explore Egypt together when he was older. With fond memories of his mother, a captivating woman who possessed expertise in archaeology and the occult, Seth couldn't help but reflect on the void her absence had created in his life.

In the midst of his contemplation, a double knock on his bedroom door disrupted his thoughts—it was his father. Opening the door but not fully entering, his father spoke in a hushed tone, "Are you up, son? You have to be at the airport by 5:30. Remember I told you about getting to the airport two hours early for international flights." Seth noticed a hint of confusion on his father's face, yet he couldn't hide the genuine happiness radiating from within him.

"Dad, I'm up! What are you talking about?" Seth responded, a mix of concern and curiosity in his voice. He recognized the subtle signs of his father's inebriation, a sight that sadly had become all too familiar to him.

Despite the hardships their family had faced, Seth acknowledged that his father had been a caring and supportive figure for the majority of his life. However, ever since his father's unfortunate dismissal from the university, things had taken a downturn. It was a result of his father's publication on the theory of ancient aliens as the creators of humanity—a concept met with ridicule and scorn from the academic and scientific communities, as well as the media. Even friends and family had joined in on the laughter directed at his father's controversial beliefs.

Observing his father's bloodshot blue eyes as he glanced around the room, Seth found himself feeling a mixture of sympathy and frustration. It was not unfamiliar for his father to stumble home after a night of drinking, and the signs were apparent that he had been at the bar across the street. Despite this, Seth held onto the positive aspects of their situation, believing in his father's inherent goodness. Whenever questioned about his father's drinking problem by family and friends, Seth would defend him, insisting, "At least he doesn't drink and drive!"

Deep down, Seth was empathetic towards his father's struggles, recognizing the impact the loss of his professional reputation had on his self-esteem and well-being. Seth's own determination to prove his father's theories and restore his name grew stronger with each passing day. He felt a responsibility to honor his father's legacy and vindicate him in the eyes of the world. In his heart, Seth believed that one day he would unveil the evidence his father had tirelessly sought, leading to the recognition and respect his father deserved.

As Seth's laughter gradually subsided, he couldn't help but express his fondness for his father. Despite the circumstances, he found humor in their situation. Seth's voice, although still filled with laughter, softened slightly as he spoke, conveying a genuine warmth. "You know what I love about you, Dad?" he began, his amusement evident but not as boisterous as before.

Curiously, Seth's father leaned against the doorway to steady himself, clearly affected by his earlier indulgence in alcohol. He looked at Seth, awaiting his response, a hint of a smile on his face.

"No matter how wasted you get," Seth continued, trying to suppress his giggles, "you're always up early, and you're never late for work!" The laughter resurfaced, and both father and son shared another moment of joviality, finding solace in the bond they shared.

Amidst the lightheartedness, Seth's father suddenly took hold of his son's shoulders, guiding him to face him directly. It was a gesture filled with love, tinged with an underlying seriousness. Seth could feel his father's grip, the weight of his words settling upon them both. "Look, son," his father began, his voice filled with a mix of vulnerability and sincerity, "I know I haven't been fully present since your mother passed away, but I want you to know that I love you, and I would do anything in the world for you."

Seth's eyes sparkled with affection and understanding as he replied, "All around the world and back, right, Dad?" Their gazes locked, a shared acknowledgment passing between them. In that moment, Seth's father enveloped him in a massive, joyous bear hug. The strength of the embrace overwhelmed Seth, feeling as if he were being embraced by a grizzly bear intoxicated with sweetness and warmth.

"I love you too," Seth managed to express, his words slightly muffled by the tightness of the hug. As Seth's ribs pressed against his father's giant frame, he realized the depth of his father's affection and the unwavering love that remained between them, even in the face of adversity.

"Dad you're squeezing the air out of me" Seth's dad realized he was probably holding the boy too tightly, so he quickly let him go and stood back trying not to lose his balance once again.

He was able to steady himself with a little help from Seth, and they both began to laugh again

"Looking at the ship shape, I'm impressed." Said Seth's father, as he finally noticed Seth's fully packed suitcases, neatly made bed, and best of all the fully dressed teenager who normally he had to shake several times in the mornings in order to get him out of bed.

"Looking good son!" He smiled at the boy approvingly. "It looks like we have a little extra time, so why don't let your dear old dad make you some bacon and eggs and your favorite blueberry pancakes." He said.

"Sweet!" Seth Said. His father leaned forward and gave him a soft kiss on the forehead.

"I'm really proud of you son." I just wish your mother could be here to see you!

Seth held back his tears. He hugged his dad tightly then took a few steps back.

" I can't help but worry that some people or even the other children will pick on you because of my last book. "Honestly, I'm still surprised they picked you." His dad said.

"Dad, listen, you don't have to say anything. I know you're right. I believe in your theory and not just because you're my dad either. History has been hijacked. And the masses are being spoon fed one lie after another." Seth said.

"Son, I'm glad you understand these things but I just want you to do well. I know you and I don't want you getting into any fights because of me and getting kicked out of the Y.A.S."

"Don't worry dad, I'll be on my best behavior I promise". He winked and smiled, and they both laughed out loud which was the way they laughed in Seth's family.

"Keep it down, you're gonna wake the neighbors, you know that old bag next door already hates me !" His dad said with a cheeky grin.

AS SETH MADE HIS WAY downstairs to the kitchen, his dad instructed him to gather his belongings and join him for some last-minute tips before the Uber driver arrived to take him to the airport. Seth gave his father a quick smile before glancing around his room one last time. He reached out and turned off the light, closing the door behind him as he headed downstairs.

CHAPTER TWO

O child of Adam! Listen unto the words of the Teacher: "I and the Father are one." "Suffer little children to come unto me, for of such is the Kingdom of Heaven."

Elle Diva, had never ventured beyond the borders of her beloved country until today. Tel Aviv, her all-Jewish neighborhood, had always been her comfort zone. Elle, the fifth child of a wealthy Jewish family, was actually born in Chicago, but her parents had repatriated to Israel shortly after her birth. Her father, having sold his stake in AI, chose to retire and devote his time to studying Kabbalah.

As she found herself at Ben Gurion International Airport in Tel Aviv, Elle couldn't contain her excitement. Leaving her seemingly monotonous surroundings behind, she thought to herself, "Finally, I'm getting away from this boring place."

Elle possessed a unique personality that stood out from her seemingly perfect family, particularly in contrast to her overbearing mother-in-law. Even as a young girl, Elle had always felt different and never quite perfect, despite her love for her family. She viewed them as religious fanatics and empathized with them, feeling a sense of pity. However, Elle was determined not to end up like them.

The concept of a God in the sky with rules to abide by amused Elle, and she questioned the rationale behind such a belief. "How could they possibly believe there is a God up in the sky, playing such a childish game?" she often pondered to herself. Critically observing her family, she couldn't help but refer to them as sheep, a sentiment she muttered under her breath.

As another announcement resonated through the airport, Elle glanced at her watch. Time seemed to be ticking away rapidly, further fueling her anticipation of the journey ahead. Amidst the bustling environment, Elle's mother's voice pierced through the noise, laden with emotion. "You are a young lady now. One day, you will have children of your own, and I hope they don't treat you like you treat me!" Her mother's tears flowed, but the display of vulnerability was short-lived as her stepmother swiftly transitioned into a smile.

Elle couldn't help but smirk at her mother's words, implying a sense of irony and skepticism. Her thoughts were interrupted by a female voice over the intercom, announcing the final call for flight 1219 to Cairo. It was time for Elle to board. She exchanged big smiles and waves with her family, acknowledging the mixed emotions within her. She knew she would miss them.

Gathering her composure, Elle turned around, picked up her carry-on bag, and began her descent down the boarding ramp. Stepping onto the plane, she located her seat and stored her belongings overhead. With a definitive sense of liberation, she settled into her seat by the window, fastening her seat belt. As she reclined her head against the cushioned headrest, a smile painted across her face. "Free at last," she uttered, relishing the newfound sense of independence.

Chapter Three

Spiritus ubi vult spiral: et vocem ejus audis, sed nescis unde veniat, aut quo vadat: sic est omnis,
qui natus est ex spiritu.
(John iii, 8)

CAIRO, EGYPT

Zamalek, an enchanting upper-middle-class neighborhood in the sprawling city of Cairo, captivates visitors and residents alike. Its streets are teeming with vibrant open-air markets and shops, offering an assortment of spices, fragrant teas, and a plethora of meats, fish, and poultry prepared in various delectable ways. The market is a feast for the senses, boasting countless options ranging from local treasures to exotic delights. Transactions in this bustling hub occur through diverse means, dependent on the merchant or the merchandise being acquired.

Asim, a native of Zamalek, began his day like any other morning he could remember. Alongside his father, he embarked on a walk to the mosque for their routine morning prayers. These moments spent with his father held a special place in Asim's heart. Sometimes, Asim's father would regale him with stories about his grandfather, a figure of great renown in Cairo, known as an accomplished alchemist, magician, and custodian of local wisdom. Growing up, Asim had heard intriguing rumors surrounding his grandfather's magical abilities: transmuting lead into gold, healing the sick, and even the purported power to summon the Jinn.

As they continued their stroll, a profoundly stirring voice reverberated throughout the air, originating from the minaret's loudspeakers. Asim couldn't help but feel a chill traverse his spine, causing the hairs on the back of his neck to stand upright; it was the call to prayer. أَشْهَدُ أَنْ لَا إِلَهَ إِلَّا اللهُ وَأَشْهَدُ أَنَّ مُحَمَّدًا رَسُولُ اللَّهِ

"Come along, son. Being late for morning prayers is a sin... Hurry up now," Asim's father admonished sternly.

"I'm sorry, I was lost in thoughts of Grandpa," Asim replied, his mind dwelling on memories and tales of his esteemed grandfather.

Amidst the sacred ambiance of the mosque, Asim's father turned to him with an expression of pride etched across his face. "You know, I am very proud of you, and your grandfather was too," he conveyed warmly, acknowledging the significance of their family lineage.

Asim's smile broadened at his father's words, though a touch of longing colored his expression. "I would have liked to know him," Asim admitted, his gaze momentarily drifting downward.

His father mirrored his smile, recognizing the unspoken desire. Adjusting his pace, he matched Asim's stride with a quiet understanding. The conclusion of the call to prayer coincided with their arrival at the mosque's steps, where they embarked together into the sacred sanctuary, a united front of familial devotion.

Due to their slight tardiness, the mosque was already brimming with congregants. Navigating through the crowd, they settled into an unoccupied space at the farthest corner of the back row. Respecting tradition, they removed their shoes in perfect synchrony before setting foot on the intricately woven prayer mats. Side by side, father and son embarked on their prayers.

Waves of haunting chants and melodic worship permeated the mosque, enveloping its every nook and cranny with an ethereal beauty. As Asim began his prayer, a pang of guilt crept into his heart, for his mind continued to wander towards thoughts of his imminent departure for the Y.A.S (Youth Archaeological Society) program. Aware of the sinfulness in allowing distractions during prayer, Asim sought to refocus his thoughts on his devotions, fervently beseeching Allah's forgiveness. as Asim's musings transformed into a riddle within the depths of his consciousness.

Chapter Four

" W*hat animal is it that in the morning goes on four feet, at noon on two feet, and in the evening on three feet?"*

FLIGHT 233 UNITED AIRLINES

AS EMANUEL LAID ON his first-class seat, contemplating the absence of the promised chocolates, his mind wandered to thoughts of his parents. They too had made a promise, one that seemed distant now. A sense of loneliness gnawed at him, amplifying the feeling of being alone on his thirteenth birthday. The plane, although not crowded, lacked the warmth and familiar faces that he was accustomed to.

Recollections of his grandparents' wisdom flitted through Emanuel's mind. They had warned him about the propensity of flight attendants to dislike passengers who incessantly pressed the call button. He pondered the consequences of such an action, replaying images from TV shows where unruly passengers were swiftly removed from planes. The thought of Americans instilled a peculiar fear within him, even greater than the fear of his own country's drug lords.

Realizing the potential repercussions, Emanuel decided against pressing the call button to summon the flight attendant. He knew it was not a wise course of action, but his desire for the promised chocolates remained strong. With determination, he extended his left hand and gently pressed the overhead button, subtly beckoning for the attendant's attention.

Emmanuel's emotions, akin to a sign displayed in a shop window, reflected his privileged upbringing in Mexico. Being the son of a Nobel Prize winner, his status as a minor celebrity among his peers and teachers at Enron Academy, a prestigious private school in Mexico City, had made him somewhat spoiled. Each birthday held a special significance for Emmanuel, a day filled with joyous gatherings, lively music, and the delectable aromas of Mexican cuisine. The backyard of their home became a vibrant space where friends and family gathered to celebrate, indulging in fajitas, chicken rice and beans, and the delightful tamales lovingly crafted by his grandmother.

Yet, in this moment, Emmanuel found himself yearning for the familiarity and love that those celebrations brought. The distance from his loved ones and the unfulfilled promise of the flight attendant's chocolates emphasized his present feelings of isolation.

As he patiently waited for her arrival, Emmanuel's mind ventured into the possibilities that lay beyond the confines of the airplane, intertwining his longing for a birthday celebration with the uncertainties of the journey ahead.

I'm sorry to hear about Emmanuel's tragic loss and the difficult circumstances he found himself in. The sudden turn of events, with his parents being taken hostage and eventually found deceased, had left a profound impact on his young life. Sent to live with his grandparents, he carried the weight of grief and abandonment on his shoulders.

Despite his daydreaming, the reality of his situation returned abruptly as Emmanuel felt the presence of someone approaching him. Looking up, he was met with the kind and concerned face of Trina, an attractive African American flight attendant. Her sudden appearance momentarily startled him, but her warm smile and genuine concern brought a sense of comfort.

Introducing herself and inquiring about his well-being, Trina's compassionate demeanor reached out to Emmanuel. Her pretty brown eyes reminded him of his mother, evoking a bittersweet sentiment within him. Emmanuel, with a heavy Spanish accent, expressed his longing for the promised chocolates and questioned whether she had forgotten.

Assuaging his worries, Trina reassured him and wished him a happy birthday once again, though her smile appeared somewhat forced. In her earnestness, she reached down and pinched his cheeks tightly, causing him discomfort and turning his face bright red. Despite the pain, Emmanuel mustered the courage to voice his discomfort, politely informing her that he was being hurt.

Trina's expression changed, reflecting surprise and remorse for causing unintended harm.

"Muchas gracias! Señorita!"

She smiled politely and headed towards the galley.

In spite of the painful assault on his cheeks, Emanuel decided that she was indeed a lovely lady. Even though he missed his parents, and had never been anywhere on his own, he felt good, also happy, but more importantly, he couldn't wait to eat his chocolate ice cream.

Chapter Five

"O people of the earth, men and women born and made of the elements, but with the spirit of the Divine within you, rise from your sleep of ignorance! ..."

DELTA AIRLINES FLIGHT 2466

SETH STRANGE FOUND himself seated in the back row of JFK Terminal 4, gate 23, surrounded by uncomfortably uniform seats. Fully absorbed in his music, turned up to maximum volume, Seth unintentionally irritated the middle-aged man in close proximity. This man, engrossed in a weighty tome, provoked Seth's bemusement—after all, who reads books anymore?

Unsympathetic to the man's irritation, Seth made use of just one earpiece to ensure he could hear his boarding call amidst the blaring music. This, in turn, amplified the discomfort for the technologically-challenged individual engrossed in his book, prompting him to relocate to the opposite side of the boarding area, seeking relief from Seth's audio intrusion.

Perplexed by the mandated two-hour early arrival at the airport, Seth failed to comprehend its necessity. Unwilling to endure idle waiting, he occupied himself by engaging in text conversations with his fellow geeks while heartily consuming an overpriced double cheeseburger and fries from the airport's Burger King establishment.

Adding his opinion to an ongoing virtual debate among friends regarding the quality of fast food establishments, Seth confidently declared Burger King as superior, but begrudgingly admitted that McDonald's indisputably offered the best fries. As he relished each bite of his greasy Whopper, he disregarded the ketchup dripping down the sides and staining his white T-shirt. The experience felt novel, as if he were indulging in a Whopper for the first time, free from his father's dire warnings about the health risks associated with meat and fast food.

Seth regarded his father's sporadic rants as indications of his genius, despite their apparent lack of direction or purpose. These tirades may have seemed pointless, but to Seth, they reflected the depth of his father's intellect and convictions.

With a glance at his watch, Seth anticipated the imminent boarding call. Rising from his seat and collecting his belongings, he was abruptly interrupted by the announcement of "Flight 2466..."

As Seth gathered his belongings, he couldn't help but overhear the lively conversation between two flight attendants near the galley as they readied the first-class cabin for takeoff. Engrossed in their gossip, they captivated Seth's attention.

The flight service manager, a slightly chubby African American named Dwayne, shared a spirited encounter with someone who had underestimated him. He proudly declared, "Girl, let me tell you, I wasn't trying to hear any of it. I told that poor excuse for a man he was messing with the wrong queen!"

Li, a petite Asian flight attendant, prepared a fresh pot of instant coffee for the first-class passengers while expressing her admiration. Reacting to Dwayne's audacity, she exclaimed, "Oh no you didn't, Dwayne! You do not play!"

Amidst their banter, Dwayne responded with a quiet laugh, snapping his fingers back and forth over his head. "Can and will and did, Ms. Thang!"

Li eagerly anticipated hearing the details of the encounter. "I know that's right, girlfriend. He must have lost his mind. I can't wait to hear the rest of this one."

Aware of their responsibilities, Dwayne signaled his intention to provide Li with the full account after making an announcement. Taking the microphone, he addressed the passengers, "Ladies and gentlemen, as we prepare for takeoff, please ensure that your seat backs and tray tables are in their full, upright positions. Fasten your seatbelt securely, and stow all carry-on luggage either underneath the seat in front of you or in the overhead bins."

As the flight attendant continued making his announcements, Seth cranked up his headphones to drown him out, like most anyone who has ever been on a flight before.

A few hours and four video game missions later, Seth's eyes started feeling very heavy, and before he knew it, he was fast asleep.

Suddenly, Seth opened his eyes, and he found himself floating in the middle of the ocean. He could almost feel and taste the salt on his lips. His mind raced, and his chest grew tighter and tighter. "Did we crash?" he thought to himself. Whitecap waves were crashing all around him.

Visions of being eaten alive by sharks attacked his mind, and then an even more terrifying thought entered his mind: "I can't swim!"

"Flight Attendants prepare the cabin for arrival, cross-check," At that moment, Seth opened his eyes. It took him a moment to realize that it was only a dream and that he was back on the plane.

"Young man, you are going to have to turn off your device now. We're about to land." Li hated having to tell kids the bad news, in the middle of their good time, but it was part of her job.

Seth, however, was lost in thought. His whole body shivered as he wondered what his dream meant. Seth shook his head, and sat up to loosen his seatbelt, and felt the air around him grow strangely cold, and he suddenly felt like someone was sitting in the empty seat next to him.

Just then, the openly gay flight attendant Dwayne came down the aisle and stopped in front of Seth. "You need to fasten your seatbelt, little man."

Seth gave Dwayne a confused look, and then looked back at the empty seat as if to say, "Do you feel that too?" However, Dwayne didn't react at all, and Seth felt the presence leave - and with it the cold too.

"Did you hear me, little man? I'm gonna need you to fasten your seatbelt."

The passengers attentively followed the instructions, preparing for the flight ahead. Seth settled into his seat, eager to embark on his journey as the cabin crew completed their final preparations.

As Seth settled back into his seat and retightened his seatbelt, he couldn't shake off the strange experience he had just encountered. Glancing once more at the empty seat next to him, he couldn't help but reflect on the peculiarity of the situation. "That was weird," he mused to himself, a hint of bewilderment coloring his thoughts.

As the plane continued its journey, Seth's imagination began to wander. The remnants of his unsettling dream merged with his musings, and a playful thought crossed his mind. "Next, I'll be running from mad mummies hell-bent on destroying the world," he chuckled inwardly, allowing himself a moment of amusement.

With a sense of lightheartedness, Seth eased back into his seat, ready to let go of the unexplained encounter and immerse himself in the comforts of the flight. Whatever the meaning behind the dream and the brief sensation, he knew that the realm of imagination could take him on thrilling journeys, even if only in the realm of his thoughts.

Chapter Six

"Therefore keep watch, because you do not know on what day your Lord will come. 43 But understand this: If the owner of the house had known at what time of night the thief was coming, he would have kept watch and would not have let his house be broken into." Mark 24: 42-43

THE AMERICAN UNIVERSITY, CAIRO, EGYPT

"GOOD MORNING, DAD!" Mary called out once again, this time with a touch of anticipation in her voice as she entered her father's laboratory at the University of Cairo. An early start had become necessary for her today due to the imminent arrival of the highly anticipated group of students for the 1st Annual Young Archaeologist Society Expedition, a project her father, Professor Wilson, had been selected to direct.

Mary was well aware of her father's high expectations and the importance he placed on academic excellence. Ever the perfectionist, he had personally chosen the best students from a pool of thousands of talented applicants. The weight of this responsibility lingered in the air, causing Mary to feel a slight unease.

But determined to impress her father and stay ahead of the demanding schedule, Mary mustered her resolve. "Good morning, Dad!" she repeated, projecting her voice a little louder this time in an attempt to capture his attention.

Yet, Professor Wilson seemed entirely absorbed in his work, paying no mind to Mary's presence. Undeterred, she pressed on, eager to engage in conversation. "So, how excited are we about meeting the children today?" she inquired, pausing for a response.

As her father turned his gaze away from the computer screen, it was evident that fatigue had taken its toll on him. He removed his wire-rim glasses and wearily rubbed his tired eyes with his hands. Mary couldn't help but express concern. "You look a little tired, Dad. Did you remember to take your medication?" she asked, her voice laced with genuine worry.

A faint smile played on Professor Wilson's lips as he replied, "Sorry, dear... I had a very long night." It was clear that he appreciated Mary's concern for his well-being.

Mary continued, emphasizing the importance of her father's health. "You need to get serious about your health, Dad," she urged, wanting him to prioritize his well-being amidst the demanding nature of his work. She understood that exceptional dedication to one's profession should never come at the expense of personal health.

As they prepared for the arrival of the students, Mary hoped that her father would not only take care of himself but also recognize the significance of the opportunity before them. The Young Archaeologist Society Expedition was not just an honor for her father, but also a chance to inspire and educate a new generation of talented students.

"Mary only called her father by his name whenever she got upset and wanted to get her point across in as few words as possible."

"OK, so... back to the job at hand, we have 44 minutes before we have to meet the children at the university library," said Mary.

"Right, of course... not to worry, we will be on time. I've saved some interesting data I pulled last night on this separate hard drive. I want to take it with us too, and if we have time, maybe you can help me finish analyzing the data, maybe run some more tests," said the professor.

Mary smiled flatly. "If you say so. And what is it for, may I ask?"

"Nothing really, just a side project I've been working on. You might even call it a hobby of sorts."

"Hmmm... Well, while you handle whatever you're doing over there with your new hobby, why don't I bring the car around front, so we can get going? You know, some of us, unlike our present company, can't stand to be late."

Mary put her hands on her hips and waited patiently for her father to reply, but again the professor never looked up from his screen. This would usually get Mary's short temper boiling over like a hot teapot without a lid. But then she remembered he wasn't exactly known for his social etiquette, and more importantly, she remembered that when her father fixated on something, there was no use talking to him. Short of the building being on fire, there was no getting his attention.

"One more thing; I want to make a quick stop before we meet our young archaeologists... Oh, and I want you to bring the students' files with us too. I need to review them on the way," the professor suddenly blurted out in one breathless rant.

Mary bit down on her bottom lip while her right hand clenched into a tight fist until her knuckles began to turn white.

Why does he always do this? He's going to make us late, she thought to herself.

"Sounds like a plan."

She gave him a perfect plastic smile, and to pretend to look out the bay window to avoid eye contact.

Mary paused for another moment till she was satisfied the rhetorical conversation was over. She turned around the way she came and slowly regained her composure, and headed out of her father's office. After successfully exiting the building without exploding at her beloved father,

She relaxed her tense shoulders finally and quickly made her way across the campus center lawn, Mary suddenly remembered how proud she was on her first day on campus. She'd never been happier. Egyptology was her life.

The thoughts faded as she reached the teachers parking lot and hopped into her late model Olive Green Land Rover. She started the engine then slowly drove around to the front of the building to meet her father.

"He better be ready..." She said out loud.

And to her surprise, as she pulled up close to the curb, there he was, set and ready to go.

She nearly gasped.

Mary stopped the Land Rover directly in front of the professor. He leaned in and opened the door and hopped into the car.

"Wonderful timing, my dear, you know how I hate waiting."

"Haha... no sarcasm there dad." Mary retorted. "Where did you want to stop, your highness?"

"You remember Dr Mubarak don't." The professor ignored Mary's sly remarks.

Here are the grammar, spelling, and content corrections:

"Unfortunately," Mary grunted. "Something about him gives me the creeps..."

"You could do worse, my darling," said the professor, and for the first time, he raised an eyebrow and tilted his head at an angle that allowed him to see his daughter over his set of thick glasses.

Mary said nothing, and the pair locked eyes, staring at each other, waiting for the first one to blink.

The professor winked first.

"Nevertheless, my darling, as your father and employer, I might need to stop by the good doctor's offices. It will only take five minutes."

"Let's change the subject," said Mary.

She reached down to the center console, turned up the volume on the radio, and drove the rest of the way without speaking.

Chapter Seven

"*The Nephilim were in the earth in those days, and also after that, when the sons of God came in unto the daughters of men, and they bore children to them; the same were the mighty men that were of old, the men of renown.*" *Genesis 6:4*

CAIRO INTERNATIONAL AIRPORT, EGYPT

After disembarking from the Boeing 757, Seth's body began to remind him that he had not been to the toilet since he left New York. He decided it would be best to find the nearest lavatory and relieve himself as quickly as possible.

Once he finished his much-needed pit stop, Seth stepped out of the bathroom stall and made his way to the wall of sinks. He washed his hands and quickly dried them under one of the strategically placed air dryers in the bathroom.

Seth left the bathroom and navigated his way down the course, recalling the instructions his father had given him. However, after some time, he sensed that he might be heading in the wrong direction. He stopped abruptly, nearly causing the lady behind him to spill her cup of Starbucks on him.

Startled, Seth quickly removed his headphones and apologized to the lady several times. The woman, however, remained silent and continued on her way in a hurry.

"Are you lost?" a deep male voice came from behind.

"Yeah?" Seth responded cautiously to the stranger.

"Sorry to surprise you like that, but I couldn't help but notice that you look a bit lost," the stranger smiled. He looked deep into Seth's eyes, and for a moment, Seth almost felt as if he knew the man. However, that made no sense since Seth had never been anywhere outside of New York before.

"Do I know you?" Seth inquired cautiously.

"No, of course not," the man replied. "Unless you are from Cairo, which I'm guessing you are not. I can recognize an American accent anywhere in the world. I thought you looked like you could use some help after that young lady nearly tripped over you. You seem to be fine, so I'll be on my way." The man smiled.

"No, wait. What I meant was, could you tell me how to get to the baggage pickup place, sir?" Seth requested.

"Of course," the man replied, still smiling.

"Just follow the signs up above you," the stranger pointed to the black and yellow exit signs above them on either side of the course.

"Oh, I see... This is my first time in another country," Seth replied.

"You're a little young to be flying alone. Where are your parents?" the stranger inquired.

Suddenly, Seth remembered his father's words, "Don't talk to strangers..."

"They are waiting for me at the baggage claim, so I better get going, sir," Seth responded, recalling his father's advice.

The man smiled, "Follow the signs around, and they will take you down the escalator to the baggage claim."

Seth thanked the stranger once again and there was a brief awkward pause. Then, Seth stepped around the gentleman and continued walking down the course, keeping his eyes on the yellow signs the stranger had shown him.

Unbeknownst to Seth, the stranger continued to take an interest in him. He remained motionless in the middle of the busy concourse, his eyes locked on Seth like a pair of laser beams.

Seth, unaware of the stranger's continued attention, headed through the concourse and put his headphones back on. Finally, he reached the escalator leading down to the baggage claim area. Before he reached the bottom, he noticed a man holding a sign with his name on it.

"Oh yeah, buddy! I'm a rockstar!" Seth thought to himself.

He quickly shot a selfie video with his iPhone and sent it to his friends through his Instagram, TikTok, and QIK ROK profiles.

"Seth Strange?" the man holding the sign called out.

"That's me," Seth replied with a big grin.

"Welcome to Cairo. Please follow me," the man said, gesturing for Seth to follow him.

Seth followed the man to a small group of children who appeared to be around his age. A young TA named Christine introduced herself as the one in charge of the YASE summer expedition in Cairo.

"I'm Seth," he said, blushing and trying to avoid looking at Christine's unusually large breasts, silently questioning their authenticity.

"How was your flight?" Christine asked.

"It was cool," Seth replied.

"It looks like you're the last one. Just follow me, and we'll meet the other students out in front, load onto the bus, and head to the hotel, OK?" Christine said with a smile.

"Any questions?" she added.

"No, I read through everything last night, so..." Seth started to say.

"Well then, in that case, follow me," Christine said, leading the way.

Unbeknownst to Seth, the stranger who had approached him earlier had followed him through the terminal. He sat down on a bench near the smoking area, still keeping a watchful eye on Seth from a distance. The stranger's pupils appeared to phase in and out, changing shapes. He reached into his pocket and pulled out an odd-looking mobile phone. Without taking his strange eyes off the children, he dialed a number and waited as the phone rang six times before a voice answered on the other end.

"I've been waiting for your call. What did you see?" the voice inquired.

"The last one arrived, but my sight has not returned," the stranger replied.

After the voice on the phone responded coldly to the stranger's report, stating that his sight not returning was unfortunate but they would proceed as planned, the call ended. The stranger with the blue cap calmly put on a pair of dark sunglasses, maintaining his vigilant watch over Seth and the group.

As he stood up, the stranger lit a gold-banded, fine-cigarette, taking a deep inhale before exhaling a cloud of white smoke into the air. His gaze remained fixed on the children as they greeted each other and gathered their luggage. The Arab driver and American student assistant assisted them in loading their belongings onto a yellow school bus, while the smell of diesel made Seth scrunch his nose.

Stepping back from the bus, still pinching his nostrils closed, Seth proudly read aloud the writing on the side of the bus, which proclaimed it as the "University of Cairo!" The stranger flicked his cigarette to the ground and extinguished it with his shoe, his eyes momentarily twinkling from red to black, then back to a deep sky blue. With one final drag from his cigarette, he quietly headed towards the parking garage, leaving the scene behind.

Chapter Eight

"The Way of Mastery is to break all the rules—but you have to know them perfectly before you can do this; otherwise you are not in a position to transcend them."

MINISTRY OF STATE ANTIQUITIES, EGYPT

As the day progressed, the sun rose higher in the sky, casting its scorching rays upon the father and daughter duo as they made their way towards the Ministry of State Antiquities. The early morning air had transformed into a stifling heat, suffocating them under its tormenting sunlight.

"Did you bring those student files I asked for?" inquired the professor.

"I've got you covered, dad. They're right there behind the seat," replied Mary, accompanied by a quick wink.

"What would I do without you, my little angel," expressed the professor, grateful for his daughter's assistance.

"Could you please roll down your window? That disgusting fly is bothering me," Mary requested, her frustration evident.

"Humor was never your strong suit, princess," chuckled the professor, finding amusement in their banter.

Following Mary's request, the professor reached up and rolled down his window, instantly creating a change in pressure that sucked the fly out of the vehicle.

"Thank you," Mary smiled and continued driving, tuning in to the political chatter on the talk radio.

Ten minutes later, they arrived at the Ministry of Antiquities. The professor remained silent as they parked in front of the building, quickly flipping through the student files on his lap before tucking them securely under his arm.

"You can wait in the car. I shouldn't be too long," he assured Mary.

He smiled warmly at his daughter, squeezing her hand before stepping out of the Land Rover. With his short, stocky legs, the professor trotted up the steps and entered the building, heading straight for Mubarak's office located in the main lobby.

When the professor reached the office the door was already open.

"Ryan, my friend, Please come in, come in Ryan!" Mubarak said in his thick arabic accent, colored rather nicely amongst Mubarak's unmistakable Oxford Educated elitist tone. Mubarak prided himself in always being the smartest person in the room. He was one of only a handful of Academics to earn two PHD's.

"It's been a spell my friend, I trust you are well." The professor entered the room, closing the double doors behind him.

"It's good to see you too, Ryan. So Tell me, How's your lovely daughter getting along now that she is all grown up, as it were?" Dr Mubarak politely inquired, smiling at the professor he turned and walked behind his desk and took a seat.

After he was seated he pulled himself closer to the desk and gestured with his right hand inviting the professor to take a seat as well.

"She's still as curious as ever." The professor chuckled.

"Well, she certainly has some enormous shoes to fill my old friend. Said Mubarak.

At any rate, you certainly have done a fine job, in-spite of that messy divorce...thing,"

"Right..." The professor said reluctantly, his face now looking blush even a little bit angry.

"You've raised her to be a first-class archaeologist. And I might add, she is a real credit to your work and reputation. You know she is quite beautiful too if you don't mind me saying so,"

"I don't know where she gets it from." The professor laughed

After a few more rounds of pleasantries, the conversation quickly became serious as they discussed the contents of each of the children's folders and the business at hand.

Ten minutes later the professor looked at his watch.

Professor Wilson stood up, and leaned over the table and shook Dr Mubarak's waiting hand. Both men felt the need to exchange a few more pleasantries, and then professor Wilson turned and left the office leaving the files behind and running down the corridor as fast as his short stocky legs could go.

After the professor was far enough out of his office Dr Mubarak opened the top desk drawer and removed a small bottle of hand cleaning soap that he generally used to scrub his hands, slowly then very quickly until his skin felt dry again. He placed the small plastic bottle back in the desk drawer and then he stood up walking behind his chair in order to look through the open blinds where he calmly watched his old friend drive away.

"Finally! We will crush the infidel once and for all! Allahu Akbar!" He said, clenching his fist and squeezing till he could see his veins around his knuckles pulsing under his skin

Chapter Nine

"*To do good to others because we want them to do good to us is essentially selfish. In time we must learn to do good regardless of how we are treated by others; as Christ said, we must love even our enemies.*"

FOUR SEASONS HOTEL. CAIRO, EGYPT

"Good morning, children. I am Professor Wilson," the professor began, acknowledging the excited group of children before him. He then turned to Mary, standing nearby, and introduced her as his assistant and daughter, praising her intelligence and loveliness.

"First and foremost, congratulations to each and every one of you. You should be incredibly proud of yourselves," Professor Wilson continued, his tone filled with pride. "Being selected for this expedition is a tremendous honor. The YASS society accepts only the very best, so take pride in your work and your induction into our elite group."

He paused for a moment, allowing his words to sink in before continuing. "Always remember our creed: 'Discover the past with dignity and gain knowledge through humility!'" The professor emphasized the importance of approaching their work with respect and humility.

"I promise you all," Professor Wilson continued, his voice filled with enthusiasm, "that the experiences each of you will gain over the next three months will not only be intellectually rewarding but also contribute significantly to the rest of your academic journey."

With the formalities concluded, he lightened the mood, signaling the start of an exciting adventure. "Now, with all that out of the way, I want to welcome you and remind you to have fun!" The children erupted into cheers, and some of the boys exchanged high-fives, brimming with excitement for the journey ahead.

Professor Wilson took a moment to enjoy the look of excitement on all the children's faces. This was the part of the job he loved most. He loved being a teacher, but he loved knowledge more than anything. To professor wilson knowledge was more valuable than money or prestige or even friends and family. Knowledge was his god and had been one most of adult life.

Soon he'd be the pupil again, He shied quietly to himself.

The professor looked down at his iPad, touching the screen with his two fingers to open up the student roster.

They look younger every year. He thought to himself.

"Each of you should have received an itinerary and a syllabus." He paused for a moment, then continued speaking. "I won't waste time going over what students of your quality should already have memorized."

"Please pay close attention, children. In front of Mary, there are 12 backpacks, each of you will be taking one of these with you to the field. Each backpack has a name tag on it." He pointed to the yellow tags that were tied to each bag.

"You will find each backpack has all the tools and supplies you will require for the field expedition."

The children responded gleefully with bright enthusiastic smiles and a short round of blissful cheers. The professor and Mary both smiled back at them. Both Mary and the professor felt a warm fuzzy feeling in their stomachs, and smiled again and then looked at each. There they were father and daughter doing what they loved, together. After a moment the professor looked away from his beautiful daughter and focused his attention back at the children.

"Right, so let's get started then. As I call your name, please come and pick up your backpacks and then go form a line in front of the bus."

"And without further ado," the professor said, attempting a broken French accent that elicited chuckles from the children. "Elle Diva, please come and collect your backpack," he called out, reminding her to ensure she had the correct name tag.

Elle's eyes lit up at the sound of her name. She enjoyed being in the spotlight and craved attention, especially since embracing her identity as a lesbian. With her dark brown eyes and long, jet-black hair framing her boyish face, she exuded both beauty and intelligence. Elle was a math wizard, a genius by any standard. She held the top position in her class at Herzliya and was the only female to receive national honors for academic excellence.

"Thank you, professor," Elle responded graciously. She walked over to the bus, picked up her backpack, and quickly fell back in line with the other children.

"Seth Strange!" the professor called out, but there was no immediate response. After a brief pause, he called Seth's name again, trying to grab his attention.

Seth, plagued by a short attention span, was lost in his thoughts, engrossed in the idea of playing another game of Halo. He had been diagnosed with bipolar disorder and ADHD at a young age, which made him a challenging student to handle. Only his mother knew how to calm him during his intense episodes.

"Seth Strange!" Professor Wilson repeated, deepening his voice as he emphasized the importance of their work that morning. "We have a great deal of work ahead, children, and I expect everyone to pay attention and not waste time. ADHD is not an acceptable excuse for students selected for YAS."

With that, Seth finally responded, "Right here, professor!"

"Glad you could join us," Professor Wilson responded, giving Seth a cold look before continuing with the roll call, shifting his attention to the next child.

Seth lowered his head and stepped forward to retrieve his backpack. He picked it up, turned around, and quietly returned to his place in line. Feeling a sense of curiosity, he whispered to the pretty African girl standing next to him, seeking an explanation for Seth's behavior.

"I don't think I understand what you mean," she replied, unaware of the issue Seth was referring to.

The professor interjected, noticing the whispering and giggling. "Okay, guys, that's quite enough," he said, addressing the whole class. "As my father used to say, we have a long day ahead, and the sooner we can escape this heat, the better." Mary, the professor's daughter, gave him a look of disapproval, signaling her lack of amusement.

Knowing his daughter well, the professor quickly smiled back at her and did the thing with his eyebrows that always used to make her giggle when she was younger. "Really, dad," Mary remarked sarcastically. The professor let out a low cough and continued with the roll call.

"Mr. John A. Dunnigan, please come and collect your backpack, if you would be so kind, sir," the professor called out.

A tall, blond, and athletic young man eagerly leaped forward. His tan cargo pants and matching cargo shirt gave off a fashionable impression, almost resembling a designer suit. Additionally, he wore a Texas-sized cowboy hat, custom-made at his family's factory in Mexico.

"One giant leap for mankind," he smirked, tossing his backpack casually over his shoulder.

The professor continued with the roll call and called out the next name, "Rachel Monroe." The sun was now high in the sky, its scorching rays reaching everyone in the vicinity. Professor Wilson couldn't help but chuckle to himself as he noticed a cute 13-year-old African-American girl, Rhonda Stone, enthusiastically waving her hand in the air as if she were the Queen of England.

"Well, a jolly good morning to you, young lady! It's wonderful to see such enthusiasm," the professor exclaimed, grinning from ear to ear. "Please come and collect your backpack."

Rhonda, who was tall for her age and had a confident demeanor, approached Professor Wilson to retrieve her backpack. Despite being a little on the heavy side, she carried herself with grace. Notably, she wore fashionable glasses that changed colors depending on the light.

"Thank you, Professor Wilson. I'm excited to be here," Rhonda expressed her gratitude as she grabbed her backpack. Seth couldn't help but notice her confident walk and spirited attitude. She reminded him of some of the girls who used to tease him back in his old neighborhood.

"I'm right here, professor!" confidently exclaimed the pretty black girl, waving her arms over her head to catch his attention. The professor chuckled warmly and tipped his cargo hat in acknowledgment of her enthusiasm.

"She's a real spitfire, that one," he thought to himself. Reflecting on the girl's spirited nature, the professor couldn't help but comment, "You remind me of another young lady," he said, glancing over at his daughter with a grin, who wasn't particularly amused by the comparison.

The children chuckled and smiled as Rachel, the confident girl, stepped forward to retrieve her backpack. However, as she reached for it, she suddenly felt an uncomfortable strain on her side, emitting a sound akin to that of a snorting piglet. It was evident to everyone that Rachel was having a hard time picking up the overstuffed bag. Standing at barely five feet and well under 100 pounds, she was much smaller and weaker compared to the weight of the backpack.

Observing Rachel struggling, John Dunnigan, the tall and fit young man known for his love of attention, immediately stepped forward. Stiffly reaching out with his hands, he offered to pick up Rachel's backpack for her. "Let me get that for you, little lady," he offered with a pseudo-gallant tone.

"I can manage it myself, actually!" replied Rachel, clearly annoyed by the unsolicited assistance. Regardless of her protest, John overrode her objections and took the bag from her.

Even though appreciative, Rachel resented the uncomfortable and unwanted attention. "I don't need any help, really," she expressed her independence. "But thank you anyway."

"Now, isn't that something? Looks like we have a real Southern gentleman in our midst," commented the professor, playfully acknowledging John's chivalrous act, while John pretended not to hear the remarks and proceeded with his gentlemanly assistance.

"You better get used to that backpack, young lady. I'm afraid it will be a very long summer if you don't. Thank you, young man," the professor remarked, acknowledging John's assistance. He then adjusted his glasses and had a bout of violent coughing, spitting out something yellowish from his mouth. After regaining his composure, he proceeded to call out the rest of the children's names.

"Charles Martin, Elizabeth Xing, Pari Kupar, Klaus Renn, Asim Ashad, Adenesh Adunga! Please come and pick up your backpacks," he announced.

Adenesh Adunga, filled with excitement, eagerly stepped forward and picked up her backpack. Being the youngest of the group and not yet 13, she thought to herself, "My goodness!" But despite the weight, Adenesh was accustomed to carrying heavy objects. In her village, the women were expected to haul various heavy items without complaint, always grateful for what they were given.

Moreover, Adenesh was thrilled to be out of her village and part of the YAS (Youth Archaeology Society). Her departure had been celebrated with a week of music, dancing, and feasting, as the entire village came out to see her off. Determined to represent her family and people in the best possible light, Adenesh daydreamed momentarily before being interrupted by the professor.

"Now, children, we're going to divide you into two groups. Once we reach the dig site, you will be assigned your areas of responsibility. Additionally, each team will be accompanied by a group leader, either myself or Mary," the professor explained, wiping the growing pool of sweat from the end of his nose.

With these directives, the expedition was set to commence, and the young archaeologists eagerly awaited their roles and the adventure that lay ahead.

"We will be accompanied by two private security officers, along with our guide," the professor announced.

"Great, that's all we need, two total high school bullies to protect us from what?" Seth muttered quietly to himself, expressing his skepticism. He playfully winked at Adenesh and whispered, "Losers."

However, his whispered comment did not go unnoticed by the professor. "Would you like to share your comments with the rest of us, Mr. Strange? We're all ears," the professor responded, resting his hand on his waist in a slightly feminine manner that reminded Seth of his mother.

"Archaeology is a serious business, young man, and the desert is a very unforgiving place," the professor continued sternly. Seth feigned ignorance, looking around as if unsure of who the professor was addressing. The professor rubbed his bushy beard up and down, emphasizing his point.

After an uncomfortable silence, the professor instructed Mary to proceed with reading off the names of each group. The first team consisted of Seth, Adenesh, Asim, Rachel, Emanuel, and Elle, who would be working directly with the professor. The remaining group, composed of John, Rhonda, Charles, Elizabeth, Pari, and Klaus, would be under the guidance of Professor Wilson.

As Mary continued giving instructions to the children, a rumbling sound emerged from the nearby horizon. Mary recognized the distinct noise of a loud Harley approaching. The motorcycle, black and oversized, rolled into the parking lot with a fury reminiscent of a bat out of hell.

"I guess some things never change!" Mary thought to herself as she witnessed the rider dismount from the vintage bike amidst the smoke and dust.

The rider swiftly dismounted from the bike, discarding his helmet and removing his sandblasted goggles. Standing before them was a ruggedly handsome African American ex-military man, towering over 6 feet tall. He donned black leather jeans, a cargo shirt, and an orange Harley Davidson scarf with white lettering wrapped around his bald head. His face sported a long braided goatee, accentuating his strong jawline.

Apologizing for his tardiness, Francis Martin explained, "Sorry, I'm late, Doc. My girlfriend and I had a bit of a disagreement."

Professor Wilson raised an eyebrow, glancing at Martin. "We can discuss the various particulars of our personal lives later, Frank," he responded.

With a slight grin, Martin remarked, "You know you're the only one that still calls me Frank."

Addressing the children, Professor Wilson introduced Martin as their expert guide for the expedition. "Hello, Mr. Martin!" the children exclaimed in unison, some of them offering half-hearted waves in his direction. Mr. Martin smiled warmly and waved back.

SETH EAGERLY JOINED the other children in boarding the bus after Mary's cautionary message. As he made his way towards the bus, he felt a tinge of embarrassment as the other children laughed and pointed at him, likely due to Mary's playful finger-shaking.

Filled with a sense of excitement, Seth couldn't help but stare at the radiant sun overhead, its brilliance captivating him. The air around him carried a foreign scent, emphasizing the unfamiliarity of the land. Lost in his thoughts, he chuckled to himself, declaring, "I'm going to touch the Sphinx."

Following the rest of the group, Seth stood in line to board the bus. Soon, he struck up a conversation with a fellow traveler named Adenesh. Introducing himself as Seth, he greeted her warmly. Adenesh reciprocated, introducing herself as a first-time visitor to Egypt.

Unfazed by whether Adenesh took his words seriously, Seth shared stories of his past adventures and explorations, pointing out that his mother was a renowned archaeologist who often took him on expeditions. Although he couldn't gauge Adenesh's level of interest, Seth remained undeterred.

After recounting several tales, Seth turned the conversation towards Adenesh, curious to hear her own experiences and stories.

Adenesh politely acknowledged Seth's stories, mentioning that there wasn't much to share about her own background as she hailed from a tranquil village where nothing extraordinary occurred. Despite this, she smiled warmly and listened attentively.

Undeterred by her modest response, Seth proceeded to elaborate on his extensive experiences in the field, continuing to indulge in sharing his adventures. Adenesh, though coming from a village that discouraged bragging, graciously entertained his tales and actively engaged in the conversation.

As they exchanged introductions, Seth mentioned that his friends referred to him as Seth, while Adenesh shared that her friends called her Red. This playful exchange led them to discover and appreciate each other's accents, resulting in laughter and a lighthearted connection between the two.

Their shared sense of humor created a comfortable atmosphere, allowing them to enjoy each other's company and find common ground despite their different backgrounds and experiences.

Chapter Ten

"*Within every man and woman is a force that directs and controls the entire course of life.*"

ABYDOS DAY ONE

Mr. Francis Martin, commonly known as Frank, was an experienced professional in the field. He exuded a rugged persona and had an undeniable sense of adventure. Instead of pursuing a football career with a full scholarship offer from the University of Texas, Frank chose to join the army due to his unwavering passion for exploration and thrill-seeking. His military background and exposure to challenges in harsh environments made him feel right at home in the field.

Frank held a deep fascination with ancient alien theory and government conspiracies, making him an ideal candidate when the university sought additional security personnel following the tragic Cairo bombing three years ago. Professor Wilson, a trusted colleague, personally recommended Frank for the job.

Engaging in conversation, Professor Wilson inquired about Frank's personal life and well-being. Frank revealed that he and his partner, Jamie, had decided to separate temporarily for the sake of their children. However, he reassured the professor that he was doing well and fully dedicated to the task at hand. In fact, he expressed enthusiasm for escaping the personal turmoil and focusing entirely on the upcoming journey.

Professor Wilson expressed relief upon hearing Frank's positive outlook and assured him that they would be undertaking dual responsibilities during the trip. The professor seemed confident in Frank's abilities and trusted him to handle the challenges that lay ahead.

Amidst the lively chatter and singing on the bright yellow bus headed towards the awe-inspiring temple of Abydos, Adenesh sat quietly, observing the animated group of young students surrounding her. Conversations filled the air, and although she couldn't understand some of the children speaking in different languages on their cell phones, she listened attentively nonetheless.

Suddenly, Adenesh was taken aback when a girl named Elle, who was sitting across from her, directed her attention towards Seth. Elle questioned if Seth's father was Dr. Strange, a former Harvard professor known for his unconventional belief that humans originated from aliens. Seth quickly clarified that his father believed humans were genetically altered by aliens rather than directly descending from them.

Elle responded dryly, dismissing the alien ancestry notion with a roll of her eyes. Meanwhile, Adenesh looked at Elle with a perplexed expression, which resulted in laughter from Elle. Intrigued, Elle leaned closer to the soft-spoken African girl and inquired about her beliefs regarding human origins. However, before Adenesh could respond, Seth impulsively decided to answer on her behalf.

Seth confidently introduced Adenesh as being from the Dogon tribe, an ethnic group residing in the central plateau region of Mali, West Africa, near the city of Bandiagara. His confident delivery and slight arrogance incited a response from Elle, questioning Seth's role as a spokesperson for Adenesh.

Coming to Seth's defense, Rhonda, who was seated beside Elle, praised his knowledge and dismissed Elle's criticism. At this point, Elle redirected her attention back to Adenesh and shared that her mother had been fascinated with the Dogon tribe, particularly their mythology, evident from the Dogon artwork necklace Adenesh was wearing.

THE EXCHANGE REVEALED a connection between Elle's personal interest and Adenesh's cultural background, sparking a potential point of mutual intrigue and discussion within the group.

ADENESH WAS SURPRISED by Seth's genuine interest in her culture, especially when he expressed fascination with the Dogon tribe. She explained that her eldest brother had made the necklace for her as a form of protection against evil spirits.

Rhonda chimed in, mentioning that she had come across information about the Dogon tribe in her readings. She mentioned their belief in originating from the area of the constellation Sirius and the involvement of a serpent god that descended from the stars to create humanity.

Elle, however, responded with sarcasm and dismissed Rhonda's reference to the Dogon belief, equating it to concepts like Santa Claus, the Easter Bunny, and religious beliefs. Elle seemed skeptical about accepting ideas that couldn't be proven scientifically.

Rhonda, on the other hand, acknowledged that not everything in science can be fully explained, leaving room for unexplained phenomena. She suggested that there are mysteries and gaps in our knowledge that science has yet to uncover.

Elle and Rhonda found humor in the exchange and playfully referred to themselves as "Ancient alien conspiracy theory geeks" masquerading as scientists. They laughed and shared a high five, finding entertainment in the diversity of perspectives within the group.

Adenesh found Elle's response amusing and acknowledged her humor, appreciating the lightheartedness injected into the discussion.

As the chaotic situation unfolded on the bus, Seth grew increasingly concerned about the reckless speed at which they were traveling. He whispered to Adenesh, trying to tune out the laughter of Elle and Rhonda in front of them. Seth's anxiety heightened as he realized even bus drivers didn't drive this fast.

Adenesh, sharing Seth's unease, glanced out the window and noticed the rapidly passing sand dunes. She agreed with Seth's observation that something was definitely wrong. They both sensed danger looming.

Seth, determined to understand the cause, decided to stand up and get a clearer view over Elle and Rhonda, who were obstructing his line of sight. When he finally saw what was happening, his heart dropped. Mr. Francis, the bus driver, had a panicked expression on his face as he looked back at Seth through the rear-view mirror.

Realizing the severity of the situation, Seth couldn't contain his reaction. He desperately pleaded with Mr. Francis, urging him to release the accelerator and apply the brakes. But Mr. Francis, equally terrified, confessed that both the accelerator and brakes were malfunctioning.

Adenesh, gripping Seth's hand tightly, was filled with fear and concern. She sought reassurance from him, asking for an explanation. Seth, unable to comprehend the full extent of the danger, looked into Adenesh's eyes and shouted a warning for everyone to get down.

The passengers on the bus, startled by the urgency in Seth's voice, began to crouch or lie down, bracing themselves for impact. Seth's realization that a crash was imminent heightened the desperate tone of his pleas.

In a heartbreaking moment, the school bus collided with the first range of sand dunes, causing it to flip and spin, indiscriminately tossing the passengers around. The violent motion finally came to a sudden halt as the bus settled on its side between the second and third row of dunes, shrouded in a cloud of dust and sand. The passengers found themselves disoriented and shaken, but thankfully alive.

Chapter 11

" **M** an, know yourself... and you shall know the gods."
LAND OF THE PHARAOHS

FRANCIS MARTIN'S SENSES slowly returned, accompanied by panic and confusion. With a burst of energy, he sprung to his feet, assuming a combat-ready position, ready to face whatever danger lay before him. However, his vision was blurred by sand, and he struggled to see clearly. The smell of smoke and gasoline confirmed his worst fears.

Shouting as loud as he could, Francis asked about the well-being of everyone else. He was relieved to hear a reply that they were all relatively unharmed, thanks to the quick thinking of the security detail from the university. They had safely evacuated everyone, including Francis, and kept him where he was due to his head injury.

Francis expressed his gratitude for the security officers and their prompt actions. It seemed that they had prevented a more disastrous outcome. The first aid kit remained on the bus, deemed inaccessible for safety reasons, but Professor Wilson assured Francis that help was on the way. Another bus was dispatched by the university, and they would be camping out for the night.

Recognizing the need to provide for the children and attend to their well-being, Professor Wilson had arranged for the security officers to retrieve their gear and set up tents. This would provide some shelter and allow everyone to rest and have a meal.

Relieved to hear that there were no serious injuries among the children, Francis still felt concerned about his own well-being. Mary, one of their companions, approached him gently, offering to bandage the scratch on his forehead. However, he dismissed her concerns, stating that it was just a minor injury.

Settling into the reality of their current situation, Francis took in their surroundings. The bus had come to a stop on its side, a few miles away from their first dig site, where they had planned on excavating for the next several days. The twist of fate had brought them to an unexpected halt, altering their course and presenting new challenges.

As Francis gazed at the sandy expanse before him, he couldn't help but wonder what other mysteries and discoveries awaited them in the land of the pharaohs. Little did he know that their journey had only just begun, and the trials they faced would test their resilience, tenacity, and unyielding spirit of exploration.

And so, armed with determination and with their survival instincts awakened, they prepared themselves for the new chapter in their adventure—a chapter filled with unforeseen obstacles, hidden treasures, and the unfolding wonders of the ancient land they found themselves in.

As the group settled in and began setting up their tents, the excitement and anticipation in the air were palpable. The sprawling mystical complex of Abydos, with its grand and ancient temple of Osiris, held a sense of wonder and mystery. It was believed to be built by none other than the legendary pharaoh, Seti I.

Professor Wilson gathered the attention of the children, expressing his relief that everyone was safe. He informed them that their first site of study would be the temple grounds of

Abydos, where many mysteries still awaited discovery. The prospect of uncovering something new filled the children with enthusiasm, and they cheered and shouted in excitement.

Seth, among the children, felt a special connection to this place. He had spent countless hours delving into maps, peculiar diagrams, and personal notes left behind by his late mother, all related to Abydos. His knowledge and familiarity with the area added to his excitement, making him even more eager to explore its secrets.

Setting up camp would be their immediate task, as they awaited the arrival of the new bus in the morning. Mary, taking charge, assigned the girls to one side and directed the boys to set up their tents on the other. With instructions given, the children split into groups and worked together to assemble their temporary shelters.

Though still feeling the lingering effects of the earlier accident, the children's spirits remained high, and their camaraderie prevailed. However, Elle, for some undisclosed reason, harbored an unexplained dislike towards Adenesh. Her dismissive remark about the wondrous nature of Abydos hinted at this underlying tension.

Amidst the setting up of tents and the growing sense of adventure, Professor Wilson and Mary provided further instructions to ensure everyone's safety and well-being. They emphasized the importance of working together and maintaining order. The children showed resilience and determination, overcoming their apprehensions and contributing to the camp set-up.

With the tents soon in place, the group looked forward to a well-deserved dinner. Professor Wilson reminded them to gather in one hour, highlighting the true spirit of their endeavor—to be intrepid adventurers unearthing the secrets of this remarkable place.

As night fell over the ancient grounds of Abydos, the camp became a hub of activity and anticipation. The flickering lights from lanterns and the buzz of conversations filled the air. Despite the tensions between Elle and Adenesh, the atmosphere of excitement and the allure of the unknown brought a sense of unity and shared purpose to the group.

As the stars appeared in the vast Egyptian sky, one question lingered in each child's mind: What mysteries awaited them at Abydos, and what secrets would they unveil in their quest to unlock the enigmas of this ancient land?

As the excitement lingered in the air, Elle expressed her enthusiasm about the prospect of finding something amazing in Egypt. She had dreamt of this moment for as long as she could remember, longing to uncover wondrous treasures within the ancient land. Being in the same group as Adenesh seemed to bring her additional joy, as she shared her excitement with her newfound companion.

Elle continued unpacking her belongings with meticulous precision, arranging everything in neat and orderly rows. She had a keen eye for cleanliness and organization, ensuring that every item had its designated place. Disorder unsettled her, regardless of its scale. Her attention to detail and preference for order often clashed with the messier nature of being a tomboy, which further accentuated her unique traits.

In response to Elle's comment about her brothers, Adenesh remained largely unfazed, seemingly unaffected by the sarcasm. The dichotomy between the two girls grew as each maintained their own focus and approach to their surroundings.

Suddenly, a voice called out from outside the tent, interrupting their personal interactions. It was time for everyone to gather and line up. Seth emerged from his tent, full of energy, with Asim following closely behind. Briefly, Seth's eyes met Adenesh's, and he couldn't help but be captivated by her beauty. Aware of his lingering gaze, he averted his eyes, hoping she hadn't noticed.

The group assembled, with Mary standing beside Professor Wilson, delivering instructions for the evening's activities. Mary's thoroughness became apparent as she meticulously walked the children through the drill, leaving no detail unaddressed. She explained the objectives and parameters of their exploration, followed by an extensive list of do's and don'ts to ensure everyone's safety and adherence to the rules.

As the evening progressed, the children gathered around the campfire, enjoying the company of their newfound companions. Conversations, laughter, and the warmth of the fire created a sense of camaraderie among the group. Eventually, it was time to retire for the night and prepare for the adventures that awaited them in the morning.

The next day, the replacement bus from the university arrived punctually, greeting the children with searing heat and glaring sunlight. Everyone loaded their gear onto the bus, ready to embark on their journey to the first dig site. The desert seemed even hotter than the previous day, intensifying their anticipation of what they would discover as they made their way towards their archaeological destination.

Once Seth reached the location, he immediately noticed it was situated southeast of the central grand temple complex. The area had been meticulously roped off, extending at least 300 meters in every direction. A surge of excitement coursed through him as he marveled at the precise arrangement of the dig site.

"This is a genuine dig site!" Seth exclaimed to himself.

"Let's begin digging and happy hunting, as I always say!" declared the professor.

The children laughed, quickly forming groups as directed by Mary, and enthusiastically started digging.

After hours of tirelessly sifting through the shifting desert sands, Seth began to worry that the task might become monotonous and drawn-out. Images of gold and treasure flashed through his mind, serving as motivation to keep going.

"There must be a more efficient way to do this," Seth muttered to himself. Suddenly, his attention was drawn to Adenesh, who wore an intriguing expression on her face. She stared curiously at an unusual rock formation that had gone unnoticed when they first arrived.

Adenesh stood near a large block of broken black granite, feeling a strange sense of familiarity with the stone.

Conflicting thoughts raced through her mind. Could it be mere imagination? Or perhaps a symptom of dehydration due to lack of water?

"The elders spoke of living stones," she said, her voice filled with a mixture of uncertainty and awe.

Curious, Seth approached Adenesh and asked, "Living stones? What do you mean?"

Gazing at the stone formation, Adenesh's eyes brightened. She replied, her voice filled with wonder, "In my village, the elders believed that the gods used living stones to conceal secret knowledge, powerful weapons, and magical devices."

Seth's imagination soared with the notion of hidden secrets, ancient artifacts, and the potential for extraordinary discoveries. He couldn't help but share Adenesh's excitement.

"Fascinating!" Seth exclaimed. "Do you think this formation could lead us to something remarkable? It feels like we might have stumbled upon a hidden treasure trove!"

Adenesh nodded, her eyes shining. "It's difficult to say for certain, but the tales passed down through generations have always possessed a kernel of truth. If these are indeed the living stones spoken of in our folklore, unimaginable wonders might be waiting to be unearthed."

With renewed enthusiasm, Seth and Adenesh examined the stone formation more closely. They marveled at the intricate patterns and mystical symbols engraved on its surface, suggesting a profound significance.

Seth followed Adenesh's gaze and noticed a small circular hole in the granite, about 3 to 4 inches wide. It appeared as though the hole had been cut using modern tools. Adenesh moved closer, determined to investigate further. Seth couldn't help but worry about the potential dangers that might lurk within the hole, considering it as a possible hiding spot for snakes or scorpions, particularly in the heat.

Adenesh, undeterred, cautiously extended her hand into the hole, searching for something hidden within. For a moment, Seth's thoughts raced with concern for her safety, pleading silently for her to be cautious.

As Adenesh's arm disappeared into the perfect cavity of the hole, she experienced a flood of thoughts rushing through her mind. After a brief pause, she confirmed that she did indeed feel something at the bottom and decided to try once more.

"Adenesh, please be careful," Seth pleaded.

Taking a moment to steady herself, Adenesh announced, with short and choppy breaths, "I think I might have... I mean, I believe there's something in here."

Seth's concern grew, but Adenesh remained determined. With a sudden burst of adrenaline, she exclaimed, "I got it!" The sheer excitement in her voice nearly took her breath away. In one swift motion, she pulled out a small gold cylinder tablet, leaving both of them astounded.

Adenesh handed the tablet to Seth, and together, they gently laid it on the sand. Without delay, Seth grabbed his cellphone and began capturing multiple pictures of the tablet from every angle, following the instructions his mother had taught him about documenting important discoveries.

Meanwhile, Elle approached the duo, curiosity evident on her face. "What are you guys doing? Did you find something?" she inquired.

In silence, Seth carefully placed the tablet inside a plastic bag. Elle's eyes widened with a mix of curiosity and envy. "Is that... gold?" she asked unexpectedly.

"Yes, it appears to be a tablet covered in cuneiform writing, and it has an ancient look to it," Seth explained, offering a glimpse of its possible historical value.

Excitedly, Elle called out to the professor and Mr. Martin, waving her hands frantically to get their attention. "Professor! Over here! I think we've found something!"

The professor and Mr. Martin hurried over, their faces reflecting a combination of surprise and anticipation at the sight of the golden tablet. The discovery had ignited a sense of thrill and wonder among the group, opening the door to a new chapter in their archaeological expedition.

"Remarkable," the professor mused. "If this is, in fact, a living stone, it could hold the key to untold knowledge and ancient technologies. We must approach this with caution and meticulous care."

News of their finding spread rapidly among the group, transforming the atmosphere at the dig site. The mundane task of digging now became an exhilarating quest to unravel the secrets veiled within the black granite.

Chapter Twelve

" A man's personal god is a shepherd who finds pasturage for the man. Let him lead him like sheep to the food they can eat. The lion who lives a life of compassion will receive it. Oh Utu, you are my judge: pronounce my judgement!"

BROOKLYN, NEW YORK UNITED STATES

PROFESSOR ABRAHAM STRANGE sat at the neighborhood bar, seeking solace from the challenges of his day at New York Community College. It seemed like everything was going wrong, leading Abraham to believe that he was trapped in a series of unfortunate events.

Determined to give himself some respite, he ordered a double gin and prepared to savor it. Turning to the short, pot-bellied bartender, Abraham requested, "Let me get one more for the road, and make it a double, will you!"

The bartender, perceptive as ever, noticed Abraham's dejected demeanor and remarked, "Looks like someone is having a bad day at work, doc?"

Chuckling wearily, Abraham replied, "Well, you could say that... My department wants to slash the funding for my research, my new girlfriend wants to explore other dating options, and to top it all off, my son finds it amusing to send me obviously fake Sumerian tablets to decipher."

Doubt etched on his face, the bartender listened intently as Abraham continued, "The funny thing is, the writing on these tablets is incredibly captivating. I can't decipher a single word, and I'm supposed to be an expert! And you know what? To add to the humor, he claims to have found them in Egypt, inside a rock near the temple of Osiris." Abraham burst into laughter, finding the absurdity of the situation amusing.

The bartender, however, gave Abraham a perplexed look, his expression revealing his lack of understanding about Sumerian tablets or the temple of Osiris.

"If it's all just a prank, well, it's a masterful one," Abraham mused to himself. "But if, by some unlikely chance, it happens to be true..."

Inspired by mischief, the bartender suggested, "Why don't you play along, buddy? Give him a taste of his own medicine. Make up a story about aliens and hidden treasures, just like the tales you've shared with me."

A mischievous twinkle sparkled in the bartender's eyes as he contemplated their plan, eager to witness Abraham's son receiving a taste of his own medicine.

"That will teach him a lesson!" the bartender exclaimed, relishing the anticipation of the prank about to unfold.

Abraham's face lit up with a mischievous grin, appreciating the bartender's cunning suggestion. "I like the way you think, Mickey," Abraham exclaimed, reaching into his pocket for his phone. "I know just the story to tell my son, and let's have another round. Put it on my tab!"

As the bartender poured Abraham another drink, he eagerly awaited the intriguing tale that was about to unfold. Abraham's fingers danced across his phone's keyboard as he crafted a message to captivate his son's imagination. With each word, he weaved a captivating narrative about ancient aliens, hidden treasures, and the mysteries surrounding the Sumerian tablets.

Taking a thoughtful sip of his drink, Abraham paused to consider the perfect cliffhanger for his text message. He wanted to ensure his son would be simultaneously bewildered and enthralled by the story. With a final touch, he pressed the send button, feeling a surge of excitement for the prank that was about to unfold.

"Now we wait, Mickey," Abraham said with a sly grin, raising his glass as if to toast their upcoming adventure. The bartender joined him, clinking their glasses together, eagerly anticipating the outcome of their clever ruse.

Chapter 13

" For our struggle is not against flesh and blood, but against the rulers, against the authorities, against the powers of this dark world and against the spiritual forces of evil in the heavenly realms." Ephesians 6:12

TABLET OF GOLD

AS THE THICK SMOKE filled the tent, Mary's patience wore thin. The stench and irritation became unbearable, and she had reached her breaking point. Frustrated, she could no longer contain her annoyance and confronted Professor Wilson, whose cigarillo had become the source of her discomfort.

"Okay, Dad!" Mary exclaimed, her voice bursting with exasperation. "You are choking me literally to death... honestly! Do you mind putting out that stupid cigar? For God's sake."

The sharpness in her tone reverberated throughout the tent, prompting heads to turn and gazes to fixate on Mary and Professor Wilson. Aware of the attention, Mary suddenly felt a twinge of embarrassment for her outburst but also a sense of relief for expressing her genuine frustration.

Professor Wilson, momentarily taken aback, lowered his cigarillo and glanced at Mary with a mix of surprise and contrition. In that instant, he realized the impact his actions had on those around him, particularly his daughter.

He swiftly extinguished the cigarillo, apologetically saying, "You're right, Mary. I'm sorry. I didn't realize how much the smoke was bothering you. I'll be more considerate."

Mary's expression softened as she acknowledged her father's apology. Letting out a sigh of relief, she responded, "Thank you, Dad. I appreciate it. I just needed some fresh air in here."

The tension in the tent began to ease as the lingering smoke slowly dissipated.

"I would certainly say that the writing is a form of Sumerian, but it belongs to a dialect I haven't seen before. However, what really caught my attention is the question: where did it come from? Discoveries like this often have a significant impact on one's career in archaeology. We all know that challenging the prevailing beliefs of mainstream Egyptology is usually met with resistance. Therefore, we must proceed with caution and avoid making radical assumptions about this find.

"Mary, I would like both you and Frank to return to my lab in Cairo and provide me with an analysis as quickly as possible. Frank, I want you to investigate the circumstances surrounding the breaks that occurred while you were there and try to determine what happened yesterday."

"But who will take care of the children? I'm not sure if that's a good idea."

"Thank you for your advice, but I am experienced in handling such situations. I will take care of the children and find a collective activity for them. Who needs groups anyway?"

"Right, I always thought it would be easier to manage!" Francis exclaimed, as if he had just revealed some hidden wisdom.

Mary and Professor Wilson exchanged looks and then turned their attention back to Francis. However, before any of them could speak, they heard a loud crash outside the tent, as if someone had accidentally knocked over some equipment.

"Knock, knock, Professor Wilson? It's Seth, Seth Green."

"Seth, you don't have to state your last name. You are the only Seth in the group," said the professor.

Mary and Francis exchanged glances, suppressing their laughter.

"Right," Seth responded timidly. Even from outside the tent, he knew when he was being teased for saying something foolish.

"May I come in for a minute? I was hoping to ask you something."

The professor swiftly picked up the ancient golden tablet and carefully placed it inside his briefcase.

"Come on in," the professor called out, a smile visible behind his thick beard and mustache.

"We were all just discussing whether we should work together to decipher the tablet. Everyone is thrilled to take a crack at it. We're all curious about what it is and where it came from.

Elle thinks it's a prank."

"Fake! You'd think we'd recognize a fake when we see one. We certainly didn't plant it. We're professional scientists, not stand-up comedians!"

"I'm just conveying the opinions," Seth shrugged his shoulders. "Rhonda believes this might be part of the curriculum. Will we be graded on our response to such a significant discovery?"

"Indeed, those are intriguing theories, young man. However, nothing could be further from the truth. I must say, skepticism is a valuable trait for a successful archaeologist.

"So, it's a test? Did I pass?" Seth half-jokingly remarked.

"No! That's not what he meant," Mary interjected, visibly agitated.

"What the professor means is that, due to the delicate nature of a find like this, there are specific protocols we must follow. Simultaneously, we must meet the expedition's goals and deadlines, among other things. Hence, we will conduct a preliminary analysis of the tablet to gain a better understanding of its contents.

Once we are confident in our findings, we will share them with you and the rest of the children."

Oh boy, the nutty professor really enjoys hearing himself talk, Seth thought to himself.

"Now, young man, if that is all... I want you to head back to your tent. It's getting late, and we have a great deal of work ahead of us tomorrow," the professor instructed.

"Okay, I guess," Seth replied as he turned around and made his way back to his tent.

He couldn't help but feel that the situation was unfair. How could they possibly exclude him from the analysis process? "That's the best part!" After all, it was his and Adenesh's discovery.

"Whatever," he muttered under his breath. Seth entered his tent, hopped into his sleeping bag, and quickly drifted off into a deep slumber, where he began to dream of a place far, far away.

Chapter Fourteen

"*O child of Adam, in reverence and awe do thou meditate upon this Tablet, for it is a thing of beauty, a being of light, life, and love, m*

anifesting its creative mission. It is the Vicegerent of God, flaming forth His splendours in the sky."

TREASURES IN PLAIN SIGHT

Seth's eyes opened to a mesmerizing sight of vast, brilliant blue waters stretching as far as the eye could see, complemented by an ethereal ultramarine sky. Overwhelmed by the unfamiliar surroundings, he let out a scream that seemed to defy the limits of his vocal cords, fueled by his fear of being unable to swim.

"OMG! I can't swim!" he wailed, consumed by panic. But before he could even close his mouth, something extraordinary began to unfold before his eyes. In a surreal twist of fate, a sudden burst of dazzling yellow light materialized out of thin air, swallowing the vast sea and sky, and Seth found himself transported inside an old Victorian Manor he immediately recognized—it was his late grandfather's house, where he used to play with his now-deceased cousins when he was just a young child.

Standing within the confines of his grandfather's private library, Seth's memories flooded back, the rare occasion when his grandfather had allowed him to enter this sacred space on his 10th birthday. His grandfather had imparted the invaluable wisdom that knowledge held more importance than material riches, a lesson that had stayed with Seth ever since.

As he absorbed the ambiance of the room, a soft, elusive voice broke through the silence, barely audible but gradually gaining clarity. Despite the muffled murmurs, Seth strained his ears, placing his hands behind them and pushing forward in an attempt to enhance his hearing. Standing motionless in the center of the library, he eagerly awaited the return of the elusive voice. And then, like a gentle breeze, it came again, this time more distinct than before.

"There it is," Seth whispered to himself, a mix of anticipation and curiosity welling up inside him.

Intrigued by the mysterious sound emanating from behind one of the grand wooden bookcases that adorned the top of the imposing stairwell, Seth ventured forth, following the unmistakable yet enigmatic noise. Slowly ascending the grand staircase, he was guided towards a secluded library—an extension of the opulent room he had just left behind. Finally, he stood before the last row of the bookcase, marked E-R, where the sound seemed to grow louder and more distinct. Beckoning to him was a book, adorned in shimmering gold—'The Golden Hermetica.'

With the determination to uncover the source of the sound, Seth reached up, his fingers longing to grasp the golden-covered book. However, despite his efforts, the book remained firmly lodged in its place, refusing to yield even the slightest inch.

Suddenly, without warning, a blinding white flash engulfed the library, causing it to vanish before Seth's eyes. In an instant, he found himself standing in a vast limestone cave, the voice he had heard echoing through the ethereal realm once again. A door materialized at the front of the cave, and anticipation filled the air as it slowly swung open, revealing a figure emerging from the shadows—it was his mother.

"Mom!" Seth exclaimed, his heart leaping with joy at the sight of her. Every instinct urged him to run towards her, but to his dismay, his legs refused to budge, as if invisible chains immobilized him to the cave floor.

"Seth, you must listen carefully. Time is short," his mother spoke urgently, her eyes scanning the surroundings as if anticipating a lurking danger. As she turned her gaze back to Seth, her face emitted a radiant, otherworldly glow, resembling that of an angel to his trembling eyes.

"You must remember," she continued, her voice filled with a sense of urgency, "all of you must awaken before it is too late. They are coming for you."

Seth's mind raced, trying to comprehend the weight of his mother's message. The urgency in her voice and the ethereal ambiance surrounding them heightened his sense of impending danger. But before he could gather his thoughts or ask further questions, the cave and his mother began to fade away, the image draining from his sight, leaving behind a profound sense of urgency and a mind filled with questions.

"Who was coming, Mom?" Seth's voice trembled with a mix of confusion and fear as he desperately sought answers. But before his question could be answered, his eyes abruptly shot open, and he found himself sitting upright at the edge of his sleeping bag, drenched in the realization that it had all been a vivid dream.

"That was bizarre," Seth murmured to himself, his hand absentmindedly reaching up to adjust his pajamas as he scratched his tousled red hair.

From beyond the confines of his tent, a familiar voice called out, snapping him back to reality. It was John, eagerly inquiring about breakfast and wondering where Seth was.

"I'm coming!" Seth replied, shaking off the remnants of the dream. He hastily dressed himself and made his way to the food tent, joining the other children.

As they settled in for breakfast, conversation flowed naturally. Someone brought up the topic of Elle, prompting a query directed at Seth.

"So, what do you think of Elle?" John inquired, his curiosity piqued.

Seth pondered for a moment, keeping in mind the wise teachings of his father, who had always emphasized the importance of speaking kindly or remaining silent.

"She seemed nice enough," Seth replied diplomatically, his father's teachings guiding his response. "If I don't have anything nice to say about someone, I should keep it to myself."

In his mind's eye, Seth could still vividly recall his father's warm touch on his small shoulder and the profound gaze that accompanied those words of wisdom. The memory of his father's advice echoed within him, and he silently cherished the sentiment it held.

With a hint of uncertainty, Seth added, "I guess it's true, as my father used to say: 'Only a fool tests the depths of the river with both feet.'"

He paused for a moment, reflecting on the cryptic dream he had experienced, but chose to keep those thoughts to himself, allowing his mind to wander into the mysteries that awaited him in the waking world.

Seth and Adenesh continued their breakfast in silence, both lost in their own thoughts. The taste of the usually delightful buttermilk pancakes had become unpleasant for Seth, leaving him with little appetite. His mind remained fixated on the unsettling dream he had the previous night, a desire to share it tugging at his conscience. However, he ultimately decided to keep it to himself, unsure of how others might react.

As the sun began to rise and breakfast came to an end, the professor called everyone's attention. Seth's confusion deepened as the professor explained that Mary and Mr. Francis would be returning to Cairo to examine the tablets they had found.

Meanwhile, the rest of the group would spend the day classifying and cataloging pottery and bone fragments discovered the day before. The professor's attempt at a smile failed to console the disappointed children, who felt left out of the more intriguing work involving the tablets.

Once the professor finished his instructions, Mary distributed bags for sampling and cataloging, and she and Mr. Francis departed in one of the vehicles, en route to Cairo. Seth, seeking to ease Adenesh's concerns, spoke up.

"Don't worry, Adenesh. Remember those pictures I took? I sent them to my father," Seth reassured her, his tone laced with a hint of mischievousness.

Adenesh appeared apprehensive, aware that the professor might not approve of their secret actions. "I don't think the professor will be okay with that, Seth," she cautioned, her voice reflecting a mix of caution and loyalty to their mentor.

Smirking, Seth replied, "What he doesn't know won't hurt him."

With a shared secret now nestled between them, Seth and Adenesh prepared themselves for the day's work, carrying the weight of their own curiosity and the thrill of their hidden endeavor. It remained to be seen what their actions would bring forth, but for now, they both carried a sense of anticipation as they joined the others in the task of cataloging relics, eager to uncover the mysteries that awaited them.

Seth's mind raced as he absorbed the astonishing revelation that not only did Rhonda share the same dream as Elle, but also the rest of their group—Asim, Elle, Emanuel, and Rachel. The hair on his arms stood on end, and his thoughts swirled like a tempest within him.

Interrupting the disbelief swirling in his mind, Adenesh posed a question, her voice filled with a mix of curiosity and apprehension, "What did you dream about?"

Rhonda's excitement bubbled over as she recounted the details of her dream with unwavering precision. The other children nodded in silent agreement, confirming their shared experience. It was a moment of astonishment for Seth, struggling to process the implications of what he was hearing.

Seth's voice quivered with a mixture of incredulity and intrigue, "Are you guys trying to prank me?"

As Rhonda continued describing her dream, her excitement growing, she relayed a pivotal moment in the dream where her father appeared, urging her to wake up quickly. It was at this point that Asim interjected, confirming the collective nature of their dreams, "We all had the same dream."

Seth's confusion deepened, realizing that this was not a prank but a remarkable and mysterious occurrence. The realization sent chills down his spine, mingling with a surge of curiosity and a tinge of fear. The significance of their shared dream and its connection to their current archaeological expedition was undeniable.

In the midst of this revelation, Seth's reluctance to share his own dream began to waver. The weight of secrecy felt heavier than ever before. Perhaps disclosing his experience would shed light on the unfolding mystery and foster a deeper understanding among the group. With a mix of determination and apprehension, Seth took a deep breath and prepared to share his own version of the dream, hoping that it would bring them all closer to the truth they were seeking.

Seth's initial laughter subsided as he realized that his friends were not joking. Their accounts of speaking to dead loved ones and the consistency of their dreams struck him with a sense of awe and trepidation. He glanced at each of them, their earnest expressions reflecting the gravity of their shared experience.

As the reality of the situation sank in, Seth's laughter transformed into a mixture of disbelief and excitement. He struggled to comprehend the magnitude of what they were experiencing. This was far beyond anything he had anticipated, reaching into the realms of the inexplicable and the supernatural.

Seth took a deep breath, his eyes locking with the others, his voice laced with a newfound seriousness. "Wait, so you're all saying that you genuinely had the same dream about speaking to dead loved ones?" Seth queried.

Elle affirmed his question, her voice steady, "Every detail is the same. We all had conversations with our deceased loved ones."

In an attempt to dismiss the seemingly impossible, Rhonda interjected, her disbelief palpable, "That's impossible."

Seth's amusement at their shared prank faltered as he observed the unwavering sincerity in their eyes. A wave of realization washed over him, as he began to comprehend the magnitude of what they were claiming. The laughter that once filled the air now paused, replaced by a mix of curiosity, wonder, and a touch of fear.

The significance of their shared dream, speaking to deceased loved ones, and now the discovery of inscribed names on the ancient tablet weighed on Seth's mind. Each thread of the unfolding mystery became entangled, intertwining the dreams with the artifacts they were uncovering.

Seth's thoughts raced, contemplating the implications of this new development. He realized that this revelation was far bigger than anything they had encountered before. With a newfound determination, he decided to delve deeper into the shared dreams, seeking answers to the mysteries that now enveloped their expedition.

But little did Seth and his friends know that their discoveries had caught the attention of others. Unbeknownst to them, they were now part of a game in which they were the hunted prey, pursued by forces that sought to exploit the ancient knowledge they were on the verge of unraveling.

Meanwhile, deep in the lab, Mary Wilson, consumed by her love for ancient history, examined the near-perfect, exquisite tablet made of pure solid gold. As she meticulously examined it, two names inscribed on the tablet caught her attention - Enki and Enlil. The significance of these ancient Sumerian deities began to stir within her, setting the stage for a deeper exploration of the tablet's secrets and the secrets of their shared dreams.

"Nothing about this makes sense," she whispered.

"If this is a coded text, then that raises the question why, and by whom, and for what purpose was it made? Maybe a royal decree or order of instructions intended for a royal ceremony or perhaps a prophecy of some kind, or it could have religious connotations." Mary thought to herself.

A noise caught her attention, and she heard the lab door latch open, and Francis appeared from behind the door, looking like he'd had a long night.

"How are things coming along, here, Mary?"

"Francis, you startled me," she said, feeling a little embarrassed.

"Sorry, I was gone so long, I was taking care of some personal business, took longer than I thought," said Francis as he entered the office, trying not to make eye contact.

"Personal business... is that what they are calling it today?" The light coming from the windows hit Mary's face perfectly. She was more beautiful than ever Francis thought to himself.

"So what are we looking at here?"

"Well, to be honest with you, a whole lot is going on here."

"The only thing I can tell you is, as far as I can tell, the tablet is some kind of code, or instructions. Maybe a religious artifact, or possibly something along those lines.

What is the most remarkable is the astonishing quality of gold itself. The composition is the purest gold sample I've ever seen; even by modern standards.

"Sweet, Jesus, like we hit the jackpot!"

Francis, you know I gave that life up.

"Come on, I was just taken the piss...my bad"

NOT FUNNY, NOW COME here and take look at this,"

"I CROSS-REFERENCED the writing over and over, but when I try to make any sense of it, I get nothing. Expect these two names, Enki and Enlil, of the Sumerian creation myth.

"Hey, I read about those two, they were brothers right?" Francis said his eyes wide now with excitement.

"I think we should contact Dr Mubarak and let him take a crack at it. He's an authority on ancient languages. Maybe he can sort it out."

"Hmmm, but shouldn't we check with the professor first, you know, see what he thinks about this?"

"I already spoke to him about it approximately 20 minutes ago. He agreed that we should let Dr. Mubarak take a look at what we found, and he should be arriving any minute," Mary said, now beginning to feel the effects of her sleep deprivation.

They continued examining the tablet, bouncing ideas off each other and discussing possible explanations for its origin and age.

Suddenly, the hallway outside erupted with a chaotic tumult, the hurried sound of footsteps echoing down the corridor.

An unsettling clicking noise reached their ears, followed by an eerie silence that quickly engulfed the room.

"Francis, what's happening out there?" Mary reached out and squeezed his hand.

"If I tell you... you won't like it."

"Perhaps it's someone sent by my father to assist us, maybe even Dr. Mubarak?"

"I highly doubt it. I've served three tours in Afghanistan, and that sound is never a good sign outside your door!"

Without warning, the double doors of the lab crashed open, and two olive-green riot gas canisters rolled in, filling the air with thick clouds of tear gas and suffusing the small room with smoke. Before they could react, three masked men armed with cutting-edge military assault rifles and dressed in black ops military gear rushed into the room.

Instinctively, Francis reached for his sidearm concealed within his vest, but before he could draw the pistol, he was shot twice in the chest. Mary heard a soft popping sound as the bullets struck Francis.

The intruders' weapons were equipped with advanced noise suppressors, emitting minimal sound as they opened fire. Frozen in horror, Mary watched as the muzzle flashes illuminated the room before her.

Francis Martin's lifeless body crumpled to the floor, reminiscent of the collapsing towers on September 11th. He had already succumbed to death before his body even made contact with the ground.

Mary's scream pierced the air as she spiraled into a state of frantic shock. She clawed at her hair in a frenzy before succumbing to paralyzing panic, her chest tightening, leaving her unable to breathe. Through her terror-stricken viewpoint, Mary observed as darkness gradually enveloped her field of vision, rendering everything black as the midnight sun.

Chapter Sixteen

"*According to the universal laws, the magician will form his own point of view about the universe which henceforth will be his true religion.*"
— *Franz Bardon*

ONE HYDE PARK LONDON, UNITED KINGDOM

"Do you have the tablet?" inquired Lord Louis S. Dottington, his presence commanding the luxury rooftop balcony and its automatic sliding glass doors, which welcomed a cool breeze into the spacious area.

On this typical English night in London, the air was often chilly and breezy, providing a fitting backdrop as Lord Dottington gazed upon the distinctive London skyline from his multi-story, multi-million dollar ultra-luxurious penthouse apartment. It was a city that held a historical connection to the dark arts, and he could sense the lingering remnants of the darkness that once permeated the land—a presence that enticed him, much like a moth drawn to a flame.

"No, remain where you are. I shall meet you in Cairo tomorrow evening, my good man," Lord Dottington spoke into his cellphone voice text, confident and composed.

The text conversation continued effortlessly, "Indeed, I possess everything as promised. I shall be in my customary suite at the Four Seasons. Let us convene sharply at 6 o'clock. We shall discuss the intricacies of our shared interest then, my old friend."

Placing his phone delicately in the pocket of his black and gold Tom Ford dinner jacket, Lord Dottington took a deep breath, inhaling through his nostrils and holding it for a count of thirteen.

The night, with all its fears and dark passions, became his ally—an inspiration for the cruelest intentions. Lord Dottington's purpose was clear as the night sky itself. He sought the annihilation of mankind and was determined to exact his master's revenge.

Lord Dottington, a Master Magician and eternal High priest of the Dark Brotherhood, known as the ageless one, originating from a forgotten time, once traversed the realms of Eden until he was betrayed by man, leading to the imprisonment of his beloved Master, Lord Enlil. Under Enlil's tutelage, Dottington harnessed the power of the left-hand path, transforming into the most feared and formidable magician of all.

Lord Dottington lowered his head and entered his library, his mind consumed by deep contemplation. As he traversed the opulent living room, adorned with the artistic touch of renowned designer D. Collins, he moved purposefully, akin to a cat stealthily making its way towards its prey. Finally, he arrived at the entrance of the two-story library and settled at a small rectangular table, approximately three feet high and four feet wide. The table's surface was draped with a velvet black cloth embellished with golden stars, silver moons, and an array of magical symbols.

At the center of the table, an intriguing sight awaited Lord Dottington—an ebony marble crystal ball positioned precisely within a perfectly round, six-inch, seven-pointed pentagram. The crystal ball rested upon an ornate silver base, adorned with intricately sculpted dragons, skulls, lightning bolts, and daggers.

With a straight posture and his hands placed flat on his thighs, Lord Dottington firmly planted his bare feet on the floor. He relaxed his shoulders through a series of deep breaths, gradually raising his chin until it reached a parallel position with the floor. Taking another slow, deep breath, he relaxed further and straightened his back. As he exhaled, Lord Dottington began enunciating a sequence of vowel sounds, directing each sound towards a different point on the dormant black orb.

After each repetition, he inhaled, steadily drawing colder air into his lungs. This ritual was performed seven times, and Lord Dottington maintained his closed eyes, purposefully pushing away any stray thoughts that attempted to intrude upon his mind until finally, his consciousness became empty—an absence of all mental activity. He sat in this state for several minutes before gradually opening his eyes, each movement deliberate and unhurried.

"Cro Maat," he whispered, his voice carrying a weight of mystique and profound intention.

As Lord Dottington stood there intently observing the crystal ball, a remarkable transformation began to unfold in the air surrounding him. A tiny speck of light emerged from the center of the black sphere, steadily growing in size and radiating a brilliant white luminescence. The ball itself flickered and shimmered, now alive with an otherworldly glow.

Within the crystalline depths of the orb, vivid images took shape and danced before Lord Dottington's eyes. He beheld the sight of Abydos, where the professor and the children diligently excavated around a large white stone. Among them stood Seth, conversing with a young African girl. Dottington watched their exchange with keen interest.

With a subtle gesture of his finger, the image shifted like wisps of smoke, turning its focus towards Rhonda and Elle, who were engaged in digging a short distance from where they had discovered the golden tablet. Lord Dottington, his voice a mere whisper, spoke into the crystal ball, commanding,

"Show me!"

In response, Rhonda sat upright, ceasing her excavation and proceeding to walk toward the very stone where the tablet had been unearthed. Meanwhile, the professor stood approximately five meters away from the stone, offering guidance to Seth and Andenesh regarding proper field measurements.

Lord Dottington's gaze penetrated Rhonda's eyes, as if he stood beside her, peering deep into her soul. He found what he sought and swiftly released his hold on her consciousness.

"Rhonda, are you okay?" he queried, projecting his voice through the crystal ball.

Pausing for a moment, Rhonda replied, uncertainty lacing her words, "Yeah, I think so. I'm not sure. I was just talking to Elle a second ago, and the next thing I know, I'm standing here."

Understanding the situation, the professor intervened, his concern evident. "Okay, maybe you should get some water and take a break, young lady," he advised, acknowledging the need for her to rest and regain her composure.

Lord Dottington observed the unfolding events, contemplating the implications of what was evident. The crystal ball showed him all he needed to know for now. And he knew what he needed to do next. All was transpiring just as he had foreseen.

Chapter Seventeen

"*From the center where the Will of God is known Let purpose guide the little wills of men - The purpose which the Masters know and serve.*"

-Arcane School

MAGICIAN'S GAMBIT

Lord Dottington stepped away from the crystal ball, feeling a little confused. He saw something unexpected in the boy's eyes. "Was someone protecting the child?" He thought to himself.

Time was of the essence, and now was not the time for distractions. Lord Dottington's carefully laid plans were in motion, with his recent appointment as the governor of the Bank of England serving as a crucial stepping stone to his plans.

Over the past two years, he had strategically positioned himself as one of the most influential figures in the United Kingdom, esteemed and widely respected.

Having assumed a new identity upon his arrival in England decades ago, Lord Dottington concealed his true heritage. His transformation from a survivor of Nazi war camps to a distinguished economist and financier was masterfully orchestrated. He had artfully charmed his way into the hearts of many, earning titles, honors, and public adoration.

The King herself had bestowed Lord Dottington with his noble titles, oblivious to the dark secrets he harbored. The public admired his charitable endeavors and handsome appearance, considering him a paragon of virtue and goodwill. His involvement in numerous charitable organizations and generous donations painted a picture of a man dedicated to uplifting the less fortunate.

The British press, enamored by his quick wit and genuine compassion for London's impoverished children, celebrated him and bestowed him with multiple humanitarian awards. Questions lingered, however, about his unmarried status at the age of 51. Yet, he effortlessly evaded such inquiries, leaving the public to speculate and gossip as they pleased.

Now, as Lord Dottington continued his path of manipulation and subterfuge, he knew that the truth behind his facade could not remain hidden forever. The revelations of Abydos and the enigma of the newly discovered golden object beckoned him to embark on a perilous journey, where secrets would be exposed and destinies entwined.

Lord Dottington could no longer afford to delay. With determination etched upon his sharp features and his piercing gray eyes reflecting a mixture of resolve and trepidation, he resolved to confront the unfolding destiny head-on.

But tonight like every night, he sat quietly in his private sanctum that lay hidden behind the far wall of his spacious master bedroom. His cold, gray eyes stared intensely and without blinking into his magic mirror. His thin lips were moving slightly as he inaudibly chanted an ancient invocation.

The eerily glowing candles around the room flickered as he uttered the last verses of the arcane magic, and the room grew abnormally still, gradually the lights dimmed and took on a reddish glow that suddenly appeared in the magic mirror. A moment later a hideous image began to form in the mirror. It was a face like a man's but larger and with horns like a bull and with a rather strange headdress. Its eyes were much larger than normal and looked like black pearls.

The glow from the mirror lit Dottington's pale white face with a fiery red hue. Spectre in the mirror, now fully formed, began to speak to him in the ancient Sumerian tongue, a language barely a handful of scholars today understand.

The being in the magic mirror continued to speak, the ornate and beautifully gothic room grew colder sending a sharp chill down Dottington's spine, a feeling he quite enjoyed.

Lord Dottington listened intently as the face in the mirror transferred secret instructions to him. After some time, the face in the mirror started to fade.

The strange red glow slowly faded, the temperature returned to normal, and the room returned to its natural state. Lord Dottington stood up and faced himself to the west, his body stiff and his back straight. He made several gestures with his left hand, then recited a closing spell in the old world Coptic tongue to end his dark invocation.

Dottington was visibly pleased with himself as he gracefully walked around his magical sanctum, and with one motion of his hand, he put out the 13 red and black candles on either side of the black painted walls. He carefully placed each candlestick back into an ornate black chest to the right of the elaborate altar at the back of the sanctum.

Lord Dottington turned and stepped from inside the hidden room, and was greeted by his trusted butler, George Reynaud.

"My lord, the brothers are arriving," he said in a cold, and lifeless tone.

"Thank you, George, I will be down shortly."

Lord Dottington closed his eyes and sent his astral body into the Akasha; He stood at a distance in the shadows to watch and listen before joining the meeting downstairs.

The brothers of the black lodge filed into the main hall of the spacious apartment one by one, each making the sign of the brotherhood with his left hand and uttering the secret password before being allowed entry into the main audience room.

The room was thick with tension and a feeling of general dis-ease. Members mottled about nervously starting short conversations with one another, each hoping to get an idea why this meeting was called, because tonight was an unscheduled meeting.

And for the brotherhood unscheduled meetings were a rare occurrence. The last time the brotherhood had an unscheduled meeting was twenty years ago when one of the brothers had given away secrets about the order to a tabloid newspaper reporter.

Unscheduled meetings indicated a violation of the sacred oath or the emergence of an urgent crisis that demanded immediate attention. In either scenario, it often led to the unfortunate demise of an unfortunate soul.

In accordance with tradition, each of the brothers purified themselves by washing their hands and faces with unholy water, then swiftly donned their black hooded robes. These robes, reserved exclusively in a special wardrobe, were distributed by the lodge's secretary. Adorning the room were portraits of esteemed past brothers and grandmasters.

kjbkm

The walls were completely covered with chilling oil paintings depicting scenes of horned demons and tortured souls. Above, a magnificent chandelier hung, radiating a mystical glow from its 99 lit candles.

At the end of a long conference table, the grandmaster's chair stood, flanked by 32 seats on each side of the colossal table positioned in the center of the room. This chair, a solemn representation, was adorned with ancient symbols and carved out of a solid walnut tree trunk. Skulls, dragons, and daggers intricately adorned each side, while a giant five-pointed pentagram was carved into the headrest.

Once all 99 brothers were seated, a bell rang, and the grandmaster made his entrance through a crimson door. He donned a crimson red robe with gold and black embellishments, peculiarly adorned with mystical inscriptions down each side.

The brothers concealed their surprise at witnessing the grandmaster clad in his high ceremonial robes, which were typically reserved for the High Holy Nights and official brotherhood rituals.

As fear swept over the room, rendering it deafeningly silent, several minutes passed before the grandmaster finally spoke. "Greetings, brothers of darkness and lords of the earth!" Lord Dottington proclaimed.

"Forgive this last-minute summoning to The Order. I am aware that many of you have traveled great distances and have had to cancel significant prior commitments, both personal and vital to The Order. However, your loyalty shall not go unrewarded," Lord Dottington proclaimed.

"The moment we have eagerly awaited is upon us. Our Lord has communicated with me, indicating that the hour has arrived! The final cycle is now in motion. Everything has unfolded just as our master foresaw. Rejoice, brothers, for our endeavors shall soon bear fruit. The darkness will reclaim its dominion over this world, granting us eternal life!"

The atmosphere in the room became charged with electric anticipation, as the air grew unnaturally cold, akin to the icy expanse of a frozen tundra. An icy frost encased the wall mirrors and wine glasses that were thoughtfully arranged on the large table where the brothers were seated.

In that moment, without uttering a word, all the brothers rose from their seats, holding their glasses high above their heads. The entire ritual seemed to be orchestrated by an unseen conductor, guiding their wicked cadence from the shadows.

As one, the brothers stood and raised their glasses, synchronizing their voices to chant the invocation of their dark lord.

He that waits in darkness He who waits alone
He that waits in darkness He who waits alone
He that waits in darkness He who waits alone
He that waits in darkness He who waits alone
He that waits in darkness He who waits alone
He who is the five-pointed star.

Oh, great lord of darkness, master of the earth and that which is below the earth!

May you rise again in blood and
Fire!
Zi Kia Kanpa(Zee-Kee-Ya-Kan-Pa)
Zi Anna Kanpa (Zee-An-Na-Kan-Pa)
Zi Dingir Kia Kanpa (Zee-Deen-Geer-Kee-Ya-Kan-Pa)
Zi Dingir Anna Kanpa (Zee-Deen-Geer-An-Na-Kan-Pa)
Hear me, O Thou Asarualimnunna
Come to me by the powers of the word Banatatu,
And answer my urgent prayer!
Zi Kia Kanpa
Zi Anna Kanp Asarualimnunna.

Chapter Eighteen

"*What you have taken, Has been from here*
What you gave has been given here
What belongs to you today belonged to someone yesterday
and will be someone else's tomorrow
Change is the Law of The Universe"

ABYDOS DIG SITE

Professor Wilson was standing 100 meters away, engaged in a conversation on his iPad, when he noticed Seth Strange and a few other children pointing and staring in his direction.

"Children, what's happening over there?" the professor shouted.

"We're okay; Elle just suggested that maybe we should dig further around the area where Adenesh found the tablet," one of the children replied.

"I didn't say anything... What are you doing?" Elle snapped, jerking her head back, clearly annoyed with Seth.

"Perhaps there are more fragments to be discovered or a clue nearby that could lead us to its origins," Seth contemplated.

The professor paused for a moment, pleased with Elle's logical deduction. "Excellent thinking, Elle!"

"Professor, I..." another student began.

"Now, gather your equipment, my little geniuses. Let's examine that rock formation more closely and see if we can find any clues about how the tablet ended up here," the professor instructed.

"Hey, everyone... listen up. I believe it's best if we keep this whole dream-like experience to ourselves," Rhonda whispered.

"Hmm, I agree. Sharing this with the professor doesn't seem like a good idea. In my village, such occurrences are considered bad omens and attributed to witchcraft," added Adenesh.

"Maybe she's right. We should gather all the facts and make sure we have a coherent story before approaching the professor. I don't know about you guys, but I don't want to be sent home early because the professor thinks I'm affected by the heat," John suggested.

"Perhaps we all had a collective hallucination?" Klaus proposed.

"Didn't Professor Wilson write a book on hypnotism and subconscious mind control?" Asim questioned.

"Do you actually think Professor Wilson hypnotized us?" Elle interjected, displaying clear annoyance on her face.

"Maybe the heat is indeed affecting us," Emanuel suggested.

"For God's sake, what would be the point or reason behind all of this?" Elle exclaimed, clearly frustrated.

Adenesh, growing increasingly frightened, stepped back from the perplexed group of children. She instinctively covered her ears and stared at the ground, feeling a sense of unease.

"I don't like this," Adenesh muttered to herself, nervously scratching her ears.

Scratching her ears was a nervous habit Adenesh developed as a result of a traumatic experience. When she was just eight years old, she suffered a vicious attack by a swarm of deadly African bees. It happened one early morning while she was accompanying her mother to gather firewood for the daily cooking needs.

Unfortunately, luck was not on Adenesh's side that fateful morning. Unknowingly, she stepped directly onto a beehive near a large tree where she was collecting fallen branches.

The swarm of enraged bees wasted no time in launching a counterattack. The first sting struck her left ear, and with each subsequent sting, Adenesh's panic grew. Running in circles and screaming in terror, she was subjected to a flurry of stings on her face and ears, barely escaping with her life.

To this day, any form of intense buzzing, loud conversations, or arguments triggers immense fear within Adenesh.

"Enough chit-chat. Let's focus, children! We have no time to waste," the professor interjected, urging them to move forward.

"We're on our way, Professor Wilson," the children echoed in unison, their enthusiasm evident in their voices.

"Let's discuss this later during our lunch break!" Seth suggested to the rest of the group, who eagerly agreed. With renewed determination, they all set off towards the location where the tablet had been discovered the day before.

As the group hastened forward, Seth glanced at his phone and noticed a text message from his father. Intrigued, he paused to read it. His eyes widened with each line, and as he finished reading, a wide grin spread across his face.

The message revealed that Seth's father had successfully translated the tablet and uncovered a remarkable secret. Deep beneath the very rock where they found the artifact was a hidden treasure. The tablet contained instructions to unlock a concealed gateway leading to extraordinary powers and eternal life!

Overwhelmed with excitement, Seth halted in his tracks, frantically composing a reply to his father's message.

Chapter Eighteen

T HE LEFT-HAND PATH
"There are many names for the place of knowledge—the Absolute, the Cosmic,
the All, God, the Divine Spirit, the Transcendent —yet the concept is one; it is the Universal Manifestation, the Spiritual Essence, that pervades all things. And, it is this entity, this Universal Oneness, that the mystic seeks to know."
-Rosicrucian Manuscript.

A FEW HOURS LATER, Mary stirred from her unintended slumber, only to be greeted by a chilling sensation against her cheek. Opening her eyes, she touched her face and felt something tickling her nose.

As her vision gradually focused, a surge of shock shot through her body. There, lying beside her, was Francis, submerged in a pool of his own blood. A numbing sensation washed over Mary as she stared at his lifeless, open-eyed expression—his eyes devoid of any spark of life.

Adrenaline coursed through Mary's veins, her heart pounding with an intensity fueled by fear. Summoning all her strength, she struggled to rise to her feet, slipping and sliding in the viscous pool that poured from Francis's chest and head.

Forcing herself to avert her gaze, Mary concentrated on maintaining her balance. With great effort, she managed to regain her footing by removing her rubber-soled shoes and stepping away from the steadily expanding puddle that encircled Francis.

The flood of emotions overwhelmed Mary, her senses consumed by an indescribable and primal fear she had never before experienced. Her voice barely above a whisper, she murmured, "My God, Francis, why?"

Tears welled up in her eyes, smudging the thick black lines of eyeliner as they streamed down her face. Acting on instinct, Mary hastily discarded her lab coat, placing it beneath her feet for stability. Blood was everywhere, and she was resolute in her determination to escape.

Surveying her blood-soaked attire, Mary deduced that Francis had been unconscious for at least ten minutes. Her instincts urged her to flee as swiftly as possible—no time for tears. Francis was gone, and there was nothing she could do to bring him back. She had to prioritize her own survival before the person responsible for his death returned to ensure she met a similar fate.

Mary's heart pounded relentlessly in her chest, its rhythm mirroring the crashing waves against a rocky shoreline.

"Pull yourself together, Mary. Move!" she urged herself, trying to quell the panic that threatened to overwhelm her.

Mary scanned the lab, her gaze searching desperately for any sign of the tablet, her laptop, notes, or samples. But they had vanished without a trace. Confusion washed over her as she shook her head in disbelief. "But why?" she muttered, her voice filled with bewilderment.

Without hesitating, Mary reached down and removed the slippery, blood-soaked socks, determined to maintain her balance and speed as she made her way to the exit. With cautious yet swift movements, she maneuvered through the lab, ensuring she avoided any further contact with Francis's blood. Once outside the lab, her steps quickened into a sprint as she navigated the narrow hallway, her sole focus on reaching the emergency exit at the far end of the floor. While there were closer exits and a set of elevators, Mary believed the back stairwell offered the safest route out of the building.

A torrent of unanswerable questions flooded Mary's mind as she descended the stairwell. "Why would terrorists target the tablet? How did they even know we had it?" The perplexing thoughts raced through her psyche, urging her to find answers.

Finally reaching the bottom of the stairwell, Mary propelled herself forward, pushing open the exit door with her foot. She continued running for another 50 yards until exhaustion forced her to halt, gasping for air, behind the building, concealed from view. From her vantage point, she spotted a white maintenance van parked near the faculty parking lot, adjacent to the main entrance's double sliding doors. Beyond the van, she could see the campus security office, knowing there would likely be an officer on duty even at this late hour.

"I need to get help. Maybe Francis is still alive," she thought with a flicker of hope, summoning the courage she needed.

Mentally preparing herself, she reminisced about her days as a high school track athlete, recalling her prowess in the 100 meters. Estimating the distance to be around two hundred meters, she closed her eyes momentarily, took a deep breath, and exhaled slowly, gathering her strength. Then, like a bat out of hell, Mary burst into a full-throttle sprint across the open parking lot, determined to reach the campus security office as swiftly as possible.

Mary's heart pounded with each stride, pushing herself harder than ever before, maybe even surpassing her personal best. The intensity of the situation fueled her determination, fueling her legs as they propelled her forward.

As she ran, the memories of her well-bred upbringing and her father's expectations faded into the background. Her brief flirtation with drugs while studying abroad had exposed her to a darker side of life, one her father would never comprehend. In this moment, survival was paramount, and Mary's past seemed distant and irrelevant.

The discomfort in her feet grew with each pounding on the hot pavement, her limbs aching and protesting. Yet, she had honed the ability to push through pain during her years of Olympic training. Amidst the chaos and exhaustion, Mary maintained her focus, fixating her gaze on the finish line as she had done countless times before.

In a final burst of speed, Mary crashed into the solid wood door of the security office, unable to stop her momentum. Collapsing to her knees, she felt the numbing fatigue engulf her legs and feet. With whatever strength she could muster, Mary raised her hand to knock on the door, only to find it swing open before her.

Desperate for anyone to rescue her from the fear that was choking her mind and body, Mary gasped for air between frantic pleas. "Help me, help me! Somebody, help me!" Her words were tinged with desperation and fear. "Someone shot Francis!

Somebody, please help me!" Her voice cracked with emotion, the urgency evident in every syllable. Mary needed help, and she could only hope that someone inside the security office would be able to offer her the assistance she so desperately sought.

Chapter Nineteen

"*O mysterious and incomprehensible Spirit!
In the depths of my heart, there is only You—You, for all time.*"

LIGHTNING STRIKES TWICE

Despite the professor's explicit instructions to wait until he arrived, a strange and irresistible urge crept over Seth. It felt as if something or someone was beckoning him, pulling him towards an unknown destination. Without pausing to think, he instinctively grabbed a small pickaxe that happened to be leaning against one of the nearby tents.

With the pickaxe in hand, Seth began walking, almost hypnotized by an invisible force guiding him forward. He covered several hundred yards until, abruptly, he came to a halt. Leaning his head forward, he noticed an oblong white marble stone at his feet, adorned with a central signet. The sight of the stone seemed to deepen the trance-like state that had encompassed him.

Without a second thought, Seth raised the pickaxe above his head and took a step back. In one swift motion, he struck the smooth stone with the pickaxe, aiming directly at its center.

The moment the pickaxe made contact, the ground beneath Seth's feet started to shift and give way. Before he had a chance to react, he found himself falling into a rapidly expanding sinkhole, the sands cascading around him.

Desperately, Seth reached out for something to grasp onto, but it was too late. He crashed helplessly to the bottom of the sinkhole, pain shooting up his right arm as he heard the sickening sound of bones snapping. Agony consumed him.

In anguish, Seth cried out, his voice echoing through the depths of the sinkhole. "My arm! My arm is broken!" This was unfamiliar territory for Seth. He had never broken any bones before, always considering himself lucky in that regard. The pain surpassed anything he had imagined.

Upon hearing Seth's desperate cries, the professor's voice thundered from above. "Seth! Seth! Dear God!" he shouted, filled with concern. "I'm down here! My arm I think it's broken!" Seth shouted back, his voice filled with agony and desperation.

"Good Lord! Don't try to move, young man," the professor instructed urgently. "Just stay right where you are and stay very still. Help is on its way." The professor's words carried a mixture of relief and urgency, as he realized the gravity of Seth's predicament could jeopardize the entire expedition.

Despite the pain coursing through his broken arm, Seth managed to adjust himself enough to lift his head and survey the situation. Relieved to find the rest of his limbs intact, he took a moment to assess his surroundings. It appeared that he had fallen about 15 to 20 feet into a chamber of sorts, but how he had ended up there in the first place remained a mystery. The memory of his actions leading up to the fall had vanished from his mind.

Amid the chaos above, Seth could hear panicked shouting and the sound of people rushing around, issuing frantic orders. Security officers had arrived at the scene, assuring him that they would work to get him out. Their words brought a measure of comfort, but the uncertainty of the situation still weighed heavily on his mind.

"Stay calm, son. You're going to be fine," one of the security officers reassured him. The voices of the other children trapped above echoed in his ears, and he could hear the professor warning them to keep their distance for their own safety.

As the rescuers continued their efforts, their shouts and the sound of debris falling filled the air. Amidst all this, Seth's attention was drawn to a sight that stunned him. With slight movements, he crossed his legs and sat up, taking in the chamber he had fallen into. And there, right in front of him, stood a large wooden door adorned with exquisite Egyptian hieroglyphs and captivating pictorial images. Above the door, a cartouche displayed a name unknown to Seth. Having learned to read Egyptian hieroglyphs from his father, he found himself well-versed in the language.

With his good arm, Seth fished out his cell phone from his pocket. As he turned on the phone's built-in flashlight, the dim light illuminated the intricate carvings on the door.

Overwhelmed by the magnitude of the moment, Seth whispered to himself, "They're not going to believe this."

As the commotion above grew louder, the professor's voice rang out, attempting to maintain a sense of composure amidst the chaos. "We're coming down now!" he called out, urgency hidden behind his calm tone. Seth's heart skipped a beat at the realization that they had discovered a tomb.

"Professor, I think we found a tomb!" Seth shouted back, unable to contain his excitement and awe at the discovery.

Relief washed over the professor's voice as he responded, "Thank God you're okay. You could have... Wait a minute. What did you just say, young man?" There was a mixture of curiosity and astonishment in his tone.

Rhonda chimed in, her voice filled with anticipation, "He said there's a door!"

"And it's sealed," Adenesh added quietly, almost sheepishly.

Instructing Seth to stay where he was and not touch anything, the professor and the security officers hastened their descent into the chamber. Seth, still captivated by the sight before him, followed their instructions, unable to do much else with his broken arm throbbing in pain.

As the professor and the officers approached, Seth's eyes remained fixated on the grand seal adorning the door. There was something hauntingly familiar about it, a sense of déjà vu creeping into his mind. It stirred a curiosity deep within him, making him wonder if he had encountered something similar in the past, perhaps in the stories his father had shared or the books he had read. But for now, all he could do was wait, an eager anticipation building within him as he yearned to uncover the secrets held behind that ancient door.

Chapter Twenty

"**N**ow there was a day when the sons of God came to present themselves *before the Lord, and Satan also came among them." Job 1:6*

WASHINGTON, D.C, UNITED STATES

"Patrick, please send everyone back, and we're ready now," the president said, his voice filled with a mix of astonishment and curiosity. As he glanced up from the phone, he couldn't help but feel a profound disbelief at the sight before him. The humanoid-like lizard creature that had shaken his hand moments ago had now transformed back into the well-dressed and dignified Ambassador who had initially entered his office.

Zagr, observing the familiar look of surprise on the president's face, couldn't help but be amused. He had grown accustomed to the reaction of humans, noting how easily they could be frightened or unsettled by the unknown. Nonetheless, he maintained his composed demeanor, understanding that the existence of different races and species required a level of adjustment and understanding on both sides.

Having acknowledged the president's astonishment, Zagr's British accent surprised the president. However, the president had been previously briefed on Zagr's Oxford education, which was part of a secret exchange program initiated after World War II.

The program aimed to foster cultural exchange and understanding between humans and the Nagas and other races living in Inner Earth, preparing governments for the eventual full disclosure.

With the president's agreement to continue the scheduled meeting, he lifted the receiver of his desk phone, and his assistant promptly responded, "Yes, Mr. President!" The stage was set for the meeting to proceed, encompassing the delicate dance of diplomacy and the ongoing journey toward knowledge, acceptance, and cooperation between different worlds.

"Patrick, please send everyone back and we're ready now." The president said, glancing up as he continued speaking the president found himself startled with disbelief as he watched the humanoid like lizard creature that had just shook his hand transform back into The well dressed dignified looking Ambassador who first entered his office just a few moments ago.

Zagr was amused by the familiar look on the president's face. He was always surprised just how easily frightened humans could be. Zagr also knew better than to let his guard down around humans.

After all, as far as he was concerned any race with a history of enslavement and mass genocide of its own kind could never be trusted.

Chapter Twenty Two

"Never forget, the words are not the reality, only reality is reality; picture symbols are the idea, words are confusion." "There is no happiness for the soul in the external worlds since these are perishable, true happiness lies in that which is eternal, within us."

WAKING THE DEAD

EVERYONE WAS STANDING around in silence as the professor studied the newly discovered seal and the unique cartouche engraved at its center. The tomb was very dark near the entrance, but there was enough light for them to examine Seth's broken arm and set it in a field splint.

Seth was greeted by each of the children, and even the local workers offered smiles and words of admiration for discovering the first unopened tomb at Abydos in the history of archaeology.

"Well, you have done an amazing thing, Seth," said Adenesh. "I'm very sorry about your arm."

"Ah, that's ok. It doesn't hurt... really!" Seth replied, sticking his chest out ever so slightly.

"So, if I do this, you won't feel it..." Elle poked his middle finger directly on the epicenter of Seth's fractured bone.

"Hey! Watch it!" Seth shouted.

"I thought you said it didn't hurt, city boy," said John.

Just then, the professor's phone rang and startled everyone, especially Adenesh, who nearly screamed.

"Now, who can this be?" The professor looked at the home screen of his iPhone with disgust. He absentmindedly read the number out loud.

He thought for a moment, but he didn't recognize the number and decided not to answer it. Then he quickly shut off his phone.

"All right, children, I think we are going to have to wait to open this door. Unfortunately, the law requires me to contact the Ministry of Antiquities and have someone from the Ministry present when we open a tomb."

"Oh man, well, that really sucks!" Seth's face was wrinkled with disappointment.

Afterward things settled down, and the professor and the rest of the children took measurements and samples of the area surrounding the tomb. Everyone was excited except for Seth.

"Man, this is real you know what. Typical mainstream archaeology... bullcrap!"

"What you just said makes no sense!" Elle said while picking up a few sample bags that were lying next to her and started adding dates and labels to them.

"If you're so against mainstream science, then what the heck are you doing on this expedition?"

"It's a free trip to Egypt, why would I not come?" said Seth. Adenesh and the other children laughed in agreement.

"Look, everyone knows the Ministry of Antiquities is a bunch of crooks and black-market thieves."

Elle rolled her eyes without responding and quietly turned away to continue making labels.

Chapter Twenty Three

" $\mathbf{W}$ hat we finally do, out of desperation ... is go on an impossible, or even forbidden, journey or pilgrimage, which from a rational point of view is futile: to find the one wise man, whomever or wherever he may be; and to find from him the secret of eternal life or the secret of adjusting to this life as best we can."

THIEVES IN THE NIGHT

"I CAN'T BELIEVE HE didn't answer. Bloody hell, why isn't he answering?" Over the next few minutes, Mary tried without success to reach her father or anyone at the campsite.

Mary had been gripping the phone for so long that her fingers had gone numb.

She was doing her best to keep her head in the game and now lost it in front of everyone at the police station.

She was afraid they might try to sedate her, and there was only one thing Mary hated more than hospitals, and that was needles.

But her fear of needles couldn't stave off the repeated images of Francis lying on the floor of the lab, his lifeless eyes, pools of blood pouring out of every point in his upper body as he lay there empty and still.

"Miss, please take a deep breath and try to calm yourself down." One of the security officers had been watching Mary and monitoring her vital signs, while the other officer was on the phone with the local police. Mary had been so deep in thought she had forgotten anyone else was there.

"You're perfectly safe now. The police are on their way, as well as an emergency medical team. I need you to have a seat and let us take a look at you. Are you sure you're okay?" said the campus security officer.

"I'm okay. Thank you," said Mary. "I'm fine physically. It's not my blood. It's my colleague, Francis Martin. He was a freelance researcher who worked for my father."

The sound of blaring sirens came from the distance and started to fill the air. Mary lost control; her stoic exterior wall suddenly cracked as she started crying uncontrollably.

"I want to speak to my father!" she tried, covering her face with her hands. "What if whoever killed Francis is going after my father as well?" said Mary.

"I'm sure your father is fine, and someone will contact him as soon as we can," said the security officer.

The officer gave Mary a reassuring smile, then gently squeezed her hand and continued. "The police are here now, and they're going to need to get a statement from you."

They're going to need to get a statement from you on exactly what you saw, Ok."

Ok... Mary whispered, still holding her head with both hands like a beach ball.

Outside, at least a dozen police vehicles pulled up, their sirens blaring to a deafening degree. A psychedelic symphony of lights flashed from every direction, creating an intense atmosphere. Streets and the campus were now blocked off with police barricades and armored personnel carriers. Swarms of police officers and members of the special terror unit, dressed in all black, were taking up positions all around the school, while people shouted in every direction.

"Is anybody hurt or in need of immediate attention?" asked an EMT.

"This is the victim, her name is Mary Wilson. She reported the murder. According to her, her co-worker in one of the labs was shot twice during what sounds like a robbery-homicide. She was knocked out by some type of gas the robbers used on them, and when she came to, she found her co-worker on the floor next to her, deceased. Some items may have been stolen, along with some research materials," said the security officer.

Mary sat staring at the floor, drifting in and out of awareness. Her mind was trying to make sense of what had just happened to her and Francis Martin.

"Hi, I'm Christina. I know this is very hard right now, but I'm going to have to take a look at you and make sure you're not seriously injured or have any concussions or fractured bones," said a female EMT.

The two EMTs carefully began examining Mary, pulling and prodding at her various body parts. They were searching for the source of the massive amount of blood covering her entire upper left side from crown to waist but found nothing.

As the EMTs continued their examination, more uniformed police officers filed into the room, making the already small office feel even more crowded. Behind them, two hard-looking men dressed in dark gray suits stepped into the room and pulled out official-looking government badges.

It was late in the afternoon when Professor Wilson finally remembered to turn on his cell phone and check his messages. He had spent the last several hours diligently preparing his reports, knowing that submitting anything to the Ministry of Antiquities required strict adherence to protocol. Taking great care, he reviewed his documents, ensuring every "I" was dotted and every "T" crossed. He was determined not to let any paperwork get in the way of obtaining the permits necessary to open the tomb he had been eagerly awaiting for so long. The excitement of the expedition had made him feel like a kid again, even though just two days ago, he had doubts about its potential.

However, amidst his enthusiasm and focus, Professor Wilson suddenly remembered his daughter, Mary. He had completely forgotten about her in the midst of his work.

"Let's hope things have gone well," he muttered to himself as he pressed a button on his phone.

A small white apple appeared on the display screen, followed by a picture of Mary and his ex-wife. The professor noticed he had missed 25 calls from Mary alone, along with a series of urgent messages.

Quickly slipping his glasses onto his nose, the professor retrieved them from his shirt pocket. One by one, he rapidly scanned through half a dozen messages, all of them from Mary, painting a distressing picture.

"PLEASE CALL ME, TERRORIST SHOT FRANCIS, I THINK FRANCIS IS DEAD! THEY TOOK THE TABLET. I'M AT THE POLICE STATION. PLEASE CALL ME!"

Deep concern etched across his face, Professor Wilson realized the gravity of the situation. Without wasting another moment, hastily dialed his only daughter's number, fervently hoping for her well-being and desperate to understand what was happening.

Professor Wilson held his free hand to his forehead, while his other hand tightly pressed his phone against his ear. He took a long, slow, deep breath and began to casually pace back and forth across the dusty tent floor. He counted six rings to himself before the phone was suddenly answered, not by his daughter, but by an unfamiliar adult male voice with an unmistakable Italian accent.

"Professor Wilson, this is Detective Garofalo," said a clearly masculine voice, with a thick Italian accent. Even when answering a simple phone call, Simone Garofalo's English wasn't perfect, but he spoke with authority despite his limitations.

Garofalo had graduated two years ago, topping his class at the Italian Police Academy, and quickly made a name for himself. He had risen through the ranks faster than any of his predecessors, making him the youngest detective in Italian police history. Now, he was in Cairo on his first assignment for Interpol. Just weeks ago, he had been invited to join the prestigious organization and had been transferred to Cairo by a director's order, which he was told came from someone high up in the organization, who chose to remain anonymous.

Garofalo had taken the job in Cairo as a stepping stone towards his dream of becoming an internationally renowned detective, working on the "big" cases with MI6 or even the CIA. He had grown up watching reruns of American detective stories on a small black and white TV set his parents had given him on his 10th birthday, and from that moment on, all he had ever wanted to be was a detective.

"I received an emergency call from my daughter, Mary Wilson. Is she all right?" the professor's voice wavered, but it was barely noticeable, even to the well-trained ears of Garofalo.

"Your daughter is ok, Professor Wilson. She is a little bit shocked, but this is normal," said the detective reassuringly.

"Thank God! What about my colleague, Francis Martin? Is he alright?" said the professor, his voice now calm and steady.

"I'm afraid he is no longer alive, Professor Wilson. It would appear your colleague was shot during the robbery," said Garofalo.

The professor felt a cold chill run down his spine. But his face said he was not surprised by what he had just heard.

"A robbery? My God, why would anyone want to do such a thing? There's nothing of any real value kept in my lab," said Professor Wilson.

He sat down on his folding chair, crossed his legs, and placed the call on speaker, continuing to listen closely.

"Sir, we don't know much at this moment. However, according to your daughter, the only thing taken was a tablet and several files she and Mr. Martin were working on when the gunmen broke into the laboratory. Can you think of anyone who would want this tablet so badly enough to kill someone for it?" asked Garofalo.

"No, and I must say, I don't know the authenticity of the tablet, let alone its value. It could be a fraud worth absolutely nothing," said the professor.

"I think we can safely say that despite your professional opinion, someone already believes that tablets are quite valuable, no?... I will need to know everything you know about this tablet, Professor Wilson, and any theories you might have would be helpful as well. Are you sure you told no one else about the tablet?" said Garofalo.

"When can I see my daughter? I need to speak with her first. They were doing examinations on the tablet!" said Professor Wilson, starting to form a less favorable opinion of the pushy Italian agent.

"The EMTs took your daughter to the hospital. They felt it was best to take some routine X-rays since she has complained of bruising and discomfort. Why don't I come to where you are and give you a lift to the hospital, so we can discuss things further? I can be at your site in less than one hour."

Chapter Twenty Five

'*A s for me, since they did not fear my name, and I have disregarded Marduk's command, so he may act according to his wishes I will make Marduk angry,*
    stir him from his dwelling, and lay waste to the people!'

MINISTRY OF STATE FOR ANTIQUITIES EGYPT

The two gentlemen hadn't been waiting long when a very young, very blonde secretary came out to escort them into Dr. Mubarak's office.

"Will there be anything else, Dr. Mubarak?" she asked gingerly.

"Yes, Anna, hold my calls. I do not... I repeat, I do not want to be disturbed under any circumstances," said Dr. Mubarak.

"Yes, Doctor," she replied.

"Gentlemen, may I congratulate you on a job well done." Normally, he would have asked them to have a seat, but today he didn't see any need for formality. They were hardened men, real professionals. To this day, he didn't know their names, nor did he want or need such knowledge.

As expected and true to form, only one of them ever spoke, which was the way he liked. He was impressed by their efficiency and professionalism.

Dr. Mubarak took the same approach in his work, so naturally, he appreciated these particular attributes of their relationship.

It was a relationship he understood well. "People are so predictable," he thought to himself.

"Forgive me for asking, but one must cover all the bases. I take it you left no loose ends?" he said calmly.

The two men in the gray fitted suits eyed him carefully. They said nothing for a few seconds, their faces expressionless, and they seemed to breathe in at the same time.

When they exhaled, the smaller of the two giants began to speak again.

"We neutralized any potential problems," said the man.

"Wonderful! You'll find your accounts have been credited as agreed. Now, if there isn't anything else, I thank you for your time, gentlemen. I'm sure you can see your way out. It was a pleasure doing business with you," said Dr. Mubarak.

Dr. Mubarak continued standing, slightly leaning forward over his desk, his hands resting on either side of the briefcase, with his fingers lightly touching the brim.

As Dr. Mubarak lifted the prayer rug, revealing the hidden metal safe underneath, his curiosity grew further. He was intrigued by the mysterious content of the briefcase, and now, discovering a concealed safe only deepened his intrigue. With a sense of anticipation, he approached the safe, his short stubby hands trembling slightly.

Carefully, he entered the combination, the metallic clicks resonating in the silence of the room. The safe door swung open, revealing its hidden contents. Dr. Mubarak's eyes widened in both surprise and confusion as he saw what lay inside.

Instead of the expected valuable documents or possessions, he found a collection of ancient artifacts. There were intricate sculptures, delicate relics, and strange symbols etched onto ancient tablets. Each item seemed to radiate a sense of power and mystery.

Dr. Mubarak's mind raced as he tried to comprehend the significance of these artifacts. He realized that they were of immense historical and archaeological value. His initial uncertainty and fear were quickly replaced by a profound sense of awe and excitement.

He carefully picked up one of the artifacts, observing its craftsmanship and studying the inscriptions. Although he couldn't decipher the writing, he knew that he held something of great importance in his hands. It was clear to him that these artifacts had a story to tell, a story that could reshape history and shed light on ancient cultures and civilizations.

At that moment, Dr. Mubarak's mind turned away from thoughts of personal gain or worldly power. His lifelong dedication to the pursuit of knowledge and truth propelled him forward. He was driven by a desire to unlock the secrets contained within these ancient relics, to uncover their hidden mysteries, and to contribute to the collective understanding of humanity's past.

With renewed determination, Dr. Mubarak carefully arranged the artifacts back into the safe, closing it securely.

The unexpected turn of events had ignited a new purpose within him, a path that merged his love for scholarship with the enigmatic allure of these ancient treasures.

As he stood there, gazing at the closed safe, Dr. Mubarak knew that his life was about to take a fascinating and consequential turn. He would embark on a journey of discovery, guided by his intellect, faith, and unwavering commitment to unravel the mysteries that lay before him.

He pressed the code on the keyboard lock, then lifted the lid open. Dr Mubarak carefully placed the tablet in the safe next to several small bundles of various fiat currencies,

He stared at the content of the safe and again thought of paradise.

He was grateful he was so fortunate. "Allah be praised!" he said to himself, then he quickly closed the safe.

Chapter Twenty Six

M otion is eternal in the unmanifest and periodical in the manifest, says an occult teaching. It is when heat caused by the descent of flame into matter causes its particles to move, which motion becomes the whirlwind. (The Secret Doctrine, Vol. 1, p. 114)

WHERE THE WIND BLOWS

Seth's eyes were feeling fatigued, and extremely dry, from the hot desert air. The sun was much brighter and penetrating than in New York City. He had never thought about it before, but he was sure it had something to do with the skyscrapers obstructing the direct sunlight, and the effect of the cities polluting the air.

He was just about to go to his tent to get some shade when from behind he heard Adenesh's soft voice call out to him. He liked Adenesh's voice.

"Seth, please wait. Where are you going? Something awful has happened. The professor is at the hospital. Something is going on with Mary and Mr Martin!"

Seth immediately noticed she looked genuinely frightened.

"What? Man, that sucks. Are we going to get to open the tomb?" Seth said as he scratched his forehead.

"I'm burnt from this sun. I think I'm gonna go lay down until the professor gets back." He thought to himself.

The hot desert wind blew like a dragon's hell-fire around Seth's face, and he felt like he was raining sweat. He wiped his forehead with his T-shirt and started to turn and walk away. Adenesh ran forward and grabbed him by the arm before he could turn around.

"Seth, I don't think you understand. I'm afraid something terrible has happened! Said Adenesh.

Her eyes began to tear up again as she let go of his hand and wiped her eyes before a tear could fall.

"Adenesh, said Seth. "I'm sure everything is just fine…where is everyone?"

"The professor called Elle. I was there when he called well; everyone was there except you. Where were you anyway?" She shouted. Suddenly felt embarrassed for being, and so direct with the cute American boy.

She was a bit surprised with herself but had no time to ponder it, so she continued and tried not to let her discomfort show.

"What were you doing? I saw you come from the direction of the tomb. You didn't go down there, did you?"

"No! Of course not. I was looking for a place to take a dump." He said. Lying was easy for Seth. Growing up in Brooklyn, lying just came naturally, even for suburban middle-class kids. Lying was part of survival in the city. You lie to your teachers, the cops, strangers, friends, your parents, and even to yourself. That's what it means to be a New Yorker.

Adenesh gazed at Seth with an inscrutable expression that seemed to convey, "I know you're lying." Seth averted his eyes and looked downward, choosing to shift the topic instead.

"Anyway, what are we supposed to do? Is he coming back?" asked Seth.

"He mentioned he would Facetime us on Elle's iPad. Elle asked me to find you. We should go over there," said Adenesh.

Both of them decided to momentarily set aside their individual inquiries, although Adenesh's intuition told her Seth was hiding something. Nevertheless, she decided to overlook it.

While she found Seth to be clever and somewhat assertive, Adenesh had never encountered an American before. She had often heard that Americans were generally loud and rude, but she did not find Seth offensive at all. In fact, she found him intriguing and refreshing, and she certainly didn't want to cause any trouble.

Seth took the lead as they hurriedly joined the other children to learn why the professor insisted on their presence, as if it were something of utmost importance.

For Seth, the only thing that mattered was what lay inside the tomb. "It's going to be incredible! Everywhere I looked, in every direction, gleaming solid gold statues—real gold, glistening in the shadows," he exclaimed. "Without a doubt, it's all covered in thick, lustrous, gleaming, beautiful gold."

Few things excited Seth as much as the sight of gold. He loved examining it and holding it; sometimes he even believed he could detect its distinctive scent. Gold, in some strange way, gave Seth a sense of power that he couldn't quite comprehend. His uncle was a pawnbroker in Manhattan, running a reputable shop with esteemed clients.

Having worked for his uncle during previous summers, Seth thoroughly enjoyed his time at the shop. He took pleasure in exploring rows of aged items, particularly gold rings, watches, and other exquisite jewelry. Seth quickly learned to discern between real and fake gold, possessing an innate ability to identify the genuine article.

Chapter Twenty Seven

"O people of the earth, men and women born and made of the elements, but with the spirit of the Divine within you, rise from your sleep of ignorance! ...

S MOKE AND STEEL
Initially, Mary found it incredibly difficult to recount her bone-chilling brush with death to her father. Her feet still felt numb, and her throat was hoarse as she forced herself to provide a detailed account.

The words tumbled from her quivering lips like a slow, steady drip from a faucet. Her narrative reached its climax with the tragic demise of Francis Martin, a father of two and Mary's one true love. He had been shot dead before her disbelieving eyes, amidst swirling smoke and gleaming steel. In a daze, Mary spoke as if she were under the spell of a snake charmer.

The officers were impressed as Mary meticulously recounted every tiny detail, a reflection of her discipline as an archaeologist.

However, Mary's consciousness began to fade, allowing her subconscious to take over the narration of what had transpired in the lab with Francis.

"My dear child, I am so sorry. Are you going to be alright?" asked the professor, his kind eyes filled with concern.

"I think it may be best for you to head home. I will take care of the children. I can call someone from the university to cover for you," suggested the professor.

"No, I'm okay. Please, father, I don't want to be alone right now. I would prefer to keep my mind occupied with work."

Everyone could clearly see that Mary was still deeply shaken.

"What was so incredibly important about that tablet?" inquired the professor.

"Why would someone be willing to rob and murder for a Sumerian tablet? There have been hundreds of thousands of tablets discovered," added Garofalo.

"How could they have known about the tablet?" questioned the professor. "I knew Frank was struggling financially, which is why I offered him the job. He got involved with a group of smugglers last year, and I know he had accumulated significant debt."

"Wait a minute!" exclaimed Mary, her voice filled with urgency.

"That's the million-dollar question, isn't it?" remarked Garofalo.

"How did they know? Someone who knew about the tablet..." Mary pondered, trying to make sense of the situation.

"It doesn't make any sense at all," she continued. "Why would he put himself in harm's way?"

"Yes, you mentioned that he reached for his gun, trying to protect you," Mary turned to the professor. "Think, professor, is there any additional information you can provide, no matter how small?"

"Try to recollect if anything else could be important," added Agent Garofalo.

"No, honestly, I can't think of anything else," replied the professor with a tone of genuine confusion. "I can't fathom any reason why this would be happening. It simply doesn't make sense!"

Garofalo scrutinized the professor, remaining silent. As an experienced investigator, he possessed a keen instinct for detecting deception.

"He's lying. But why?" Garofalo contemplated silently, his gaze fixed on the professor as he embraced his daughter tightly.

Chapter Twenty Eight

"*He who knows the fire that is within himself shall ascend unto the eternal fire and dwell in it eternal. Fire,*"

AIR FORCE 1, SOMEWHERE OVER THE ATLANTIC OCEAN

General John Smitherson's distinguished career of 40 years in military service had provided him with valuable insights and a hardened perspective. Among the lessons he had learned was the absolute necessity of never trusting the Reptilians. Smitherson was well-versed in their history, particularly their insatiable bloodlust and their cunning ways of navigating diplomatic waters. He was always mindful of the fact that humans had once been the primary food source for the reptilian species, and he suspected they wouldn't be averse to returning to those dark days.

Despite his deep-seated mistrust, Smitherson remained committed to his role as a career soldier. He had learned early on that following orders until instructed otherwise was the key to securing a proper pension. Personal feelings or even his contempt for the Nagas, for example, never interfered with his duty as a soldier. Not even his tumultuous personal life, including his three ex-wives and four children whom he rarely saw, could sway his unwavering loyalty.

Although the hour was growing late, Smitherson was summoned to a special meeting concerning the repercussions of the day's market crash and the president's upcoming meeting with Ambassador Zagr. The general's first encounter with Ambassador Zagr had taken place over 30 years ago when he assumed the highly coveted and ultra secret position of commander of the Earth Alliance and special liaison to Inner Earth Zone 5.

The command group and alliance General Smitherson belonged to comprised not only Reptilian forces but also a few alien races that had migrated to the southern region of Inner Earth over 100,000 years ago. This alliance was, in fact, the underlying reason behind America's remarkable technological advancements in the early 21st century.

As the general reviewed his notes, he prepared to debrief the newly elected president and determine how well the meeting with the Inner Earth race had gone. Previous incidents involving other presidents and their initial encounters with alien races had resulted in unfortunate outcomes. In some cases, presidents had to be sedated, and regrettably, one president had to be terminated due to the traumatic nature of the experience.

During the first meeting with the Reptilians, it was customary for the reptilian ambassador to reveal his true form to the surface government representative. As General Smitherson waited, he noticed that he had been kept waiting for nearly an hour. Finally, a male aide emerged from the back room of the plane and informed the general that the president was ready to meet with him.

Smitherson greeted the president, expressing his pleasure at seeing him again, and inquired about the outcome of the meeting with the ambassador. The president, sounding unsteady and visibly shaken, candidly admitted that nothing could have prepared him for what he had witnessed or how he felt during the encounter. Impatient to share his thoughts, the president quickly indicated his dedication to truth and the urgency of disclosing the existence of aliens to the American people and the world at large.

General Smitherson listened attentively to the president's account, remaining patient and understanding of the president's overwhelmed state, as it was typical for human beings to experience shock and confusion during their first contact with extraterrestrial beings.

General Smitherson skillfully masked any emotional response as he listened to the president's unexpected declaration. The president's firm belief that the American people deserved to know about the existence of aliens and his intention to initiate the process of disclosure throughout his tenure left the general taken aback.

In response, General Smitherson chose his words carefully, acknowledging the president's conviction while expressing concerns about the potential consequences of such a disclosure. He emphasized that unveiling the truth would violate the longstanding treaty the United States had with the Inner Earth Alliance, and therefore, it would not be in the best interest of the country or its citizens.

However, the president remained steadfast in his decision, viewing this disclosure as a significant achievement and his potential legacy. He issued a direct order for the general to collaborate with the ambassador to devise a feasible plan for complete disclosure within the next four years.

General Smitherson, compelled by his military training and sense of duty, accepted the order, assuring the president that he understood his intentions clearly. Internally, though, he realized the gravity of the situation and contemplated the challenges ahead. The thought of potential complications resonated with him, evoking the iconic phrase, "Houston, we have a problem."

As the meeting concluded, the president, mindful of his early experiences in politics, sensed some unease in the general's demeanor. He questioned whether there were undisclosed matters that the general was withholding, recognizing the significance of body language even during seemingly casual conversations.

Chapter Twenty Nine

" As above, so below, as within, so without, as the universe, so the soul..."

THE LAND OF THE NAGAS

Deep within the Earth lies the mysterious realm known as the inner earth, also referred to as Agharta or Shambala by ancient civilizations. This ancient world is far older than the one inhabited by human beings, characterized by vast valleys, teeming oceans with peculiar creatures, expansive Amazonian-like rivers flowing through endless forests, and fossilized forests adorning volcanic highlands. A maternal inner sun bathes these lands, sustaining a unique and thriving ecosystem.

Agharta is a land of rich green forests, rolling hills, and extensive networks of tunnels that span hundreds of miles beneath the Earth's surface. It is adorned with majestic mountain ranges, mighty rivers that lead to emerald oceans, and golden islands inhabited by a variety of mythical creatures and formidable beasts. Three significant races dwell within Agharta: the Nagas, the Nordics, and the Asktamar.

Towards the southern end lies a forbidden territory known as the black lands or the desert barrier. According to legend, this land was created by the gods to imprison the followers of Lord Enlil, who harbored a deep hatred for humanity and sought to destroy mankind, flooding the Earth with rivers of human blood.

Mornings in the inner earth, particularly in Area 1, are hot and humid, with temperatures averaging around 60 degrees Celsius. This fiercely tropical region is inhabited by the Nagas, also known as the Reptilians by those who dwell on the Earth's surface. These mighty creatures once ruled the surface as kings and warriors of the earth, sea, and sky. However, they were eventually driven underground by the Anunnaki who arrived and exerted their dominance over them.

Though many treaties were made to bring peace between them, the deals were often broken, more often than not before they could even be signed or enforced.

In the time before human beings the Anunnaki forced the Nagas and all their kind off the surface with weather weapons which terraformed the planet surface and its air, making it uninhabitable for the Nagas for long periods of time.

But instead of fleeing the surface, many tried to fight back and were annihilated but the gods in a great deluge of fire, and finally ice. Those who survived were forced into the underground.

The Nagas have the ability to shape-shift. Some are supposed to have the ability to change into giant flesh-eating beasts, while others take the shape of birds and sea creatures. It is even said that some of the priests of the Nagas can assume any living form and also make themselves invisible to the untrained eye.

Ambassador Zagr was a Reptilian of the first order. As the ambassador to the surface governments, he spent most of his time in the shape of a middle-aged, white male diplomat.

He'd long forgotten the poor soul he devoured to absorb his essence. Eating the victim's flesh is how the reptilians of the first order acquire the raw DNA material needed to take on the shape of other life forms, by ingesting their brain's and devouring their DNA, then assimilating the DNA into their own.

Zagr hated the way humans looked, but they smelled and tasted just like bacon. Zagr loved the smell of bacon, he even sometimes absent-mindedly sniffed his own arm or fingers when he was in human form.

Ambassador Zagr dismissed the random thoughts swirling in his mind and refocused on the task at hand. Having just boarded the transport for the return journey to Agarath, he knew he had to make his report to the Ministry of Human Affairs. However, before initiating the transmission, something caught his attention.

Glancing at the viewing monitor, Zagr saw his reflection and realized he was still in his human form. Determined to rectify his oversight, he closed his eyes and directed his will inward. In an instant, his skin began to roll and twist, revealing green and leathery scales. Feathers resembling those of a bird fluffed out in every direction, only to swiftly retract, simultaneously changing color and texture.

Upon opening his large, yellow and green eyes, Zagr noticed the flickering of the long black slits that had replaced his pupils. His teeth, elongated and jagged, were as razor-sharp as ever. His snake-like tongue flicked in and out of his formidable mouth. Instead of ears, he had small openings in their stead, while gill-like structures adorned each side of his neck, facilitating his breathing. With a lengthy neck, sturdy legs, and a robust upper torso, Zagr now resembled a towering, two-legged creature—an extraordinary blend of a dinosaur and a lizard, with avian attributes.

"Much better," he thought to himself, momentarily slipping into vanity. Though he had always considered himself appealing, the extensive time spent in human form occasionally caused him to forget just how striking his true form was. "All right, I must not allow myself to be distracted any longer."

With a press of a button on the control panel of the cloaked flying disc, the vehicle began to ascend gradually into the air. Seemingly weightless and soundless, it surpassed the confines of Area 51 Hangar 13 with ease.

He commanded the navigation controls to plot a return course towards the Inner Earth base, and instantly, the now cloaked flying craft lifted into the air, ascending above the desert and into the vast expanse of the starry night sky.

Ambassador Zagr was well aware that King Sargon would not take kindly to the proposition put forth by the President. However, this did not bother him. Right from the moment he laid eyes on the conceited and small-faced politician, Zagr harbored a strong dislike towards him. It wouldn't be the first time they had to eliminate a president or any human, for that matter. But as he made his way to the Inner Earth base, the aroma of bacon invaded his thoughts once again. He couldn't resist the temptation and let out a slight moan. How he loved the enticing smell of bacon.

Zagr waved his disproportionately small left claw-hand, causing a small headpiece to descend from above his command chair. It hovered just above his head as he carefully positioned it over his ear opening. Speaking in his native reptilian tongue, he initiated communication.

"Yar nan sa taka, Hun kasa ta sa kambe et so fan te!" he uttered. Reptilians were telepathically connected and did not require verbal communication at close distances.

"Welcome home, Ambassador Zagr. Please relinquish control. We have you securely locked on and will guide you through the barrier," responded a moderately slow hissing voice over the ship's communication control speaker.

"THE AMBASSADOR IS AWARE of his majesty's displeasure," responded the voice. "Understood," acknowledged Zagr. "Inform his majesty that there has been a change in the plans." With another wave of his hand over the control surface, Zagr disconnected the communication.

Taking several rapid and shallow breaths, the ambassador relished the anticipation that had been building up within him for years. Flicking his forked tongue in delight, he knew that the moment he had been waiting for was finally at hand. The taste of human flesh was something he truly savored, and now it was only a matter of time. The thought of bacon crossed his mind once more, causing a smile to creep across his scaly green face.

Chapter Thirty

" Close your eyes and let the mind expand. Let no fear of death or darkness arrest its course. Allow the mind to merge with the Mind. Let it flow out upon the great curve of consciousness. Let it soar on the wings of the great bird of duration, up to the very Circle of Eternity."

TOMB RAIDERS FAIR

"Everyone is present, Professor Wilson," Elle announced, panning her iPad's FaceTime camera slowly from left to right, giving the professor a clear view of the gathered individuals, as he had requested. She then turned the iPad around, observing a pleased expression on the professor's face.

"Thank you, Elle!" expressed the professor gratefully. "It's good to see everyone. Now, let me begin by addressing the tablet we discovered..." He paused momentarily, nibbling on his upper lip.

"I believe it could hold considerable value, which is why we have sent it to Dr. Mubarak's team for further analysis. However, we will proceed with our plans to open the tomb. It appears that what we previously believed to be a missing tablet was actually just misplaced," explained the professor.

Seth and the other children appeared puzzled and remained silent, processing the information. Finally, Seth spoke up, seeking clarification. "When will you and Mary be back?"

"Mary and I will be returning tomorrow morning," the professor assured. While lying was not his preferred approach, he understood that sometimes difficult decisions required such actions. He reminded himself to justify it as a necessary step.

Revealing the truth about what had happened to Mary and Francis would only needlessly frighten the children and potentially derail the expedition. That was something he couldn't allow to happen.

"Mr. Martin, unfortunately, won't be joining us, as he unexpectedly fell ill. Instead, Mr. Garofalo will accompany Mary and me back," the professor disclosed.

"Now, I want all of you to get some rest and avoid venturing beyond the perimeter of the camp," Mary interjected, pointing towards the roped-off area surrounding the campsite. "We have a substantial amount of ground to cover tomorrow, and it's important that we start fresh at dawn."

Having concluded their conversation, Mary, Garofalo, and the professor made their way towards the professor's tent, ready to retire for the night.

Seth's revelation left Adenesh intrigued, her eyes fixed on him with a mix of curiosity and concern.

"You shared the pictures with your dad?" she whispered back to Seth, remembering their earlier conversation. His nod confirmed her question.

"He responded with a message claiming that the tablet contains a secret code about a trapped god and a key that can release it from its confinement. He also mentioned a tomb with a map written in the form of spells, leading to the location of the key," Seth disclosed, his voice filled with anticipation.

Adenesh stayed silent, absorbing this new information.

Seth continued, sharing his thoughts. "Honestly, I have a gut feeling that we should pursue opening the tomb and finding these keys, before the professor takes complete control over everything."

As if on cue, the professor's voice interrupted their conversation through the FaceTime call. "Okay, kids, thank you for being understanding during this minor setback we're facing. We'll meet you at the tomb entrance after breakfast tomorrow. Goodnight."

Adenesh mulled over Seth's suggestion, her mind racing with possibilities. "Maybe we should inform the professor about what your dad told us. What if they have already deciphered the tablet as well?" she proposed, expressing her concerns.

Seth, however, remained resolute. "So what if they have? If we reach the tomb first and uncover the truth, we'll have evidence on our side. I can't shake the feeling that they're hiding something from us. We need to take matters into our own hands."

The decision weighed heavily upon their young shoulders, the consequences unpredictable. But their determination to uncover the truth propelled them forward, regardless of the risks involved.

Seth's frustration grew more evident as he passionately defended his dad's expertise and the significance of his translations. He believed that the professor and Mary deliberately omitted mentioning the information his father had shared with him, suspecting ulterior motives.

"The tablet and the tomb must be connected, and I'm certain this discovery could surpass even King Tut's gold," Seth insisted, his face reddening with intensity. "They just want all the credit for themselves, or maybe they're planning to sell everything on the black market."

Elle, noticing the hushed conversation between Seth and Adenesh, intervened, demanding an explanation. Rhonda and John also joined in, voicing their curiosity and concern, echoed by the nodding agreement of the other children.

Adenesh attempted to defuse the situation, starting to explain Seth's revelation, but Seth quickly interrupted, desperate to avoid revealing too much.

"Everyone knows my dad is an expert on symbolism and ancient writing," Seth blurted out. "I sent him pictures of the tablet before we handed it over to the professor, and he translated it. It's a treasure map."

Elle's curiosity led her to inquire further, seeking clarification. "So you're suggesting that it's strange the professor didn't mention any of this to us?"

Seth nodded emphatically, hoping to convince the others. "Exactly! It's odd that he would keep such crucial information from us."

Elle offered a possible explanation, attempting to give the professor the benefit of the doubt. "Perhaps he had his reasons for not discussing it over the phone. It could be a matter of discretion."

Emanuel chimed in, questioning the professor's motives. "Even if there was another reason, why would he deliberately hide it from us?"

The air filled with uncertainty and suspicion as the children grappled with the conflicting narratives presented before them. Their trust in the professor began to waver, and the realization that there might be hidden agendas at play left them questioning their next steps.

As Seth's ambition to claim the glory of the potential treasure grew, he urged the group to seize the opportunity to make history and secure a place in the annals of archaeology. He emphasized the immense size and significance of the tomb, comparing it to the grandeur of King Tut's treasure.

Rhonda quickly interjected, expressing concern about the consequences of engaging in unauthorized excavations. She reminded Seth that they were part of a structured program and warned against jeopardizing their positions, being expelled from the Y.A.S program, and potentially facing legal repercussions.

Adenesh echoed Rhonda's sentiments, emphasizing the need to follow proper protocols and involve the authorities before entering the tomb. She emphasized the importance of maintaining integrity and legality in their endeavors.

Seth, undeterred, proposed a plan to trespass into the tomb without detection. However, Asim pointed out the presence of a seal on the chamber door, suggesting that any attempt to open it would likely be noticed. Additionally, the professor had instructed the security guards to protect the entrance until he returned with the necessary permits and authorities.

Elle reiterated the practical obstacles, reminding Seth that bypassing the guards and breaking the seal would be nearly impossible. Nevertheless, Seth was confident and excited, assuring the group that he had a plan in mind.

Adenesh voiced her apprehension about Seth's plan, but Seth insisted they trust him and eagerly raised his hands to gain their attention. Elle, unafraid to challenge Seth, cautiously embraced the conversation, recognizing his determination and appreciating his spirited nature.

Intrigued and slightly skeptical, the group gathered around Seth, their curiosity piqued. They focused their undivided attention, prepared to hear Seth's master plan and assess its viability. The allure of adventure and the desire to leave their mark on history danced in their young minds, awaiting Seth's proposal.

Chapter Thirty One

"*I*t's *better to be a live dog than a dead lion.*"
    -Old Testament

CAIRO POLICE STATION

"I WANT YOU TO KNOW I have real concerns about you posing as a member of this expedition team." The professor tilted his head to look in the rear mirror, searching for a response from Agent Garofalo.

Garofalo didn't look up, so the professor continued. "But for the children's sake and to avoid any undue panic from their families, I have no choice but to go along with this."

"I couldn't agree with you more, doctor. Or is it a professor?" Garofalo said sarcastically.

It's a doctor, but he prefers professor, said Mary.

"Of course, I say that with all due respect, as I care to remember you mentioning, you minored in anthropology," said Professor Wilson.

"None was taken!" Garofalo hastily replied, still not looking to acknowledge the professor's repeated attempt at eye contact.

Garofalo was unable to focus on the professor due to a very involved and very intense texting conversation on his iPhone judging by the feverish movements of his thumbs across the phone's keyboard.

The professor wondered who Garofalo was communicating with and, more importantly, what exactly the discussion was concerning.

"I think we need to calm down. Just because Agent Garofalo isn't an archaeologist, We don't need archaeologists for Christ Sake we need someone who can find out what the hell is going on!" said Mary shouted till her face had turned bright red and the veins on the side of her temple flared up like earthworms below the surface skin.

"I am calm. I am simply expressing my concerns and hoping for some words of encouragement from the good special Agent. I mean Frank is dead for god sake! We could all be in great danger." Said the professor.

There was sudden, awkward silence, and the professor drew his eyes quickly away from Agent Garofalo's face and over toward Mary's and then back on the road. He could sense his daughter's deep-seated hostility towards him suddenly rising in her blood. Agent Garofalo too must have detected the impending eruption as well, cause he quickly intervened.

"Please professor; you are both right. You are without question right to be concerned about the children, and Mary is correct to believe I am capable of handling this assignment as well. But rest assured, if I weren't qualified the agency wouldn't have sent me here," Said Garofalo.

"Of course," The professor agreed.

"I'll be straight with you both. We believe the theft may spring from a terrorist group set on using a nuclear bomb somewhere in America. We have been monitoring the group's activities for the past six months. We have an agent working undercover within the suspected cell." Said Garofalo.

"Well, that would explain why an agent from a top secret government agency is here investigating a homicide-robbery at a university," said Professor Wilson.

"You would be correct, professor!" said Garofalo.

"But if that is true, why are you going with us and not after the terrorist. That's what I want to know," said Mary.

"We are!" said Agent Garofola. I'm here, unofficially. I have a hunch, and in my experience, my hunches are always right."

"And what exactly is this hunch you're following?" Asked the professor.

What I don't understand is why they are unwilling to find or recover the object themselves." Said Garofalo.

"But why us? It makes no sense! We're not important at all. We are school teachers at a university. We have no political connections of any kind, no radical views," said Mary, now frowning, and visibly upset.

"'That's exactly why I believe you are the perfect mark. Who would connect the dots for such a strange reason? It's possible, but not too much, I think!" said Garofalo.

"This is starting to sound like some crazy conspiracy theorist Anonymous meeting," said Professor Wilson.

Garofalo suddenly stopped texting and looked up from his phone, and this time he made eye contact with the professor, and without speaking they silently acknowledged to one another, at least for now, they would trust each other.

"I don't expect you to understand everything; I can only ask you to trust me for now." Said Garofalo.

Chapter Thirty Two

*"*H*omage to Thee, O Great God, Thou Master of All Truth!
I have come to Thee, O
my God, and have brought myself hither, that I may become
conscious of Thy decrees. I know Thee and am attuned to Thee and
Thy two and forty Laws, which exist with Thee in this Chamber of
Maat.*

PANDORA'S BOX

Lord Dottington arrived back at his apartment well before 6
p.m. Which wasn't very unusual for him. It was his habit to arrive
at important events at least 30 minutes early.

"Gentlemen, how very nice to see you all in good health. I
trust you helped yourself to my best Russian Vodka?" He sported
a clever grin and raised his bushy blonde eyebrows

.

The group of well dressed middle-aged businessmen all
nodded in unison, each man raising his glass to a slight tilt
forward as a toast to their generous host. Dottington appeared to
be pleased with their response.

Nothing better than a finely aged Brandy . Gentlemen.

"Indeed, you are also a gracious host Lord Dottington, " said
one of the gentlemen who appeared to have an American accent.

"You are too kind, Very well then gentlemen," Said Lord
Dottington. "Shall we begin?"

Dottington loved this part of the game. He could barely
remember a time he felt such pleasure watching so purely evil
unfolding in all its dark beauty and hellish glory.

He could see it as clearly as the room he was standing in. He could see wonderful death everywhere, and he, yes he, would be the cause of it all.

He relished the thought, the thought of it often made him weep with pleasure, but not tonight. There was no place for tears on this night. There was very important business that required his cold hearted attention.

He could see the darkness to come, raging rivers of blood and human suffering. Surely his master would give him the secret of eternal life and the power of a god he promised him. He looked at the Muslim fanatic and was quietly amused. He watched his lips move slowly as Dr Mubarak decided to speak first.

"As you see, I have delivered the tablet as our arrangement stated. Do you have the device you promised us? And how do we know if it's guaranteed?"

Lord Dottington gave a faint smile, his private amusement growing with each passing second. He remained still, without answering.

Doctor Mubarak, trying to hide his discomfort with Dottington's silence, adjusted himself in his chair, never letting his eyes fall away from Dottington.

Dottington reached into his gray suit pocket to reveal a small circular device which appeared to be fashioned from some sort of quartz crystal. He tossed it on the table, and it bounced about silently.

Light as a feather it seemed to float, suddenly stopping, an inch above the table.

Mubarak and his two well-suited security men turned and looked at each other with eyes wide and mouths partially open in amazement.

I assure you, gentlemen, this technology is not known to any government or security agency. It is, I guarantee you the device is entirely undetectable and carries enough destructive power to level 10 city blocks.

The well-dressed security man on the right stood up and reached across the desk, knocking over his chair as he did. This was a big man, in a lovely suit that fit him like it was made at the finest English tailor's shop.

The man had seen a lot in his line of work. He'd often been surprised by the deadly secret operations that went on in the name of freedom. And, generally speaking, he didn't care— he was just in it for the money. But whatever was floating on that table was better than false freedom, Whatever It was, he wanted it.

He grabbed the device in his hands, and as it tumbled through his fingers, he felt nothing but a faint tingle. For a moment he thought it was alive.

Dr Mubarak looked in the direction of the man on his right.

"Did you get a reading?"

"No, it's not registering at all," said the other oversized security guard.

"Gentleman, I assure you, you will not be disappointed!" said Dottington.

" I imagine you would like to see the tablet now?" said Mubarak.

"I thought you would never ask!" Dottington pressed a button under the desk, and a white-haired elderly butler entered the room almost immediately.

"George, if you would bring me a silk cloth." Said Dottington.

The butler returned after a few minutes; he was holding an expensive looking black silk cloth. He laid it out on the table in front of Lord Dottington. Then left the room, closing the door behind him. Dr Mubarak placed a small box on the table and removed the lid.

Lord Dottingtom said nothing as he examined the golden tablet and carefully placed it back down on the silk cloth.

Dr Mubarak thought Dottington's intense interest in the tablet was a bit odd, primarily since he'd never known Dottington to be a collector of antiquities. "A beautiful piece indeed," He said.

"Are you satisfied," Lord Dottington?"

" We are quite pleased indeed, Dr Mubarak. "

Dottington took the tablet and placed it in a locked drawer behind him, then sat back down quickly.

"I presume you have the files I requested from you, doctor?" Said Dottington.

Mubarak said nothing but reached down into his briefcase and pulled out the folder Professor Wilson had given him and handed across the table to Lord Dottington.

"As for the device, It's quite simple to use. All you have to do is place your thumb and forefinger in the middle on either side. Press down and at the same time and say, "I am dead" the device is voice activated, and will only work in that order."

"Very theatrical!" said Dr Mubarak.

"Yes, My personal touch, I thought you might appreciate a little drama!" said Lord Dottington.

The man on the right coughed and covered his mouth with his hand.

Where did you acquire this kind of technology? Why would you give us such a weapon for an old tablet?

"I believe our agreement was no questions asked," said Dottington, a look of displeasure growing on his face and in his body language. He felt his blood running hot. He smiled. "It's natural for one to inquire, and as you can easily imagine, the greatest care was taken to deliver my end of the bargain. The party I represent is not up for discussion. So, gentlemen, I believe our meeting is over."

Before Dottington could press the hidden butler ringer, the man on the right pulled out a 9-millimeter pistol from under his jacket. He was surprised Dottington had no security or weapons check before allowing them to enter his apartments.

He pointed the gun directly at Dottington's face. Simultaneously, the man on the left pulled an identical weapon and pointed it straight at Dr Mubarak.

Lord Dottington did not move but intently observed Mubarak's facial expressions, now he was

truly amused. " An unexpected pleasure." He thought to himself. He could see Mubarak's expression was genuinely one of shock and confusion.

Mubarak was starting to panic as his mind raced to understand what was happening. He'd been preparing to die for months but he wasn't prepared for what would happen next.

"Nothing personal, Sir," said the man with the gun pointed at Mubarak. Mubarak realized it was the first time he'd ever heard him speak, But, before the man could even blink again, Lord Dottington like lightning raised both of his hands, gripping at the air, his hands, and fingers transformed in seconds into red, glowing claws.

Sparks of red-yellow flame danced around his fingertips. The man on the left and the man on the right dropped their weapons hard onto the desk, cracking the marble top where they fell.

Dottington's eyes turned red like rubies, and his pupils turned to large black pools. The men began to choke and howl. They tugged and grasped wildly at their throats. Their faces turned white, and blood began to pour from their eyes, ears, and throats. Lord Dottington sneered and licked his lips as he watched the two men writhe and moan in pain.

The horror show went on for another few minutes before the man on the left and the man on the right finally went limp.

Chapter Thirty One

DEAD MAN'S GAMBIT

THE TWO MEN SAT STILL covered in their own blood, remaining somehow suspended in the chairs. Until Lord Dottington quickly lowered his hands, causing the two now lifeless bodies to hit the table with a loud, heavy thump of dead weight.

A thousand horror movies and murder scenes raced around in Dr Mubarak's mind as his life began to flash before his eyes. Allah had delivered him to a demon Jinn. He had seen many marvelous and supernatural events in his life; he'd done his PhD in occult studies and esoteric phenomena at Oxford.

He'd witnessed yogis levitating off the ground, Chinese masters enduring incredible pain, and monks healing patients with chi, Big Om chanting. He'd even seen the occasional exorcism.

But what he just witnessed tonight was beyond anything his previous experiences could have prepared him for.

His face was white with fear. He felt his hand gripping his chest and felt sure he was having another mild stroke, like the one he had just a year ago upon hearing about the tragic death of his only son.

"Dr Mubarak. There is no need for alarm, I have no intention of harming you. At least not today," said Lord Dottington.

Dr Mubarak was frightened and fascinated. His instincts told him to run, but after what he just witnessed, he'd deduced running would be a fool's errand. He began to recite prayer from the Holy Quran.

"Dr Mubarak, it's unfortunate we had to end our business in such an unpleasant manner. But sometimes necessity overrules even the best of plans, don't you agree." Dottington said calmly.

Of course, Lord Dottington. Dr Mubarak swallowed and continued.

"May I ask how what I just saw was possible?"

"A FAIR QUESTION AND a very good question indeed. And, under different circumstances, I would be happy to tell you, but today is not that day." Dottington grinned and then suddenly raised his left hand from the table and pointed his forefinger directly at Dr Mubarak.

"Let's just say you will see the light soon enough." Said Dottington.

Suddenly Dr Mubarak's eyes rolled back in his head, and his jaw went slack, and he was in a deep trance.

A few moments passed as Lord Dottington did his dark work implanting a set of special instructions into Mubarak's subconsciousness.

When he was finished Lord Dottington, instructed Dr Mubarak to repeat the instructions which he did verbatim, including the instructions to forget everything he had seen and heard.

Dottington slowly lowered his finger and lowered his arm back on the desk, lightly folded his hands and smiled with satisfaction.

"It was a pleasure, Dr Mubarak. Again, it has been wonderful doing business with you as usual. I wish you all the blessings of Allah in your cause."

"The pleasure is all mine, Lord Dottington." He stood up from his chair and reached out his hand to Lord Dottington.

Mubarak's eyes passed directly over the bodies on either side of his chair, but he did not react to the horrible, twisted remains of the two dead men slumped over the table next to him. Lord Dottington gave Mubarak another faint smile and reached out his hand to Mubarak giving him a warm but firm handshake.

"Don't bother to call your man. I can see myself out," said Mubarak.

"Of course," Dottington nodded.

Doctor Mubarak turned and walked out of the drawing room casually, ignoring the freshly dead bodies on the floor next to him as if they were invisible.

A few moments later, Lord Dottington leaned back in his desk chair and pressed the button for his butler to enter the room.

"You rang, My lord" said the elderly looking, but surprisingly fit for his age Butler.

"Remove this mess before it stains my floor permanently, and dispose of them properly," said Lord Dottington.

The old man's dull blue eyes suddenly had a twinkle as he gazed directly at the two bodies as if he was sitting down for a sumptuous meal.

The old man leaned over and with one arm lifted the first body in the air, and then with the other arm as if he was raising a stuffed animal.

His blue eyes turned blood red, as his face became disfigured and his teeth grew into razor-sharp fangs like werewolf monsters in your nightmares.

"Will there be anything else, master?" George said, snarling and grunting like an animal as he spoke.

"YES, HAVE, MY DRIVER brings the car around and collects my luggage. I have a crucial summit I must attend in Sweden." Said Dottington.

"Very well, Sir," he said. "I hear the weather is charming this time of year, my lord."

"Yes, it is, indeed," Dottington said with a wicked grin. And George, I'll be needing a new desk as well!"

George smiled then turned and left the room.

Dottington sat, quite slowly rubbing his fingers at the tips. He liked all beings, had strange habits. Leaning forward, he removed a black velvet cloth from the object on his desk. He breathed deeply three times and then fell into a dark trance.

His eyes suddenly went black. His head fell back and then forward again. His lips, though barely moving, chanted "ZAHRIM" he who slew 10,000 of the hordes in the Battle. Zahrim, the Great Warrior among Warriors. Zahrim, he who can destroy an entire army if the Priest so desires. Zahrim, Zahrim, Zahrim. His Word is 'MASHSHAGARANNU'.

The black orb glowed silently like a new moon, eerie and cold.

Lord Dottington looked into the orb and watched Dr Mubarak getting into his car. He could see and hear the doctor speaking to his assistant, who'd been waiting in the car.

"Where are your security guards?" She said,

"I sent them on another emergency task. Nothing to concern you, miss Goldberg. I've received a call from the home office. I must go to see professor Wilson. We'll have to reschedule the

London Museum meeting, for another time. After which, I want you to book me on the next flight to Washington DC."

"And where will you be staying, sir." Said asked.

"I won't be needing accommodations. This business shouldn't take very long, and I don't plan on staying," said Dr Mubarak.

His assistant continued going down the usual list of questions, but he didn't hear her. He could only listen to the voice of the master in his head telling him what he must do. Dottington could see himself in his mind trying to say no, but he could not stop. Someone or something had taken over his body and was speaking for him. Someone was taking him where he didn't want to go. He was trapped inside his mind. He could see and even feel everything, but someone else was controlling his body.

Dr Mubarak watched in horror as his body was completely taken over by elemental beings called forth and under the control of Lord Dottington.

Chapter Thirty One

" *The Company of the Gods rejoiced, rejoiced at the coming of Horus, the son of Osiris, whose heart was firm, the triumphant, the son of Isis, the heir of Osiris".*

DESERT OF DREAMS

The day had gone well Seth mused to himself . He was standing in one spot for longer than he was consciously aware. He suddenly became aware of his body reacting to the unbearable heat " I'm probably dehydrated, He thought to himself. He tilted his head back and looked up at the smoldering sun that hugged high over the desert floor.

"It's so freaking hot here!".

"I've only known them for three days," he thought to himself, but he knew something was telling him he had to do this. Deep down inside Seth knew he needed everyone's help to pull it off his master plan.

"Look, guys. We're all on the same team, so why not do something awesome and surprise everyone? I've read several accounts, including the discovery of king tut's tomb. They were able to enter the tomb and disguise the entry point." Seth said.

"I think our dreams are connected to the tomb or maybe even that tablet. Said Seth.

"We all had the same dream, that can't be a coincidence." Said Rhonda.

"He could be right. Something unusual is going on, and the dreams are the link that connects us all— whatever it is exactly is going on...I mean,"

Emanuel said with his soft, pensive voice.

"Suppose you're right: how do we get in the tomb without anyone knowing and more importantly before the professor gets back here tomorrow?" Elle said in protest.

All the children stood for a moment looking back and forth at each other, As if they were all waiting for someone else to say what they were all thinking.

And to everyone's surprise, including her own, it was little shy Adenesh who whispered capriciously.

I know how we can get in the tomb, I think,"

Right of course you do, Elle sarcastically retorted.

But before Adenesh could say anything, Seth shouted out "Wait, wait, I know what to do!"

We do what any smart tomb robber would do. We made a small hole in the wall. One of the walls had a large pile of rocks and loose rubble. We'll make it look natural by covering it back up." Said Seth.

"Hmmm. It could work!," said Asim. "I like it!"

"Why not," said Elle.

"What about the two security guys?" said Elizabeth.

All the children looked at the pretty girl from Ireland, and for a good reason. They were all quite sure this was the first time she had spoken since the roll call at the hotel.

"John, doesn't your dad own the security of the company or something?" said Seth.

"I see you did your homework bud!" said John laughing out loud.

"What are you talking about?" Elle said. "Those guys work for my dad's company." John laughed.

" Oh come now, A billionaire's son in the Middle East on a field trip and you dud rounds thought the security was for you? That's rich!" he said with a loud chuckle and grin.

"Whatever, rich boy!"Rhonda said, angrily.

"The point here is you can use your influence to get the guards out of the way— heck, maybe even help us." Said Seth.

"In my village, my aunt has a shop, and her employees do lots of personal errands for her all the time, and they enjoy doing all they can for her because they want to get promoted," said Pari

"I'll tell them we are doing some more cleanup before the professor gets back and ask them to stand guard outside," John suggested.

"Sweet!" Seth shouted.

"John, you go talk to the guards. We'll get the gear, and everyone will meet in front of the tomb," said Seth.

"Is it possible we eat lunch first?" Emanuel said. "I'm mucho hungry!"

"I second that motion,"said Rhonda.

"OK, so it's settled then," Seth looked at his watch. "Operation Tomb Raiders" starts at 13:00 hours!" Seth put his right arm high in the air, and the other children formed a circle and clasped hands.

"Amerikaner sind sicher verrückt!" ("Americans are sehr crazy") Shouted Klaus.

As the children walked across the hot sand to the food tent they discussed ancient alien theory. Seth and Rhonda were rambling on at a mile a minute comparing one theory against another.

They spent most of their entire lunch discussing various alternative history theories especially those of authors like David Icke, anZachariah Sitchin, who Seth admired a great deal.

"Just because you can't prove something doesn't mean it isn't possible. You people used to believe the world was flat and black people should be slaves," said Rhonda.

"What are you talking about?" Said Elle, "Why must you people always play the race card?"

"Whatever, why must your people always play the anti-semitic card?"Said Rhonda rolling her eyes from side to side.

"What she means is you are basing your information on old data. There's so much new evidence now that questions the current scientific theories of our evolution, like in the case of many of Einstein and Stephen Hawking's theories, that have been proven to be wrong!" Seth said.

"Whatever," said Elle. "Can't you just shut up and eat your peanut and jelly sandwich for christ's sake!" said Elle.

Everyone laughed out loud, then continued to enjoy the bag lunches.

One hour later, all the children met in front of the place where Seth discovered the tomb.

John followed the plan and told the security guards the story, and, as expected, they fell for it. He found it amusing they even offered to help, but John told them it was better if they waited outside so as not to contaminate the area. "Not to be bright, those security guards," John said jokingly to everyone.

After some deliberation, mostly between Elle and Seth, the children agreed to make a small hole at the bottom of the left wall where the natural cave walls met, mainly because there were already piles of broken rock and debris covering the area. They all agreed it was ideal for their plan.

After working together, the children were able to create a small hole just big enough for one person to crawl in there. They carefully placed the debris aside to use for repairing the hole.

"We did it," said John. "Let's get in there."

"Wait a minute," said Elle. "What if the air inside there is toxic? We don't have any gas masks."

"She's right, there is a possibility the air can be toxic when first opening an ancient tomb like this," said Emanuel.

"Great, so what do we do? We just said none of us has any gas masks?" said John as he sneezed into his hands, and then wiped them clean on his shorts.

"There's plenty of ventilation in here guys. I say we wait a few more minutes and let the air flow out, then go in," Klaus suggested with his thick German accent.

The children all left the chamber and waited outside for a few minutes.

One by one they reentered the chamber, and once inside they decided to draw straws to choose who would go in.

They agreed no more than two of them could enter, to avoid damaging anything, or accidentally making the hole they made in the sidewall any bigger.

After the lots were drawn, it was Seth, and Adenesh won the draw.

Seth took his flashlight and his iPhone flashlight and scanned inside the opening. It was very dark, and he couldn't see much beyond the focus of the beams of light.

"Well, do you see anything? What are you waiting on? Go in already!" Said Elle, rather excitedly.

"Shh, keep your voice down. The guards might hear you," said John. Although he was born with a silver spoon in his mouth, he was a tough cookie. He liked a good fight and was very competitive no matter what the game. "I got those dudes in check, but let's not push it," John added.

"Yes, I can see something," said Seth. "Looks like there are a lot of black boxes and lots of jars and furniture. I can see hieroglyphics everywhere all over the walls." Seth was unconsciously rambling at breakneck speed.

Seth's heart was racing, his eyes wide open and his mind and body were alive with exhilaration. He couldn't believe what he was seeing. He smiled while scratching his forehead wildly back and forth until his forehead started to feel sore and red like a rash.

"Yo, this nuts! Like, we just found a completely intact tomb!" said Rhonda.

"Bloody hell!" said Elizabeth. "This is brilliant!"

"I'm gonna get that scholarship now! Thank you, Jesus!" said Rhonda as she threw her hands up over her head like she was about to jump in the air.

"Go ahead already, you guys. Get in there!" Said Elle.

Seth knelt down on all fours, being safe not to place his knees on the sharp edges of the broken rock and plaster. He looked inside for a moment more, then turned back to look at Adenesh.

She sure has been pretty quiet. Seth thought to himself.

Then he thought again how pretty she was. "I wonder if she even notices me?"

"I'll go first and give you the all-clear before you follow me inside," Seth said.

Adenesh nodded in agreement but didn't move an inch. Instead, she was frozen with fear, and suddenly she started crying.

Seth looked back at her.

"Adenesh it's ok, I'll be right next to you. "There's nothing in here that could be alive after 5000 years."

"That's not all." she said. "I just don't think I can go in there." Adenesh's mind raced back to when she had been kidnapped as a little girl. She was only five years old when they came for her family.

A group of rebel bandits had raided her village and took her and several other little girls from the village. The bandits locked them in small cages for many days before they were rescued by NATO troops. She could not bear small spaces ever since then.

"Adenesh, you have to try. This is a chance of a lifetime," said Seth.

He slowly reached out his hand toward her.

Chapter Thirty Two

"*Homage to Thee, O Great God, Thou Master of All Truth! I have come to Thee, O my God, and have brought myself hither, that I may become conscious of Thy decrees. I know Thee and am attuned to Thee and Thy two and forty Laws, which exist with Thee in this Chamber of Maat.*"

A LIGHT IN THE DARK

"Come on, Adenesh. It is fine, I promise, there is nothing to be afraid of, I've been in here for 5 minutes. If the air were poisoned or cursed I think I'd be dead already," Seth chuckled.

"I'm sorry. It's not that I don't want to go, because I really do, It's just."— She paused for a moment. " I'm afraid of the dark!" she blurted out. She couldn't bring herself to tell the other children something so personal. She thought they might think less of her if she did.

"I can't go in there. I can't. I'm really sorry, Seth,``said Adenesh.

"I'll go!" John said quickly as he made a quick dash towards the opening.

"Wait a minute. Oh, no sir! Nothing has changed. Everyone has to draw just like before, bro!"

Said Rhonda.

The rest of the children quickly agreed, so once again they drew straws.

This time Asim won the draw, and he didn't wait for anyone to say anything before he was squeezing his small frame through the very tiny hole they'd made, as fast as he could. Nonetheless, it took a few extra minutes of sweating and grunting before he was on the other side. Once inside, Asim stood up and turned his light to the wall where Seth stood staring at a wall of hieroglyphs.

Asim's additional light lit up the whole wall well enough for them both to read the text.

Seth decided to read it loud enough for everyone to hear. The other children huddled around the tiny entrance to listen to him. Seth had no problem reading the Hieroglyphs. He learned hieroglyphs alongside his ABCs. His parents taught him to understand and interpret the ancient symbols ever since the time he was a little boy, in fact, it was one of his earliest memories. He probably was able to read hieroglyphs before he could understand English, he thought to himself.

As Seth began reading the ancient writing out loud, and all the children crowded around the small opening.

No one made a sound as they listened to a tale beyond imagination!

"In the time before time which is not known to the human beings of this age lies a hidden place of knowledge and power long forgotten to the races of men.

It was there in the darkness; The All did speak the universes and all the worlds into existence.

And it came to pass through longing and desire The All spoke again and created laws and pathways everywhere above and below.

And it came to pass The All, through imagination filled, creation with gods, demons, angels, men, beasts, far more marvelous things, and even me.

And it came to pass that all manner of life appeared multiplying after its kind — Behold creatures of all sorts which live in the seas, mighty beasts that walk on land, flying things that walk on air, and the human beings.

Through their desires they did all evolve, growing ever upward as time passed generation after generation, ever feeding the fire, each creature playing the alchemic role of building and destroying, shifting and constantly turning, perfecting the races of beings.

And it came to be that the Elohim did command Thoth of Udal to be chosen from among the children of men, to keep a record watching over and teaching the races of men the wisdom and knowledge of the children of stars. According to its kind, The All gave unto each race its unique gifts and abilities.

And it came to pass by divine providence before the cycle of the new earth that Thoth— the teacher of men, keeper of wisdom and servant of Enki — and his Half-brother Enlil—Lord of the command, and firstborn of the great god Anu, were sent to the seventh planet (earth) to mine precious gold needed to repair the atmosphere of their homeworld Nibiru. But the labor was hard and the task too great. So it came by destiny that they chose to ease their burden, and the Elohim did create the human being, made to serve and worship them as gods. And in time, the gods chose priests-kings from among the races of men which they had created.

Thoth chose from among them 12 priest-kings whom he initiated into the mysteries and knowledge of the gods and ordered them to travel through the darkness and become children of the light. The priests taught the children of men to create civilization and to worship the gods, and it came to pass that the priesthood became very powerful and safeguarded the secret knowledge for only a chosen few.

Thoth's priests faithfully passed down the occult and arcane knowledge to their seed, and their seed, after their seed, by true bloodlines.

Thoth commanded unto the firstborn to safeguard the knowledge of the gods until the time of the new heaven and the new earth, even until the end of the ages.

And it came to pass by destiny that Lord Enlil grew weary of the children of men. He began to despise that which his brother had made from blood and clay.

Enlil, in his anger and by fate, allowed a great deluge to come upon the surface of the Earth to destroy all humanity forever.

But his brother Enki, who greatly loved the children of men, did purpose in his heart of saving his creation. He deceived his brother Enlil by preserving a remnant of the human beings from the destruction.

When Enlil saw what his brother had done, he vowed to destroy all humankind and raise his hand against his brother. Enlil's rage drove him deep into madness, and the dark magic which once nearly destroyed Nibiru was set in motion once again.

And so it was that a great war raged on earth and in the heavens, as in the time before time. Hatred pitted brother against brother until Enlil, in his madness, unleashed a weapon of terror, causing an evil wind that moved across the land, killing all in its path.

The evil wind spread across The Eden and could not be stopped, and the gods fled The Earth and returned to the heavens. The evil wind poisoned the land and the water, driving earth's intelligent races, and magnificent creatures deep into the inner earth, where they dwell even to this day.

For many months, the sky was covered in darkness and the moon glowed dark red. The darkness poisoned the hearts of the priests of Enlil, and they gained great power by feeding on the spirit of darkness growing in the hearts of men— all manner of wickedness and blasphemies did they master and teach humankind.

The dark priest taught men to hate and to despise one another, to steal, to desire, to lust, to kill and to make war. The children of earth learned the art of war and how to destroy, and to desire power with a lust as only mankind can."

"Did you guys hear all that?" said Seth.

"Heck yeah, we sure did!" Said Elle, John and the others.

"It's incredible," Asim said. His voice was shaking with excitement.

"It's not good," said Adenesh.

"There's more here!" Shine your light this way." Seth said to Asim. Asim centered his flashlight on a set of hieroglyphs to the right of the room where Seth was pointing.

Seth again began to read it out loud so everyone could hear.

"And it came to pass by divine providence that Enlil was finally defeated by his brother Enki, who then imprisoned him in the Halls of Amenti.

Enki charged his servant Thoth and his priesthood to guard the keys of Amenti, to hold Enlil and bind him in the darkness of the Halls of Amenti, where he could do no more harm to any beings until the time of the judgment before the All.

Time passed, and the races of earth separated and inhabited the four parts of the land. Thoth and his priests then founded a great city, and they called it Atlantis. The mighty city stood out beyond the vast sea. Atlantis was a marvelous sight —the golden and emerald skyline was spectacular, and a wonder to behold. From Atlantis, Thoth ruled and guided all the races of men.

In time Thoth returned to the stars. But before he departed, he commanded the watchers to monitor quietly over the races of men until his return.

"Then it came to pass that a rebellion arose splitting the priesthood into the brotherhood of the light and the brotherhood of darkness.

It is written that the brotherhood of darkness will return to fulfill its master's desire to seek revenge upon Enki and destroy all humanity forever."

"Allah be praised!" said Asim while the other children verbalized other varying degrees of oh's and ah's.

Seth was tingling all over. His knees were shaking; his palms were sweaty and warm.

He felt like the words came forth as if he had written them himself.

At that moment, Seth just happened to look down and saw something shining down by his feet. It looked like a ring, a golden ring at that. He looked over at Asim, who was intently staring at a set of hieroglyphs on the wall behind them.

Seth instinctively knelt down as quickly as he could, and picked up the golden ring, cupping it in his hand to conceal it from Asim's view. But before he could slip it into his pocket, Asim turned to look at him with a big smile.

"Amazing!" said Asim

Seth smiled and continued to hide the ring in his left hand.

"Can you see anything else?" Elle asked.

"Guys, I think It's getting kinda late. I say take pictures of everything you see, and we can look through them back at the camp," said John.

"Did you see an inventory scroll?" said Emanuel in his thick Spanish accent. Emanuel's area of expertise was ancient burial practices. "There is always a scroll containing a complete inventory," he said

Seth headed toward the sarcophagus. "Can you see any writing on it anywhere?" said Elle.

The two boys turned to get a closer look at a huge polished black granite sarcophagus in the middle of the tomb. It was quite large considering the room. Seth guessed the chamber to be about 25 by 50 meters, give or take his best guess.

"I can't see any writing," Seth shouted.

"Wait, I think there is something on top. It looks like a vessel of some kind, maybe a burial vase," Seth continued.

"Maybe I can get up there and take a closer look," said Seth.

"Asim, can you help me get up there?" asked Seth.

"Sure, but do you think we should? I don't think we should touch anything," said Asim.

Suddenly there was the sound of someone approaching from above them; it was the security guards trying to look into the hole below.

"Is everything all right down there? We thought we heard some shouting," said the African-American security officer.

"We're fine!" "Can Y'all please stay on the lookout for the officials and that antiquities officer person or another?" said John.

"Just checking Mr Dunnigan, Will do." Said the officer. Both the men stepped back away from the entrance and returned to their posts.

After they were sure the security guards had left, Elle suggested scrapping the idea of climbing onto the sarcophagus. Everyone agreed it was better to be safe than sorry. After all, they had just come very close to getting caught illegally breaking into a tomb against the authority of the Egyptian government and the Council of Antiquities.

Nevertheless, Seth and Asim continued meticulously exploring the rest of the interior of the tomb as quickly as they could.

There were stacks of golden furniture, 12-foot tall mirrors covered in gold leaf frames, statues of the gods covered in gold and encrusted with priceless jewels, amethysts, emeralds, and diamonds. They could see strange shaped vessels and cabinets covered in ancient hieroglyphic writing. There were baskets full of dried grains and food, cages with mummified sacred animals including snakes, cats and jackals. Between the two of them, they were able to take pictures of nearly everything they saw in the tomb.

They were careful not to move or touch anything.

John started becoming concerned about the time. He knew the guards would be back soon, and suggested they start working on sealing the hole again.

Hours later, It was nearly dinner time, and everyone was now complaining of hunger and deathly thirst.

Seth and Asim crawled back out through the hole. The group of children worked quickly repairing the hole with plaster and sand. Once that was done, the children carefully placed rocks and piles of sand in front of the opening.

The children stepped back and inspected their handiwork. With a few minor adjustments to the rocks arrangement, they were finally satisfied.

Everyone agreed it looked perfect, which generated a few rounds of thumbs up and high fives amongst themselves.

The children left the tomb area one by one. Seth trailed behind a few steps back from the group.

"Seth, come on buddy... We need to see those pictures," said Elle.

"I'm coming. I need to tie my shoe," said Seth.

He stopped and started to bend down as if to tie his shoelaces, but as he did so, he slipped the gold ring into his pocket.

Seth finished pretending to tie his shoes and then caught up with the other children.

"Bro, that was amazing," said John.

"Hey, Seth, send us those pictures you took. Asim already sent him to the group. Great stuff, I have to admit" said Elle.

After having dinner, some of the children along with Seth sat by the campfire discussing the tomb and their mutual love of all things Egypt and archaeology.

"It's the tomb of Thoth. This proves Thoth was a real person and the Egyptian gods did come from ancient Sumer, said Seth.

"You can't say that we haven't proven anything yet. It could very well be a tomb dedicated to the god Thoth for some ceremonial reason," said Rachel.

"She's right!" Rhonda added sharply.

"We haven't seen if there is an actual mummy of Thoth intact in the tomb," Elle said.

"I'm telling you, I read the hieroglyphs and I know Asim agrees. He was inside, too." Seth looked with his cellphone's light at Asim. His face looked surreal in the artificial light.

"Reading ancient languages isn't my strong point, but from what I could see, this could be pointing to the name Thoth inside the tomb itself," said Asim, his Arabic accent making it difficult for Seth to understand him in his excitement. Seth decided to keep that thought to himself; he didn't want to come across as mocking Asim's Muslim culture.

He took off his Yankees baseball cap and lightly brushed the dust out of his hair.

From behind a flashlight came closer, the light beam was pointing at John.

"It's time to wrap things up. Lights out in 10 minutes people," said one of the security guards. "Everyone should be in their tents and zipped in by the time I'm back over here. No exceptions" said the security guard in a harsh military tone.

"Yes, sir, drill sergeant!" said Seth. Everyone laughed.

"My dad says that all the time when he thinks someone is pushy," Seth said to Adenesh, who apparently did not get the joke.

"Don't forget to put out your fire properly. Remember, safety first," said the security guard as he turned to continue to walk the perimeter.

"Ten minutes," he shouted as he disappeared into the pitch black night with only his small flashlight.

"Anyway," said Seth, "I know I'm right, and I'm gonna prove my dad was right and get him his job back at the university!"

"Of course you will," Said Adenesh.

He looked at her and smiled. She smiled back, then lifted herself off the sand with both arms then headed to her tent.

Seth remained seated as he watched her walk toward her tent.

"Good night, Adenesh," he whispered under his breath.

Suddenly from behind, John and Asim slapped Seth on the back of his head with the palm of their hands.

"Good night ADENESH!" the other boys howled as they all fell into laughter together.

"Screw you, too!" said Seth. He immediately jumped up and fumbled his way back to his tent as quickly as he could in the pitch-black night. Just before entering his tent, Seth looked up at the night sky. He could see the stars were brighter than he'd ever seen before.

What is going on here? He thought to himself, as he entered the tent and hopped into his sleeping bag, quickly falling asleep.

Chapter Thirty Three

"*Come Thou forth, and follow Me: and make all Spirits subject unto Me so that every Spirit of the Firmament, and of the Ether: upon the Earth and under the Earth: on dry Land, or in the Water: of whirling Air or of rushing Fire: and every Spell and Scourge of God, may be obedient unto Me!*"

-Steigenberger

MASTER OF PUPPETS

Out of the night sky suddenly piercing a through group of thunder clouds A brand new sleek Gulfstream jet landed smoothly on the runway at the private Swiss airport, just before rising over the snow covered mountains. Lord Dottington stopped and breathed in the clean mountain air as he de-boarded the plane, despite his lack of sleep over the past 48 hours, he'd never felt better. His years of planning were finally bearing fruit and he was ready to reap.

HIS PERSONAL VALET loaded his bags carefully into the waiting, state-sponsored limo.

"To the Grand," said Dottington without looking up.

He was engaged on his phone the entire drive. Before he knew it he had arrived.

Lord Dottington's driver pulled the vehicle into the Grand-hotel Belvedere private VIP entrance. The black two tone Rolls Royce wasn't just another pretty car among a pool of expensive automobiles that always frequented five star luxury hotels such as La Grand; this one belonged to the Queen herself, On loan to Lord Dottington as a gesture of confidence for his outstanding service to the crown and country. Not to mention the generous donations he routinely made to her majesty's various charities.

Before the car came to a complete stop, a handsome young blond bellman was already opening the rear passenger door for Lord Dottington.

"Good evening, sir and welcome to the Grand Hotel Belvedere," said the young and fast-talking blonde valet.

Dottington never looked at the boy as he got out of the luxury limo. But with a quick hand gesture, he tipped the young man 50 euros.

Dotttington was known among the service-workers across the world as an exceptionally generous tipper, but also very short on cordiality.

Dottington arrived early to give himself time to review the folders Dr Mubarak had given him. The files contained the background information on each of the children.

After checking in to his suite and tipping another 100 euros to the other blond bellman who was attending his luggage, Lord Dottington sat down at the desk in his suite and began meticulously going through each of the children's files.

"Seth Strange," he read aloud to himself. "I've waited a long time to meet you, young man." He scanned through the small stacks of paper, then found what he was looking for.

He sat the other pieces of paper aside, reaching in his jacket pocket he pulled out his favorite Waterford pen, and wrote down the boy's place of birth, time of birth, and date of birth on a small yellow note card and placed it on his desk.

He smiled and sat back to ponder the boy's natal information for a minute.

Dottington, was a master astrologer, He quickly went to work casting the boy's chart.

He repeated this process until he had cast the charts of all 12 children. He sat back in his chair again and smiled in quiet amusement.

Dottington casually stepped over to the wall and pressed a button which automatically closed the wall-length privacy blinds to his suite.

He took off his jacket and tie and his shoes, then stepped into the bedroom. Dottington looked around for a few moments, then found the perfect spot near the center of the room. He took several long, deep breaths until he had placed himself in a deeply relaxed state. Next, he drew a circle with his left hand.

Standing in the center of the magical circle of protection, Dottington raised his hand and made a pentagram in the air at each point of the four cardinal directions casting magical spells of protection.

After setting his magical shield, he stood silent for a moment. Again, he took several more long negative breaths. A red aura began to glow around him. He raised both hands and began reciting an inaudible chant.

"I DO invoke, conjure and command thee, O thou Spirit N., to appear and to show thyself visibly unto me before this circle in fair and comely shape, without any deformity or tortuosity; by the name and in the name IAH and VAU, which Adam heard and spake, and by the name of GOD, AGLA, which Lot heard and was saved with his family, and by the name IOTH, which Jacob heard from the angel wrestling with him, and was delivered from the hand of Esau, his brother, and by the name ANAPHAXETON which Aaron heard and spake and was made wise; and by the name ZABAOTH, which Moses named and all the rivers were turned into blood; and by the name ASHER EHYEH ORISTON, which Moses named, and all the rivers brought forth frogs, and they ascended into the houses, destroying all things; and by the name ELION, which Moses named, and there was great hail such as had not been since the beginning Of the world; and by the name ADONAI, which Moses named, and there came up locusts, which appeared upon the whole land, and devoured all which the hail had left; and by the name SCHEMA AMATHIA which Ioshua called upon, and the sun stayed his course; and by the name ALPHA and OMEGA, which Daniel named, and destroyed Bel, and slew the Dragon; and in the name EMMANUEL, which the three children, Shadrach, Meshach and Abed-nego, sang in the midst of the fiery furnace, and were delivered; and by the name HAGIOS; and by the SEAL31 OF ADONI; and by ISCHYROS, ATHANATOS, PARACLETOS; and by O THEOS, ICTROS, ATHANATOS; and by these three secret names, AGLA, ON, TETRAGRAMMATON, do I adjure and constrain thee. And by these names, and by all the other names of the LIVING and TRUE GOD, the DARK LORD ALMIGHTY, I do exorcise and command thee, O Spirit N., even by Him Who spake the Word and it was done, and to Whom all creatures are obedient; and by the dreadful judgments of GOD; and by the uncertain Sea of Glass, which is before the DIVINE MAJESTY, mighty and powerful; by the four beasts before the throne, having eyes before and behind; by the fire round about the throne; by the unholy angels of hell; and by the mighty wisdom of GOD; I do potently exorcize thee, that thou appearest here before this Circle, to fulfill my will in all things which shall seem good unto me; by the Seal of BASDATHEA BALDA-CHIA; and by this name PRIMEUMATON, which Moses named, and the earth opened, and did swallow up Kora, Dathan, and Abiram. Wherefore thou shalt make faithful answers unto all my demands, O Spirit N., and shalt perform all my desires so far as in thine office thou art capable hereof. Wherefore, come thou, visibly, peaceably, and affably, now without delay, to manifest that which I desire, speaking with a clear and perfect voice, intelligibly, and to mine understanding.

Chapter Thirty Four

"Ye are gods, but you shall die like men for your unbelief"
-New Testament

ASTAROTH

"Appear unto me oh Mighty Strong Duke Astaroth!" He shouted.

Suddenly, a small spark appeared in mid-air directly in front of the magician. A foul odor filled the room. The air became stagnant. Ice formed on the furniture in the room.

The point of the spark grew more massive, and the room seemed to disappear and collapse within itself. The circle rose and surrounded Dottington, his eyes now glowing red hot.

"I command thee, Astaroth. Appear here before me now!"

The magician steadied his mind, focusing his immortal will, and overcoming his feeling of fear. Even for a magician of his skill, any sign of fear would be fatal.

Astaroth was a terrible duke and greatest amongst the demons, a powerful ally and an even more dangerous foe.

A cloud of white smoke and blue flame started to form in front of the magician outside the circle Lord Dottington had mentally created to protect himself from his mighty, demonic servant. Normally, Dottington used his magical sword and other magical tools to ensure the stability of his circle before summoning the beast, but necessity called him to take the risk, as time was of the essence.

"I am not afraid," he thought to himself. Sweat now pouring from his forehead.

Suddenly, a frightening, hellish figure appeared before him, a hideous beast frightful yet beautiful like an angel of darkness surrounded by the shadow of night. Its pale white skin shimmered. Its ghoulish face and arms were covered in scales and hair that looked like pointed spikes, its teeth were long like fangs and sharp as nails. The demon stared at the magician with its recessed glowing red eyes.

The magician had tricked the demon into servitude many centuries ago. The demon boiled with hatred and disgust at having to obey the magician it so very much despised. Astaroth was sworn to revenge for the loss of its freedom.

They both knew sooner or later the magician's soul would belong to the king of demons, but until that time, the demon was bound by the laws of magic, forcing it to appear before the grand magician and do his bidding.

"Soon you will be mine, you human wretch! I will enjoy your suffering for 10,000 years," said the demon lord.

"Be silent, demon. It is I that command thee in the name of my master, who you still are ever bound to. You will do as I command thee or be torn apart by cosmic law."

"What is your desired master?" Said the demon.

"Our dear, soon to be departed friend Dr Mubarak has exceeded our expectations. I have been able to confirm from the natal charts of all the children that they are as you said they would be," Said the magician.

"I am everywhere, human. Do you not think one such as I would not know the children of the light have returned?" said the demon. "They threaten your useless plans, human. The Brotherhood of the White lodge even now takes steps to awaken the children of the light. If they should succeed, it is written they will altogether destroy you, and your master." The demon smiled, then paused, looking for any sign of a fearful reaction from the magician.

"I must stay focused, the demon is a liar," Lord Dottington said deep in the center of his mind.

"Their bloodlines are confirmed. I will deal with them, demons, and you will make the deep magic and prepare the temple as our master instructed," He said. "Once the children have unlocked the chamber of Thoth, we will have the map to the monoatomic gold —enough to power the Omni Path. We will cause a negative shift in the earth's core energy, opening the gate and setting my master free."

"As you wish, Magician," said the demon. It studied the magician for a moment longer, its eyes burning with unholy hatred.

The room grew even colder as he sensed the slight vibration of doubt in the magician's aura. He could taste the scent of fear in the magician.

"You are an old man and weakened by time like all your kind, with each passing moon magician you become mine. I smell the fear you try to hide. I grow stronger with each passing moment! Soon I will destroy you, human. I will delight in your sweet, bloody, and rotting flesh, I will tear the flesh from your bones until I devour your rotten soul," the demon hissed with a devilish and frightening grin.

"Silence, vile beast. You shall not speak. I command you, and you must obey!" Said Dottington. "Now go from whence thou came, and do not return until all that I have commanded is done," he said out loud. With that, he began the invocation to depart:

"O thou spirit, because thou hast diligently answered unto my demands and hast been very ready and willing to come at my call, I do here license thee to depart unto thy proper place;

without causing harm or danger unto man or beast. Depart, then, I say, and be thou very ready to come at my call, being duly exercised and conjured by the sacred rites of magic. I charge thee to withdraw peaceably and quietly, and the peace of god be ever continued between thee and me! AMEN!"

The magician finished his magical rites, and the beast began to fade as the temperature in the room returned to normal. Lord Dottington carefully closed the circle and ended the invocation according to the laws of Solomon. Once he was sure, all was as it should be.

He returned to his paperwork and files to prepare himself for the G-10 summit he would be speaking at in just a few hours.

Suddenly, he felt an icy cold chill return to the room.

A face appeared in the mirror behind him. For a moment he was startled. The face in the mirror began to laugh with a hideous growl.

"Soon, magician, and very, very soon!" Said the beast. Then the dark horror vanished, leaving behind only a foul smell, and fine black ash that lingered in the air for a moment, then softly fell to the floor.

Dottington, though taken by surprise at how the demon was able to reappear, regained control of himself by quickly taking long deep positive magical breaths.

"You will have no power over me, demon. My master has promised me eternal life. You will never have my soul. It is you who will be my servant for eternity, demon!" Dottington sneered in defiance. "It is I who will destroy you, demon," he muttered under his breath before returning to his work.

Dottington began thinking of how he'd taken control of the demon, of the sacred rite. He believed it was destiny, not fate, which caused his parents murder and sacrifice by the brotherhood nearly five centuries ago. Dottington, however, was spared and taught the ways of the Dark Brotherhood. He embraced the black arts with all his mind, body and soul.

During that time he gained the respect of his captors; they taught him how to master the secret of the key of Solomon and other, even darker arts— the universal laws and magic that allow a mortal to control demons. And it was by the power of this magic that Lord Dottington not only gained control of the Brotherhood of Darkness but also gained the ability to extend his own life for nearly five hundred years.

It was after raising the demon to his service that the beast revealed to him the secrets of creation and of the gods of Nibiru, the people of the Inner Earth and the worlds beyond this dimension.

Through the demon's power, he found a way to communicate with the great god Enlil, who promised him eternal life in exchange for freeing the god from the prison his brother Enki and the traitor Thoth had bound him in for the last 12,000 years. He decided right then and there he would be the evilest man the world had ever seen. Dottington felt in his heart he had already been abandoned by the light. Therefore It was his destiny to be evil, and he would become the greatest evil the world had ever known.

Chapter Thirty Five

O child of Adam! Listen unto the words of the Teacher: "The Father and I are one." Suffer little children to come unto me, for of such ii the Kingdom of Heaven."

MYTHS AND MYSTICS

"Wait!" Seth shouted. "Guys, there's no way anyone can send pictures to anyone! Seriously, we'll be seriously trending on social media before lunch is over.

The other children laughed and pointed at each other. Making Seth all the more frustrated about getting his point across.

Hello, earth to get a clue camp. We literally broke into, like, a fully intact Egyptian tomb. I thought this was the smart kids camp or am I missing something? " Seth said his face had turned bright red with an exasperated look on his face.

"Really, Seth? Do your delusions of grandeur ever cease? Rhonda snapped back. We set up a private encrypted email on the dark web with a folder we all are sharing," She made a flip motions with her wrist in Seth direction, and said

Do try to keep up if you can Red.

"Maybe you did get on the wrong bus after all, I think you're looking for the technology challenged expedition." said Elle laughing out loud, as the other children joined in one by one. "He makes it so easy," she thought to herself.

"So can we assume we're done?" said John.

"Yes we're done here, so let's get cleaned up and then meet up at the food tent for dinner," said Elle

"I'M JUST BEING CAREFUL. We're all taking a big risk, and I don't think it's worth it, really." He said.

"What do you mean? It was amazing! My grandfather would have jumped with joy to be here now and see what we have seen" said Asim.

"What does your grandfather have to do with anything?" Rhonda asked.

"My grandfather was the keeper of the history of Egypt. He told me many times of a hidden tomb of wisdom where Thoth hid his secret, and that in the last days it would be found," said Asim.

"OK," said Elle. "And what exactly happens when this secret Thoth thing is found? And why didn't you tell the professor all this interesting folklore?"

It says there are 12 keys from the original tribes, and in the tomb lies the master key of Thoth and the secret of eternal life!

Elle suddenly busted out laughing so violently that the other children began laughing out of control along with her. After a few more minutes the laughter subsided and everyone decided to drop the subject for later. As fascinating as the discussion had become Seth suggested they table the table idea due to seeing the security guards heading in towards them.

"We just got a call from Professor Wilson," said the African American security guard. His voice was thick and low." He said he wants you kids to stay away from the tomb area. He wants everyone to remain within the tent area. No digging or exploring until they arrive in the morning. Oh, and the cook says the hot dogs are ready."

A brilliant "Yes!" erupted from the children, as they happily followed the two security guards, who Seth noticed were now carrying 9 millimeter assault weapons.

"I don't know if I'm ever going to get used to this constant sweating," said Seth. He was talking to Asim as they browsed through the tomb pictures for the 100th time.

"I'm from Germany, and I'm not complaining," Klaus chuckled.

The children spent the rest of the evening taking turns, mostly the boys, eating seconds and thirds of chili dogs, and baked beans and potato chips.

After dinner, they all gathered around the fire roasting marshmallows for dessert. They took turns looking through the photos Seth had taken earlier of the inside of the tomb. Although most of the images were very blurred and off-center, what they could see left them speechless.

"Seth, you are terrible at taking pictures!" said Elle.

"Right, well you try taking pictures in the dark, while illegally sneaking into an ancient tomb. See how well your pictures turn out."

"Yeah, my point exactly!" said Elle.

Chapter Thirty Six

" *The matrix of the universe and of all that it contains appears not to have been itself born, holding however, within it, potentially, all Nature.*"
HEAR NO EVIL, SEE NO EVIL

The following morning professor, Wilson, Mary and Agent Garofalo arrived back at the dig site camp. They pulled up in a dusty black Range Rover just outside the perimeter. They exited the vehicle at once and walked briskly toward the center of the camp to meet the children.

"Looks like the children are up and ready to go," Said Mary

" The joys of youth" the professor chuckled back at Mary. "Well, I imagine they are expecting to go into the tomb today, Unfortunately, I haven't heard back from the antiquities department. I'm not sure we'll be getting in the tomb anytime soon after what's happened."

"Don't worry, professor. Our agency has already spoken to the minister. He will be here before noon," said Garofalo. "We think it's best to move forward, and not to alarm the children. He continued. Whoever is behind this is expecting that tomb to be opened. I want to get in there and secure the tomb before they find out you have discovered whatever it is they are looking for."

"I'm still very concerned about the children's safety," said Professor Wilson. He was deep in thought as he looked at Garofalo, his eyes narrowing tightly.

"I gotta get in this wise guy's head, I know there's something he is not telling me," Thought Garofalo.

"The professor is here everyone" shouted Adenesh.

"We have eyes!" said Elle, slowly rolling her eyes at Adenesh.

"Good morning, my amazing little archeologist!" Professor Wilson said proudly. "I can't begin to tell you all how happy I am to see each of your happy smiling faces this morning, a fine thing indeed."

"What happened? Where's Mr Francis?" Seth asked.

"I am sorry to have to say this but we had a bit of unexpected trouble. But everything is fine now, children, and there's no need to spend valuable time discussing it any further," said the professor.

He looked over at Mary, who was having a bit of a time staying in character. She still had a worried look on her face. He gave her a quick gesture with his hand, that meant to get herself together.

Garofalo, sensing the awkward moment decided to take charge and started softly speaking to the children, diverting their attention away from Mary.

"Good morning, children, my name is Mr Garofalo. I'm here on a special assignment from the Department of State. I've been assigned to accompany you for the rest of the expedition as an observer and to assist professor Wilson and Mary with security, safety measures, and of course the cataloging of any items recovered from the tomb later today." Garofalo explained.

Nothing to concern, this is normal when there is a rare fine such as the one you have uncovered.

As Garofalo continued, another vehicle pulled up outside the encampment. The wheels of the all terrain vehicle were kicking up as the cloud of dust behind moved across the desert road that settled in the air around the campsite area.

Seth sneezed violently several times.

Bless you Said Rhonda.

"Yes, sir, we're seriously getting into that bad boy today!" Seth raised his fist in celebration.

"I hope you know what you are doing," Said Adenesh. She wasn't sure how to feel about her new found friend's reckless behavior and overly rebellious nature.

"It is soooo... on! This totally kicks butt!" said Seth. "You worry too much. We did a perfect job. Trust me...I can't even tell!" said Seth.

"Is there something you want to share with the rest of us, Mr Strange?" Said the Professor.

"just saying we had a great day yesterday, professor." Seth gave the professor a sly but genuine smile,

"Anyway, let's get started, shall we?" said the professor.

The professor turned away from the children and headed towards the Vehicle to greet their nearly arrived guest.

The three passengers got out of the car, Dr Mubarak, and two representatives from the Egyptian government.

"Dr Wilson, How good to see you," said Mubarak. He reached towards professor Wilson's already extended hand and shook his hand as they greeted one another.

"You remember Mary of course." Said the professor. v

"How could I forget!" Said Dr Mubarak, while watching Mary out of the corner of his eye, as covertly as he could. Even though he was a devoted married Muslim, he was still a man, and Mary was without question a looker. "Always nice to see Dr Wilson's lovely and brilliant daughter."

Mary nodded and adjusted the small gold ankh around the neck. Her mother had given it to her as a child.

"Nice to see you again as well!" Mary said coldly, looking away. Mary never felt uncomfortable around Mubarak. She just did not like the man.

"He really gives me the creeps every time I see him!" she thought to herself.

To Mary, he was the dirty old man type, in her opinion. Always polite on the surface, but she found his compliments condescending nature. She often wondered why her father thought so highly of him in the first place.

"Are you OK?" said Dr Mubarak. "I heard there was an incident at your office. I got a call from security, but the police aren't releasing any details. What exactly happened?"

"Let's talk about all that later, shall we?" said Professor Wilson.

"Right, of course. So why don't you introduce me to this fine group of archaeologists." Said Dr Mubarak.

Professor Wilson introduced all the children to Dr Mubarak, and for the children, it was quite the honor, especially to Asim and Elle. They all had grown up watching the countless History Channel documentaries, with the good Dr Mubarak always appearing as the definitive authority on all things Egyptian, so for the children, Dr Mubarak was a genuine celebrity. Although he was much shorter than most of them had imagined, not necessarily obese but pleasantly plump. He had a faint Arabic accent and what could be considered a somewhat cliche manner of dress. Nevertheless, the children were thrilled to meet someone as famous as the head of Egyptian antiquities.

Seth, however, was visibly hostile toward Dr Mubarak, who was widely known as one of the most outspoken critics of Seth's father's work.

"What a fraud!" Seth thought to himself as he watched the other children fawn over the good doctor. He said nothing, but inside, he had no respect for him. Seth being the typical Scorpio always hides his true feelings. Like most Scorpios, Seth preferred to mislead his adversary into underestimating him, until it was too late to do anything about it.

Chapter Thirty Seven

"They wander in darkness seeking light, failing to realize that the light is in the heart of the darkness"

THE GREAT WHITE LODGE

Hidden high in the Himalayan Mountains sits the Great White Lodge, ancient as time itself, the palace of wisdom and the mighty fortress of the philosopher's stone. Its glistening towers silently glow unseen by human eyes. The lodge is visible only to the highest Adepts and grandmasters.

The temple is populated by The Elect, composed of those masters chosen from the beginning of time. They are the children of men, chosen by divine providence, who have shown themselves worthy to receive the highest state of enlightenment on this plane and being able to plastically see all that cannot be seen in the visible or invisible worlds. They have escaped death and rebirth and only incarnate on the material plane when called upon by the divine providence.

The Great White Lodge is neither in this plane nor any of the nine universes. It was placed between the worlds by providence as a doorway between the nine realms of the cosmos. The dark ones move in angles; they cannot reach it. It is everywhere and nowhere.

It is said the grand masters represent the great houses of the nine realms and gather continually at the Great White Lodge. From this high place, the adept collect and focus the universal energies, directing and controlling them and their vibrations in the cosmic consciousness, to shape and guide all living beings inhabiting every kingdom, to the will of the All. This is called the Great Work.

Thoth sat in the mystic pose, feet flat on the floor, head and back straight, eyes forward and hands resting on his thighs. He was in the Chambers of Amenti, unable to interfere with the children according to cosmic law. He learned from the watchers that there was a way, but it was dangerous. He stared into the ether with his astral eyes, the divine cosmic mind where all things past present and future can be viewed if one is worthy of the sight. He was not looking into it— instead, merging with it, as he began to vibrate. He released his consciences from its physical form and joined with the ether itself, then in the emptiness, he reformed in his astral body. His conscientiousness was no longer in the physical world. His body had become an empty shell.

"It is finished," Said Prince Atrea, of Agharta.

The 12 brothers of the light in all stood around the empty shell of Thoth. All at once, they raise their arms and join hands. They were all dressed in shimmering white robes. All of them appeared as old men, some with beards, some with not, except for one— Prince Atrea. He seemed very young although he was centuries old, His hair was golden, and his pale blue eyes and pointed ears made him appear much like an elf of lore. His cloak was forest green with golden trimmings, and his hands were long and thin.

"So mote it be!" Again, said Prince Atrea.

The Brotherhood of Light stood quietly around the inanimate body of Thoth. The giant demi-god looked like a statue transported from the sands of Egypt. He was motionless, as still as the colossus of Rameses.

All at once, they raised their arms and joined hands. They invoked a light of protection around the shell of Thoth, to protect his physical body from psychic assault.

After the magicians completed their magical work, they left the room one by one and headed in separate directions from the temple hall.

"Your Majesty, may I have a word with you?" said Gabriel.

"Gabriel, you need not be so formal, my old friend!" The prince said cheerfully as he turned to face him.

"What is on your mind?" he asked.

I must warn you, we believe the reptilians have amassed a vast army and have formed an alliance with Enlil and the dark brotherhood. Their designs are on revenge and destruction.``

"Yes, our spies have reported the matter to the high council."

"They already have identified the key," said Gabriel.

"You mean the boy?" said Atrea.

"Let us hope so, my old friend! I have sent instructions to our spy at the children's camp on what to do." Said Prince Atrea.

"So mote it be!" Said Gabriel. The master adept bowed his head and continued on his way.

Chapter Thirty Eight

"*Watch close the gates of thought. Sentinel desire. Cast out all fear, all hate, all greed. Look out and up.*" -*Arcane School*

LOST TOMB OF THOTH

"I think we're ready down here, Dr Mubarak, Please be extra careful. The ladder is a bit tricky at first," said the professor.

It was midday as the last of the group, except for the two security guards and the police detail that accompanied Dr Mubarak entered the tomb area.

The desert was windy and much hotter than the past few days. The sand was starting to move and rise into the air, creating clouds of heat everywhere. Once inside the cave, Seth noticed it actually felt cooler.

Elle and the other children stood in front of the area they had repaired. Seth felt confident it couldn't be seen, but they all decided it was better to be safe than sorry.

Seth watched as the professor spoke to the group of adults, telling them about the details of the fantastic find.

"So, which one of the children, did you say, found the actual tablet?" asked Mubarak, eagerly looking around at the children, curious to see who would come forward.

"It was Seth and Adenesh that found the tablet, I believe," said the professor."

Mubarak laughed. "I meant, which one of them pulled it from the rock?" said Mubarak, still looking directly at the group of children.

Seth, overhearing the conversation, but without thinking raised his hand and said, "I pulled it out."

Dr Mubarak smiled at Seth.

"You are an extraordinary young man." What is your name again, young man?"

"Seth Strange," said Seth with an awkward voice. He looked to the right and noticed Adenesh's frowning face.

Suddenly, he wondered what she was thinking,

"Please don't say anything," he thought to himself.

Dr Mubarak and the professor continued back to their conversation about the details of opening the tomb and removing the seal.

Seth nervously watched to see if Adenesh was going to throw him under the bus. He looked at her, putting on the most innocent looking face he could muster, he looked at her and shrugged his shoulders. He texted her, "I'm sorry I don't trust that guy."

She texted him back, "It's OK, it doesn't bother me. I don't like the attention anyway."

"I think we're ready gentlemen." Said Mubarak.

A small team of local workers already were waiting by the entrance, they were brought in to lift heavy objects and to help bag and catalog the expected.

Seth was having a hard time dealing with the body odor that was coming from some of the men. The smell was choking his nostrils.

He tried holding his breath in order not to throw up.

The men muscled around and took positions, and Seth watched the professor as he held the seal in place and gingerly squeezed down on the metal bolt cutters. A hush came over the chamber.

Suddenly, cameras and cell phone flashes went off from all directions.

An assistant caught the primary seal as it was released from the dry hemp rope that no longer holds it in place, sealing the tomb for over 12,000 years. The Arab assistant placed the great seal in a bag, tagged it, then set it aside.

"Before we open the tomb, I'd like to say something to the children," said Professor Wilson.

"Children this discovery exceeds the wildest expectations any one of us could have imagined. Most archaeologists spend entire careers hoping for such an opportunity. And yet, by the hand of faith here, we stand this morning!" the professor said proudly.

"I think we all get it, professor!" said Rhonda jokingly.

"Well, then I think we can all agree this will be the summer none of us will ever forget. So without further delay, shall we open the tomb?" said Doctor Mubarak.

The children collectively gave a true thespian performance as they pretended to be anxious, and appeared to look surprised. From the corner of his eye, Seth could see Adenesh covering her eyes with one hand, cell phone clinched highly in her other hand. Seth resisted the temptation to text.

"There will be no texting or sending of data of any kind. No exceptions, no texting of any kind is allowed. If anyone is caught texting or sending pictures, everyone's devices will be taken away until cleared by myself or Dr Mubarak." Said professor Wilson.

"Come to think of it, I have a better idea!" said Mary as she opened a black backpack and removed some of the needed items in it. She quickly took them out and placed them on the side near the cave wall.

"Everyone put your cell phones, iPads, etc., in this bag," she said sternly. "You will get them back after we are finished."

The children frowned and pouted to no avail. Mary stepped around the room and gathered every single device, then zipped up the bag and tossed it over her shoulder.

"Ok, now I think we're ready, gentlemen!" Mary said with an awkward smile.

The doors of the ancient tomb were slowly and very carefully pulled open. The cave was filled with the smell of musty stale air.

"Don't mind the smell, children, it will go away. If you feel any faintness or nausea, it should pass quickly," said the professor.

Seth watched as Mubarak and the professor directed the workers, who were setting up bright spot lamps throughout the tomb.

The walls were entirely covered with texts of spells, rituals and details concerning the creation and the origins of the gods.

The tomb was more massive than Seth had imagined in the dark. The tomb went on for more than 50 yards. In the front and the rear of the room appears to slate to a point creating a triangle effect. Quartz crystal pillars lined the walls evenly. Seth counted 12 in all. They too were covered in hieroglyphs in the old-kingdom decorative style.

Seth looked up at the ceiling. It was painted entirely with stars, some of which looked like solar systems, and even galaxies. He noticed in the center was an amazingly detailed relief clearly representing our solar system. He could see the sun, the earth, Saturn, the rest of the planet's, and one odd planet that seemed to have an elliptical orbit outside of the rest of the planets.

Golden, miniature statues of the gods lined the walls, as well as baskets full of tablets and papyrus scrolls.

"This is outstanding," said the professor. His eyes were wide as he and the rest of the students and onlookers stood in awe of the wonders before them, a spectacular find, equal to, if not greater than, the famous King Tut's treasure. Gold lined nearly every surface of the chamber.

"Children, please, do not touch anything. Remember this tomb has been sealed shut for a very long time. We must take great care as we begin our work of tagging and cataloging. Some of the items could possibly disintegrate now that they have been exposed to air," He said.

In the center of the room was a massive black marble tomb. It was at least 12 feet in length and 6 feet high. They saw no writing of any kind on the outside to identify who or what was sealed inside.

The professor instructed Mary to separate the children into two groups, and they began the task of dividing the tomb into sections. They carefully started cataloging and tagging everything.

Dr Mubarak and a photographer from the ministry followed professor Wilson through the tomb, discussing various objects as they took photos.

Seth tried listening as best as he could to hear what they were saying. They had started taking pictures near the small hole he had entered through. Seth couldn't help but think what he might say if they noticed and confronted them. But, he thought, they can't prove the tomb was entered into by someone before. Egyptian tombs by nature are often robbed, but he was still nervous, but he tried his best to look normal.

"Seth, can you come over here for a second?" said the professor.

"Who? Me?" Said Seth. He looked around and then back at the professor.

"Yes, your name is Seth!" the professor laughed.

Seth put his hands in his pockets and slowly walked over to the wall where they were standing.

"I hear you are pretty good at reading ancient languages," said Dr Mubarak.

"I'm OK," said Seth.

"We were looking at this wall and noticed something exciting as we read the hieroglyphs. Can you see what we are talking about?" Dr Mubarak asked.

Seth's heart started to race. He stared at the wall and at the place where the hole was, scanning his eyes back and forth. He didn't know if it was a trick question. He could definitely read it. "No, I'm not sure what you mean."

"Try rereading it," said Dr Mubarak.

Chapter Thirty Nine

"The very elements, though each is meant
The minister of man, to serve his wants, conspired
against him. With his breath, he draws a plague into blood; and
cannot use Life's necessary means, but he must die."
-Cowper.

THE TALE THAT TIME FORGOT

There were giants on the Earth in those days and the greatest of the races of giants was The reptilian race. They were tremendous in height and ruthless predator and mighty creatures. Humans were their favorite delicacy until the Annunaki came and created great devices that terraformed the earth and drove the reptilians underground, no longer able to survive on the surface.

The gods lived among the children of men and had shown them secrets of civilisation, the arts, agriculture and medicine. And even after a time, the gods chose among the people they found worthy the mysteries of science and magic and cosmic law.

But one day, the gods became tired of mankind and decided to allow humanity to perish in the great deluge. But one of the gods, Enki, had mercy on humanity and saved a remnant, sending his servant Thoth to Kemet across the sea to hide the mysteries. His half-brother Enlil was enraged and raised his hand to destroy mankind with the weapons of mass terror, and he would have succeeded, but he was defeated by his brother, with the help of the other gods. They imprisoned Enlil in the Inner Earth and charged Thoth and the brotherhood of life, to guard the prison, lest Enlil should ever escape and carry out his dark desires.

The key was hidden among the 12 high priests, who have guarded it safely for thousands of years.

Now it is said the Brotherhood of Darkness has found the secret of the key and makes plans to steal the key, to use it to free Enlil to destroy mankind and wage war on Nibiru for imprisoning him. And in return they might receive the nectar of the gods, granting them eternal life.

Lord Enki placed the key in the flesh and passed it down from generation to generation.

Let him who has an ear hear, I Thoth have placed here the amulet of Enki.

In it, I have contained the knowledge of the keys of magic and the sacred science.

Let him that hath understanding hear my words. By my wisdom, I have spoken into the Akasha the names of the 12 keys. It shall know them, and they shall know its voice.

I shall call my sheep, and they shall I teach.

I shall meet them through time and space, and they shall make war against the rulers of darkness and the beasts of the air, for I, Thoth, have prepared for the coming days when gods and men will meet in the darkness.

Let him that hath an ear hear.

Take ye the golden tablet which is found by Isis and the amulet which is hidden by Osiris and place them in the bowl whereby ye see the philosopher's stone.

Eat neither strong drink beer for three days before the new moon.

Wash and clean thy body with the sacred water.

Lie down in the sarcophagus in the Omni Path. Say ye these spells while visualizing my form.

I will meet him there in the darkness, and I will initiate him and show him wisdom and magic. And he will teach them the 12, and they shall some be with the light and some with the darkness, and there will be sorrow and great pain in the knowing.

Let him that hath an ear hear, for the hour is at hand. Seth stood silently musing the inscription he just read aloud, then looked over, at the professor and Dr Mubarak.

"Quite a tale, isn't it son?" said Dr Mubarak, smiling while putting his hand on Seth's shoulder. Dr Mubarak was much taller than Seth, which made his hands feel heavy on Seth's shoulder. He stepped back and shook his head.

"This is what true archaeology is all about, a discovery of the great myths of ancient times, " said Dr Mubarak.

"Yeah cool stuff," said Seth.

"OK, you better get back to work with your group, we've got a lot of work to do," said the professor."

"Right!" said Seth. He turned around and quickly walked back over where Adenesh and Elle were working on tagging a chest full of vases and ceremonial bowls.

"That was weird," said Seth, picking up a handful of tags and a magic marker.

"What was that all about? Why did they ask you over there? What did they say?" said Elle, her long hair completely covering her face as she knelt on the ground, lightly dusting an alabaster vase.

"There's another story about Thoth, and this thing called the Omni-Path. You have to not drink or eat for three days, and then Thoth gives you superpowers."

"That's it!" said Elle. She looked over at Adenesh who seemed indifferent to the conversation and was much more interested in the emerald green box she was examining, carefully turning it around in her small hands and admiring the beautiful design. It had written all around its four sides, covered with golden inlays that glowed softly. She couldn't take her eyes off it and felt the urge to open it.

"My dad wrote about the OmniPath in his book. He said there was a myth of a device used to control the minds of human beings. It was the device the gods used to make everyone speak a different language. You know the story of the Tower of Babel in the Bible," said Seth.

"What is the OmniPath?" Adenesh said, looking up from a box she'd been admiring. It had a strange aura around it. Adenesh could see the aura of most any object. It was a gift, her mother told her. She stared at it one last time, then gently set it down and gave the description to Elle who was taking down the log.

Seth scratched his nose at the tip and leaned over placing a small tag with a catalog number 22 on the box. Strangely, Seth liked the sound of the snapping rubber band.

He stood up and enthusiastically scratched his nose up and down right near his nostril. A nervous twitch he always tried made to look normal.

"Well, that's just it, no one really knows. That's why it's sort of like a myth.

"I think the tablet has something to do with the OmniPath. They must be connected." Said Seth.

"What's connected?" said Garofalo, who had suddenly come from behind Seth.

"You are Seth, right?" he said.

"I was saying I think the tablet might be connected to this tomb or the people who built it." "And what makes you say that?" said Garofalo, using a voice and posture as he would with any suspect in an interrogation.

"The tablet and some of the writing in here are the same," meaning I can't read them. The tablet had Thoth's seal, as did the tomb. Oh, and the tablet is depicted in that scene behind you. Thoth is placing it in the rock, you see?" Seth had a look of surprise on his face, as did everyone else. Because no one had noticed the relief until that moment.

Garofalo looked at the images for a moment, thcn walked directly in front of the scene. It covered the entire western wall.

"Professor Wilson!" he shouted." I think you're gonna want to see this." Garofalo waved his hand to invite the professor, who was still discussing the East wall with Dr Mubarak.

"Found something interesting, I hope," he said half-jokingly as he walked over and stood next to Agent Garofalo. The professor leaned in and carefully began reading the hieroglyphs.

"This is extraordinary!" This seems to relay the history of the creation of humankind. I'd say it is nearly an exact retelling of the ancient Sumerian text."

"Astonishing," said Dr Mubarak as he removed his glasses with one quick and deliberate motion, so dramatically executed it almost looked rehearsed.

Mary, who had been intently listening from near the tomb entrance, suddenly heard a noise from the cave entrance above.

She thought she heard what sounded like a scuffle. She turned around and looked toward the tomb door. To her surprise, three armed men in black military assault gear were suddenly standing in the doorway.

"Oh my god!" said Mary.

Before anyone could react, two of the men threw two small army green canisters into the middle of the tomb and before anyone could respond, they quickly shut the door.

Seth held his breath as long as he could, but his mind overcame his will, and he breathed in deeply. Instantly he felt dizzy and weak. Seth saw Adenesh falling to the ground as if she was fainting, her eyes rolling back in her head. He smelled a sour odor around his nostrils, Grunting and reaching for her with all his might, he tried to catch her. Then everything went black.

Chapter Forty

TRIAL BY FIRE
"Mary, wake up" she heard a voice say. She didn't know where she was until she felt the sand underneath her fingers.

"Mary, Are you all right?" repeated the voice.

This time she recognised the voice. It was her father, Professor Wilson.

She opened her eyes and saw her father's face, Agent Garofalo, Mubarak and several of the workmen standing over her. They all seem to have overly worried, with frightfully desperate looks on their faces. She touched her face immediately and was relieved to know nothing felt missing, nor any scars.

"I'm all right, I just feel a little dizzy and disoriented. Where are the children? Are they all right?" She was surprised to hear herself express such motherly concern for children just days ago she didn't want to meet at all.

"They're gone. I'm very sorry. I believe we were all gassed, and while we were unconscious, children were taken," said Agent Garofalo.

"All of them, OMG! But why?" Mary said, grasping and placing her hand over her mouth. She thought about Francis and the gunmen she watched shoot him and steal the tablet. Were they the same men? She considered the thought. The more she thought about it, the more frightened she became.

Mary felt her eyes tearing up, she turned her head away, trying to regain her composure.

"Yes, I'm afraid they are all gone." Said Agent Garofalo. He held his hand out to help her off the sandy floor.

Mary didn't look up, but she couldn't help but notice how handsome Garofalo was. He had that smooth Italian charm and a manly, good-looking face. She took his hand and, still looking down and away, she quickly tried to dust herself off. Her white blouse was covered in dust and clay. Her hair and face were also spotted with dirt. It appeared everyone had been lying on the floor for some time. For how long she couldn't tell.

She looked at her watch. It was 11p.m. Again she was alarmed. "What the hell is happening?" she thought to herself.

"Why would anyone want to kidnap those children? I don't understand why this is happening. Are they terrorists?" Mary's voice shrilled to a high-pitched vibrating the air around her lips, everyone could sense her oncoming panic, which indeed wasn't normal behavior for Mary, she was known for her stoic demeanor. But, with everything that was happening, on top of seeing Francis murdered, was finally taking its toll on her icy composure.

"Mary, let's try to stay calm here. There's no need to panic just yet. Letting our emotions get the best of us will only make things worse."

"My apologies, it's just"— Mary paused and regained her composure once more.

"I'm a professional," she said to herself.

"It appears the men overcame the guards and then used incapacitating gas on all of us. There doesn't appear to be any blood. My guess is they are terrorists and have kidnapped the children and will be demanding a ransom within 48 hours."

"Has anything been taken?" Said Mary.

"Unfortunately, we have no real way of knowing, but best we can recall, everything appears as it was."

Suddenly there was the sound of an approaching vehicle coming from outside the cave.

"Everyone get behind something and be quiet. I'll go check it out," said Garofalo. He reached into his shoulder bag to pull out his handgun.

Mary and the rest scattered behind a row of boxes in the main tomb, near the rear of the room.

Garofalo knelt and slowly walked toward the entrance.

He could hear the sound of a car engine shutting off. He waited and listened carefully. Next, he could listen to the sound of a car door opening and closing.

His experience told him only one person exited the vehicle, but he had no way of knowing if the person was alone or what type of weapon they could be holding.

He stepped into the shadow behind the main door, where he could come up from behind whoever might enter.

He switched off the safety and cocked his gun, holding it tightly with both hands.

It has been two years since he fired his last shot. It was during a routine bust outside of Venice. It was dark; he remembered he could see a thing. Before he couldn't get his bearings, he had lost sight of his partner.

Suddenly there was a rain of fire, two shooter's bullets flying from both directions. The only thing Garofalo could see was the quick burst coming for the muzzles. His instincts and a sudden rush of adrenalin forced his reflexes to pull the trigger again and again. Minutes later when backup arrived, the gunman and his partner lay dead on the floor. Ballistics determined he not only killed the suspect but his own partner as well.

He didn't know if he could pull the trigger ever again.

"OK, Garofalo, get your head back in the game," he muttered under his breath. He took a deep breath and exhaled slowly. He could feel His muscles, and the tension around his jaw relax.

"Hello? Hello, Is there anybody here? I'm Dr Strange Seth Strange's father.

"Didn't expect that," Said Garofalo as he stepped out from behind the door and slowly lowered his gun and put the safety back on.

"I'm afraid we have some horrible news, Mr Strange. Your son and the rest of the children appear to have been kidnapped,``said Garofalo.

Chapter Forty One

"*This is the truth, the whole truth and nothing but the truth:-*"

G-10 EMERGENCY SUMMIT, GENEVA, SWITZERLAND

Lord Dottington looked at his expensive Cartier watch. He had only two more hours before he needed to be seated at the conference. But there was one more important thing that required his attention.

He got up, placed his phone on silent and sent a text to his PA that he should not be disturbed for the next hour.

He walked into the bedroom and pulled out a small, red leather suitcase.

Placing it on the table in the living area, he moved the furniture out of the way, giving himself room to do what came next.

From the suitcase, he pulled out a large black cloth and laid it on the floor.

He took off his shoes and socks and the rest of his clothing and neatly laid them on the bed in the other room.

Next, he removed his watch, his signet ring and his eyeglasses and neatly set them in his posh Gucci case. Neatness and order were always crucial to Dottington. Order and exactness were one of his strengths and perquisites for magical success.

Entering back into the living room, he stepped into the center of the black cloth, which had a white circle embroidered on it with another outer ring decorated with 12 magical symbols embroidered in the most beautiful black silk from the East.

Standing silently for a moment, he set himself into a deep trance. His breathing and pulse nearly came to a stop. The room began to shake and bend. He raised his left hand and with his finger. He drew a door in the air in front of him.

"Door, door; Open to the place name I must enjoy. Go, go; I chant this now. So mote it be."

"Door, door; Open to the place name I must enjoy. Go, go; I chant this now. So mote it be."

"Door, door; Open to the place name I must enjoy. Go, go; I chant this now. So mote it be."

He lowered his arms and opened his eyes. And before him, a door appeared. Gazing steadily at the ever opening doorway, Dottington could see the great hall of the reptilian king Sargon. He lowered his hand and listened carefully before stepping through the magical door.

Chapter Forty Two

"Homage to Thee, O Great God, Thou Master of All Truth! I have come to Thee, O my God, and have brought myself hither, that I may become conscious of Thy decrees. I know Thee and am attuned with Thee and Thy two and forty Laws, which exist with Thee in this Chamber of Maat.

GREAT CITY OF TAG-JART, THE REPTILIAN MINISTRY OF INTELLIGENCE

Ambassador Zagr had climbed the white, polished limestone steps of the Ministry of Intelligence before, but not like today. Today his clawed feet had a spring to them that they had not had in a century. "How do humans say it?" he thought to himself. "I feel like a million bucks! " He said.

"What is a million bucks, is it a food source?" he heard a passerby say as he reached the top of the stairs to the entrance of the building. A tall venomous-looking female reptilian was reading his thoughts as he was coming up the stairs. Zagr had been away among the humans for the past year. He had forgotten to control his feelings when back among his own mind-reading species.

He stopped in stride and stood still, breathing in deeply from his throat gills, and his mind went into focus to a single point in his mind. He exhaled, but this time through his mouth.

Releasing the breath, his mind closed, and he headed back up the steps and entered the ominous building.

"He entered a conference room where other ambassadors from the other surface government's stood before the throne. In the center of the palace sat King Sargon, ruthless and as fearsome as he appeared.

Even for a reptilian, he was frightening to behold with sinister snake-like eyes and green skin harsh like leather covered in feathers and scales. His hands were 10-inch claws, and his mouth had two rows of razor-sharp fangs. His breathing was a low unnerving hissing sound. That brought chills down Zagrs spine.

His tongue flicked and swirled around his mouth unconsciously. He was a towering creature, his body was thick and muscular built for battle and the hunt. But most fearsome of all was Sargon was a channeling of the highest degree, he could mimic any life form once he ingested its DNA.

" Ambassador Zagr, so glad you decided to join us." Hissed Sargon.

"Forgive me, your majesty. Fate decreed a change of plans. It became necessary for me to deal with something of great importance before returning, your majesty."

Sargon flicked his tongue and leaned forward from his throne. He extended his right claw and pointed it facing up. "SHARE!" He shouted, and at once Zagr stepped to the center of the room and knelt before the King' throne. He reached out his right claw to place it on the left hand of the king.

Instantly, all Zagr had seen and heard was transferred to the mind of the king.

"It would seem you have done well, Ambassador Zagr, you have done quite well indeed."

"Yes, you have done quite well indeed," Sargon repeated. Repeating something was how reptilians expressed disappointment or approval, depending on the inflexion. It was often quite difficult for even a reptilian to tell the difference between the two meanings. In this case, luckily for Zagr, it was meant as "well done."

Sargon was known to rip those who disappointed him into pieces, Before eating them in front of the entire court.

He hissed gingerly and smiled in the terrible way that only a reptilian could do.

His yellow and green eyes darted back and forth as if searching for someone. The reptilians were well known for their poor sight. However, they more than made up for it with their keen senses of smell and hearing.

He hissed and flicked his fire red, forked tongue in and out of his fanged mouth. The creature fixed its death-like gaze on General Daat, head of the Reptilian Imperial Legions.

"General, how long before our troops are in place and prepared to strike?" Said Sargon.

"Your Majesty, we are on schedule and will have our ships positioned at every surface entry for when the time comes. We have deployed a cloaked fleet in orbit over the Americas. All the final preparations are being completed as we speak. We are on schedule as you commanded. Your majesty."

Suddenly, in the middle of the room, there appeared a tiny ball of black smoke that quickly spun and grew into a figure of a man dressed in a hooded, red and black robe.

"What is the meaning of this intrusion, magician?" the beastly Sargon snarled and hissed angrily.

From inside the tower of smoke, out of the form Lord Dottington's image took shape and stepped into the great hall.

"Greetings, mighty Sargon, I bring glad tidings!" said Lord Dottington.

"My Master has a need for thee," Lord Dottington mischievous wicked grin, his eyes burning like coals on the fire.

"How dare you presume to appear before this court uninvited, making demands, Lucifer." Said Sargon. Lucifer was Lord Dottington's real name. A name feared by many he had been called directly for ages— except King Sargon, who was immune to most magical influences except the very high magic known only to the ancient one.

"I come in the name of our master, Enlil. It is by his authority have come. He commands that you go to the surface, and there you will deal with humans once and for all.

The court was stunned at Lucifer's statement. The members began to roar and hiss, flicking their tongues and showing their teeth in the most frightful of ways.

"Silence," hissed Sargon.

"What of Thoth? He is a powerful Magician with weapons even I cannot withstand. What you speak of is not an easily accomplished magician."

Dottingto smiled then quietly said, "I thought you'd never ask your majesty. Have I mentioned My master promises you shall taste human flesh again and rule the earth as in the time before the Annunaki drove you and your kind deep into the Argatha , your majesty?"

The king sat back on his throne, tongue flicking side to side. "I'm listening. Tell me more about this plan. Magician, tell me more of this plan Magician, but be warned." Sargon snarled, his eyes lowering their gaze directly into the eyes of the great magician, hissing and flicking his tongue and mouth as if suddenly violently aroused.

"And if I am displeased, it is your flesh I shall feast on this very hour, magician," Said Sargon.

"As is your right, great Sargon. But in any case, as you will soon see my master granted me the authority to speak in his name, my master, who in the time before time did rule the Earth and made peace between you, great king, and the Annunaki.

Was it not my master that granted thee and thy people this very land within the inner Earth? Was it not my Master who was given rule over this earth by the very gods of Nibiru?

"It is in his authority and promise I have come before you. All that was promised shall be done according to his great desire. You shall be rewarded, and greatly cover the face of the surface once again.

In return for your loyalty, you shall be appointed Lord of the Earth and the children of men shall once again be thy food and thy slaves, as it was before the great calamity."

"Your talk is sweet, magician, but without the key of Thoth, no magic can activate the great power plant and restore our atmosphere. We are powerless until the surface is made fit to its natural state before the Nibiruan king terraformed the world and forced my people below the ground," Hissed Sargon. His clawed fingers tapping loudly on the arms rest of his throne of skulls.

With a low steady tone Dottington replied

"That is my concern, Your majesty."

Dottington had faced Sargon before and knew full well the king was a shrewd as well as a formidable foe to contend with if things were to go against him.

There was silence in the great hall, and Dottington spoke again.

"Make your men ready to strike. Before the new moon, I will use the tablet to turn on the power plant at Giza and activate the OmniPath, which will lead us to the weapons of terror, and begin the process of terraforming the earth. Your great people will rule the Earth once more and strike a mighty blow to your sworn enemies of Nibiru," Said with a confidence that even impressed the mighty Sargon.

And in the moment Dottington knew he had won.

The magician with a sinister smile.

"So be it, So be it magician, So be it, So be it magician." I have over one million of my troops ready to strike the surface." Sargon grunted, spitting and growling in an awful way. "We will lay waste to human civilization and their gods."

"So Mote it be!" said the magician. Lucifer turned and stepped back through the magical doorway and disappeared. The outline of the invisible door became visible, and in a flash of light and blue and black smoke, he was gone.

"My lord, why should we trust that human magician?" He is but meat for the belly, said Zagr, flicking his tongue in disgust. His eye slits twitched rapidly at the thought of the pleasure of ripping into the flesh of the magician. "Magical humans had such sweet taste" he snarled and hissed.

"I trust him no more than I trust you?" said Sargon coldly. "Be warned, fool. I had foreseen the magician would come. My spies and the adepts have watched the magician's progress for many cycles. Even now he grows closer to the key." Once he activates the Omni Path, we will siege control of it and destroy them all.

The council chamber filled with murmurs and hissing.

"He will restore the surface, and we shall march on the humans, and then we will destroy the Annunaki once and for all! We will rule the new Tiamat once again! The king stood up, raised his claw to his chest and breathed in deeply through his flaring green nostrils.

"Generals of the realm, prepare the dragon warriors for war!" he said, raising his voice as he spoke.

The hall erupted into a chorus of loud shrieks, grunts and hissing sounds. The creatures roared and shouted at each other into a frenzy, ripping and clawing at each other, cutting each other's flesh, ripping and tearing until they bled.

In the midst of the frenzy, the king gave a loud, resounding hiss, and instantly the room grew deathly still.

"Now go," said Sargon. And with that, the reptilian king, his generals and the rest of the royal court left the bloody hall, their long, thick tails drawing waving trails of blood behind them.

Chapter Forty Three

"*Hark ye O old man and list to my warning:*
be ye free from the bondage of night.
Surrender not your soul to the BROTHERS OF DARKNESS."
WITHOUT A TRACE

"Kidnapped!" Seth's father shook his head and stepped back nearly losing his balance . For a moment Seth's father wondered if he'd misheard Garofalo. After all it had been a long journey and he was undoubtedly jet lagged. so he asked Garofalo again, but this time slowly measuring each word carefully.

"Did you say kidnapped?"

Garofalo recognised the high-stress reaction building internally in Seth's father's body. His experience told him the shock would soon turn to anger.

Garofalo, in a precautionary move, reached into his pocket and showed his badge along with his credentials to Seth's father in an effort to calm him down.

"Special Agent Garofalo," he announced. "Mr Strange, I know this is a terrible shock, but you have to stay calm. As far as we know, the children are unharmed."

How could something like this happen? They're just kids on an expedition?" Said Seth's father. His right cheek twitched up and down several times, then he wrinkled his upper lip to touch his nose, which oddly enough was a genetic trait he inherited from his mother.

Garofalo continued to observe Abraham Strange closely. He watched the confessed father's every gesture for signs and clues into the personality of the subject. It was what he was trained to do.

He was an expert at reading a man in 30 seconds or less.

He was impressed with what discovered. "Smart, fit looking body, clearly a military background. Has seen some action. Garofalo could see it in his eyes. "

It's always in the eyes," he thought to himself.

"I tried to get here as soon as I could. But, Seth's phone was turned off, and I couldn't reach anyone at the university offices," Seth's father said while looking at professor Wilson.

"Abraham, what do you mean you knew this would happen?"

"You know him?" said Garofalo.

"Yes, of course, Abraham is a former colleague from the university," said Professor Wilson, with a tone Garofalo had not heard from the Professor before.

"Ryan Wilson and Abraham Strange once were colleagues. before Abraham was dismissed from the university," said Mubarak.

"I see...Said Garofalo.

"You mean before you dismissed me," Said Abraham, diverting his eyes from looking directly in Mubarak's direction.

Seth's father curled his lip to his nose again but with more intensity this time making his blond mustache look like an overweight beaver crawling into his nose.

"That's a rather interesting little trick you got there, you must be popular at parties" Said Garofalo, half-jokingly.

"Gentlemen, please, we have children missing!" said Mary. She stood glaring at them with the rage of a mama bear ready to charge.

"What are we going to do to get those children back safely?" Mary said, calmly folding her arms across her breast.

The first thing we need to do is call for backup, said Garofalo. He reached into his pocket for his phone, but it was not there. He searched through all his pockets and scanned the ground around him.

"My phone is gone!" said Garofalo. "Do one of you have a phone?" The others searched for themselves as well.

They all quickly scattered across the tomb searching.

"It looks like they took all our devices," Said Mary.

"I have a phone." Seth's father said in a low voice, But before Garofalo could reply, a phone started ringing.

"Over there, It's coming from over there!" Said Mary.

"Everyone stay back from the entrance!"

"It could be a bomb!" said Garofalo.

Everyone quickly trotted out of the tomb into the cave entrance.

Garofalo carefully walked toward the sound of the phone ringing. He saw the phone on the floor and picked it up. He hesitated for a moment before answering it.

"Special Agent Garofalo," he spoke calmly into the phone. He waited to see if he was still alive.

Then a voice spoke through the phone.

"Bring the key to the Great Pyramid three days before sunrise. Absolutely no police or all the children will die," The voice said.

Then there was only silence. He stood for a moment immobilized. Garofalo had been in this situation before, but never involving the lives of innocent children.

He hung up the cell and looked around. "Definitely not a bomb," he shouted. "I'm coming out." He placed the obviously encrypted phone in his front pocket.

He wiped his forehead. The sweat dripping into his eyes was really starting to bother him now. He never liked the desert, In fact, he hated everything about the desert, especially the scorpions. He'd had more than his fair share of midnight creeping things in Iraq.

"Agent Garofalo! What happened? Did they answer? What did they say?" The professor nervously muttered out a slew of unrelated questions.

Seth's father looked on, still playing with his lips, saying nothing.

"I don't know who answered, but yes, someone did."

"What did they say?" Mary asked gingerly.

"She's a real fit bird," Garofalo said to himself. He smiled and continued "The voice is difficult to understand and distorted, but I believe it to be male. He gave me instructions to deliver the key to the pyramid." He paused and looked away, then down. "Or the children will be killed."

Garofalo swallowed quietly, a trigger he used to hide his emotions. He would merely imagine swallowing any unwanted emotions to his first chakra and release them out of his body.

No one said anything for a moment. The desert wind was the only sound you could hear. Small tears welled up at the corner of Mary's eyes. She slowly wiped them one by one.

"Good news is we know they are still alive. These guys sound like textbook terrorists. If we give them what they demand, they will release the children."

"But what key are they talking about?" said Mary.

Chapter Forty Four

"Many shall ye find, the stones in your pathway: many mountains to climb toward the LIGHT."

BELLY OF THE BEAST

"The purpose of evolution is to attain understanding of the necessity of doing good and living in harmony with Cosmic Laws;

and to express your Divine Nature in everything you think, say and do."

—Rosicrucian Manuscript

PRESIDENT RONALD T. Johnson was glad his very long day was finally over. He had reached his tipping point and he could feel it from his throbbing migraine down to his aching feet from standing for hours. Not to mention Everything he ever believed, or whatever truths once cherished, he now realized they were all complete lies.

He was the son of a born-again Southern Baptist preacher. He virtually grew up in the church and was "saved" by the time he was 9 years old. Donald had dedicated his entire life to serving the Lord. He'd done his fair share of sinning, mostly telling white lies, but he was a true believer in his Lord Jesus Christ.

"We're here, sir," said the driver. "Will you need me anymore this evening, Mr President?"

"No... that will be all for me tonight, Henry."

A small detail of security personnel appeared and opened the president's door to escort him through the white house stateroom's private entrance.

Donald entered the presidential suite, and walked into the main sitting room, and poured a drink. He wasn't a big drinker but did enjoy the taste of a good Irish whiskey once in a while to take off the edge days like this one.

He took off his jacket and neatly placed it on the opposite chair in the sitting area. He could hear his wife, the first lady, lightly snoring in their bedroom.

She's always been a sound sleeper. He thought to himself as he took another healthy sip of his expensive whiskey.

His mind drifted back to his super top secret meeting earlier in the week with the reptilian ambassador Zagr.

"Hell, I don't know if I should be laughing or crying." He whispered to himself. He knew somebody was always listening to the White House.

He took another sip, then reached over to the bottle he had sat on the table and poured himself another.

Shaking his head a few times before he killed the rest of his drink.

"Awe, hell. I gotta do what is right, no matter what the consequences," he said out loud this time.

"That's what my old man would do!" he said in a moment of holy, righteous indignation. He'd lost his father to stomach cancer while he was on the campaign trail earlier that year. He could still see the look on his father's face; it was the look in his eyes. He didn't look afraid, and it scared him genuinely. But he never told anyone. In fact, he'd convinced himself his father died bravely, but he loved his father and missed him terribly.

He poured another, took a sip, still only looking straight ahead, he sat up straight in the chair and sighed.

After a long, thoughtful pause he sat his drink down on the table and folded his hands, and began to pray.

"Dear lord, I'm going to tell the American people what we are up against in the world!" Lord Jesus guided my hand and gave me the words to say. amen"

He leaned back in his chair and took several quick sips, but this time straight from the bottle.

Chapter Forty Five

" Their reward is that they are not believed when they tell the truth."
-Aristotle

THE SLEEPING GIANT

It was late afternoon, and the heat inside the tomb was becoming unbearable for everyone, especially for Dr Mubarak, who though at age 63 had seen better days, and from the amount of sweating pouring down his face, one might think he had just taken a shower with his shirt on.

"Been awhile since you were out in the field for more than a photo op!" Mary said jokingly.

"Or... ruin someone's career." Seth's father quickly lashed out, fixing a cold dead glance at Dr Mubarak, making it clear to everyone who he was directing his comment.

"You are right, and we wouldn't be here now if I had my way, and neither would you, for that matter," said Dr Mubarak in defiance.

"Cool your horses, gentlemen. We need to stay focused!" said Agent Garofalo.

Every one dropped the subject and pressed on with searching the tomb carefully from top to bottom for the mysterious key the kidnappers were demanding.

"We've been searching for hours, and we don't have a clue what we are looking for," Mary said, her voice shaking, and she looked exhausted."This is impossible."

She stopped and sat down on the sandy floor, and she noticed a very tiny emerald green box— the same one Adenesh happened to be looking at before the kidnapping.

Mary picked up the box and turned over a few times in her hands. She was trying to make out the strange mixture of Sumerian and ancient Egyptian writing. The piece was puzzling to her, unlike anything she had seen before.

"Dad, come look at this!" she shouted, trying to hold down her excitement.

"Did you find something, Mary?" Said the professor, as he walked towards the other side of the tomb.

Seth's father also turned to look at the object Mary was admiring in her hands, as did Dr Mubarak.

What they saw stopped them in his tracks.

"That's it!" they shouted in unison.

"The secret box the text spoke about in the book of Thoth," said Seth's father. "According to the Book of Thoth, Thoth hid the knowledge of the gods and the secret wisdom in a box that held the keys to open the secret chamber of the Halls of Amenti and the key power to control the OmniPath."Seth's father said.

"There's no time for theories, Abraham," said Dr Mubarak. He was careful to measure his words so as to not appear as if he was merely acting out of spite toward Seth's father, who had been rather unfriendly toward Dr Mubarak since he arrived at the excavation site.

"Clearly even if you can see through those ardent academic lenses, something is clearly happening here!" shouted Seth's father.

He regained his composure and paused for a moment. "May I see it?"

Don't worry, son. I'll find you, Seth's father thought to himself.

"Please do... I've never seen a piece like this— brilliant, really."

She said, handing the small box to Seth's father.

Garofalo noticed the extra moment they took exchanging the strange-looking box and started to feel strangely jealous.

"Maybe Seth's father isn't the quack here!" Garofalo thought to himself. He kept his eyes moving around, looking for any signs of approach. He knew they were still vulnerable. The terrorists could return or could be watching them even now.

"It's very intriguing, indeed," Said Professor Wilson.

"Definitely Sumerian origin, most certainly." Said Dr Mubarak.

"Can you make out the inscription, Abraham?" The professor asked.

"It says here, the chosen can find the keys to the ring of Isis, the ring of Thoth and the ring of Osiris," said Seth's father.

"I, Thoth, keeper of wisdom, and protector of mankind, It is for him to meet me In the chamber. I have built the core of the power plant, the secrets of the OmniPath, and the weapons of terror. The gods of Nibiru will return in the last days, before the final judgment.

There will be grinding and gnashing of teeth. Take the ring and its power to activate the OmniPath.

Only the hand of the children of the stars can be made worthy to hold the rings and unlock the keys to Amenti, less Enlil is set free, and the children of men are no more."

"Really?" sneered Garofalo. Garofalo grew up in a Catholic home. He loved his heritage, culture and history, But it was at university he became an atheist.

He preferred facts and had an unnatural distrust of everyone, especially anything to do with religious people. As far as he was concerned, they were the worst of the lot.

"The ring could possibly be in that box," said Mary.

"Let me get this straight," said Garofalo. ``You're saying that box, and some rings are keys to jump-start the Giza pyramid-like it's some kind of power plant device?" said Agent Garofalo.

"Yes, it's in my book," Seth; dad's said with a smirk. He looked at the box further, looking for a way to open the box. He couldn't locate any particular switch or see any latch, some kind of mechanism to open the lid of the box. What he was sure of was the box clearly had a cover, indicating some purpose of opening the box.

"Maybe if you try rubbing it real hard and clicking your heels three times that might do it," laughed Garofalo.

"What agency did you say you were with, again?" Mary said dryly. She turned her shoulders slightly away from him, with a gesture that said she wasn't interested in his answer.

"According to the myth, Thoth's ring is in this box," said Seth's father.

"Can you open it?" Said Mary.

"No, I mean, I thought I could. According to the book of Thoth, the box can only be opened by the chosen."

"Of course, that makes perfect sense, great job!" Garofalo clapped his hands three times to dramatize his sarcasm "What a performance. Bravo," he laughed.

"How about you let me use your phone, Mr Strange, so while you are doing your forbidden archaeology episode, I can get us some actual help out of here."

"What about the children's parents, we are going to have to tell them," said Mary in a deathly serious tone.

"I would like to suggest we head back to the university," said Professor Wilson.

"Your lab is a crime scene. Everything has been damaged or destroyed," said Mubarak. Feeling more and more fatigued from the heat of the enclosed chamber.

"Are you all right, Dr Mubarak?" said Mary, handing him a tissue from her backpack.

"I'll be fine," he said, wiping off the flood of sweat pooling up around his forehead and upper lip.

"We are not going to the lab. We're going to my office to take another look at the data I have in my tent," said Professor Wilson.

Professor Wilson turned to look at Seth's father who seemed to be deep in thought. "He is connecting the dots," he thought to himself.

"You're talking about the chamber you discovered using the ground radar," said Mubarak, still sweating but appearing to get his second wind.

"The entrance to Amenti! You found it!" Shouted Seth 's father.

"I don't know, but it appears we're about to find out!" Said the professor.

Gathering all their belongings, they headed out of the tomb and into the open desert.

They could see Garofalo with his arms flailing in the air as dust swirled all around him a few hundred yards away.

Mary covered her ears to mute the thundering sound of the wind and the hot desert soup churning under the rotating blades. A few hundred yards away from them was a flat black, military-style helicopter with no visible marking.

Chapter Forty Six

"Now I give unto thee the knowledge,
known to the MASTERS,
the knowing that conquers all the dark fears.
Use this, the wisdom I give thee.
MASTER thou shalt be of THE BROTHERS OF NIGHT."

NEPHILIM

When Seth opened his eyes, he thrust his hands out in front of himself as if to catch himself from falling. But nothing happened, and he wasn't falling at all. Seth slumped himself over against a cold limestone wall. He decided to slowly open his eyes until they quickly widened in surprise. He sat up with a terrible feeling of confusion and fright.

"What is going on? I know, these guys are probably aliens or maybe CIA, or worse some religious fanatics, Seth mused to himself.

"Where the hell Am I?" he said, loud enough to be heard if anyone was listening. He was in a small cell of some kind. Seth backed up against the wall and then looked around for a camera.

To the right, directly above him, a camera followed his movements. The red blinking light centered at the top of the camera seemed to stare into his head.

From out of the silence, he heard the sound of keys rattling outside the door. Seth braced himself and tried not to panic.

"Stay calm, Seth," he said to himself.

"Fight or flight, fight or flight," he said, every inch of his body, every muscle fiber growing stiff and ready to burst. He was prepared to fight as he watched the cell door slowly open.

"Well, hello again, young man," said a shadowy figure. Seth couldn't make the person out until he stepped back away from the light blinding Seth from getting a good look at him.

Seth put his hand up over his eyes to see better.

"Wait a minute. You're the guy from the airport, aren't you?" said Seth

"It would seem you have lost your way from the airport baggage claim. I warned you to follow the signs."

The man's once short hair white hair was now blue-black and flowing over his shoulders. His face was as pale as a bucket of fresh milk. He wore a finely made black cloak and hood which covered his eyes from a clear view.

"Who are you, and what do you want?" said Seth, his fist clenched tighter now. Thoughts of crazy cult murder headlines flashing on the screen of his mind's eye.

"I am called Shern," said the very odd-looking, very tall being.

"Keeping breathing, Seth," he said to himself.

"You need not fear me, It is not I that seeks your blood, young master.

It is destiny that has brought you and your comrades here." He raised his head, allowing Seth to see his luminous white eyes.

Shern raised his long muscular arms to place the forefingers of each of his equally long but meaty hands on either side of Seth's small head. Seth felt an ice cold child quicken his spine like a blast of winter wind.

Seth felt Stern breaking into his mind as if the front door of his mind had been blown completely open.

Seth felt the clock of his mind unfolding backwards. He saw lifetimes from epoch to epoch pass before his mind's eyes. Darkness closed in, engulfing all matter and space around him. And suddenly in a deep hypnotic trance. He could see nor hear a sound.

Shern studied the fragile red haired boy. His glowing white eyes flashed as he slowly removed his hood to release his long red hair that reached to the small of his back

.

Shern was a sight to behold, and the last of his kind. The last surviving War Maker, created for only one purpose by God King RA 12,000 years ago after the deluge. during the dark time when the gods were at war.

Shern and his kind were created by Marduk after stealing the tablet of destiny from Enlil. They were created perfect killing machines impervious to the magic of gods and men. Even the gods fear them.

After the wars were over the gods left the earth scorched and in chaos The gods sent the death dealers of Nibiru to hunt down The War makers and remove them from the face of the earth.

In one final battle the Nephilim mercilessly slaughter Marduk and his legions of warmakers.

Shern was left on the scorned blood stained battlefield weak and dying and was left for dead. But as destiny had decreed. Shern was rescued and brought back to health by a strange priest, who offered him a chance at revenge for his loyalty and service.

"Must trouble for such a puny human," Shern said to himself.

And with that he pulled the hood back over his head carefully adjusting for his long hair as he did so. He then turned leaving Seth still lost in a deep hypnotic sleep.

The cell door shut and locked by itself; telekinesis was one of the many genetically engineered abilities of the War Makers.

Shern came to the next door, which had a small viewing slot at the top center of the metal door. However, Stern had no need of it, as he was engineered with the ability to detect thermal and ultraviolet light.

He could see all 12 of the chosen ones with his genetically modified sight. He caught a sense of strange energy vibration coming from one of the cells containing one of the females.

The sense was so powerful he stopped to take a closer look.

"I haven't felt such energy since the time before the great war!" Shern thought to himself.

Then the main door to the dungeon opened, and three of the dark brothers stepped into the chamber.

"My Lord, We've been ordered to move the children to the ceremonial chambers, and the others are arriving soon." He said gracefully.

Shern did not respond. His attention was still on the girl, but the vibrations were fading.

He turned to look at the gentlemen, also dressed in black robes and hoods. However, they bore shining, beautifully embroidered markings around the borders of the hoods and sleeves. Each wore a gold and emerald signet ring with the face of the dragon carved into the surface of the stone.

"What of the demon?" Said Shern. He drew his attention away from the young girl.

"Lord Dottington has commanded the beast to work the deep magic, and we have the keys, my lord," said Theron. He was the pupil of Lord Dottington, and the Chief priest of the Temple of the Brotherhood of Darkness. Under his hood, Stern could see his solid black eyes, black and empty like the magician's soul.

Theron was of average height, and slightly overweight, with sandy blonde hair and a sharp pointed nose.

He spoke with an American Southern drawl, Stern found quite amusing.

"And what of Sargon's Army? The deep magic will only hold the gate open for so long. It will collapse quickly. Thoth's failed safes will close it."

"Lord Dottington has met with Sargon. The dragon army is marching toward the OmniPath as we speak."

"And the Grey's, what of them? They are not so easily inclined to make alliances against their masters, I assure you," said Shern.

"The heretic's apprentice should have already arrived on Mars. We expect his report at any time, my lord, said Theron.

"Then let us make ready, shall we, magicians," Shern said bluntly. He could sense the fear vibrating from the magicians. If it were not for Dottington, he would have slaughtered them long ago.

Sharon was rather impressed with Dottington, at least as far as one could be impressed with inferior beings.

He related it to the way a master is impressed with an exceptional dancing monkey. Nonetheless, cosmic forces, once set in motion, cannot be undone. "All that has begun must now continue to its inevitable conclusion. Such is the law of all creation." Said Shern.

The three hooded men turned and headed down a short tunnel made of smooth limestone. There were no torches or lamps. Dim, iridescent light came from all directions, glowing through the limestone pores.

The tunnels were cut perfectly straight to laser precision 250 feet below the Great Sphinx.

Chapter Forty Seven

"*N ow unto thee, give I my magic.*
　　Take it and dwell on the pathway of LIGHT."
AGHARTA, THE RED TOWER

"The reptilians are mobilizing the dragon army. We have reports from across the domains in the South and in the outer forbidden zone," said Prince Atrea to his father and King of Agharta. The kind name was called, An Shar which means "He who rules from below" and whose number of power is 9.

His people were once on the surface, just as the reptilian people were once on the surface. In those days they were called the Atlantans, a name his father sorely missed.

He was seated to the right of his father as was customary in El Shar. An emergency meeting of the war council had been called by his father during the time of silence. Such a thing had not occurred in over 12,000 years in the kingdom, not even since the great deluge.

The meeting was held in the Red Tower at the center of the city. Around the round table sat 10 tall and beautiful Nordic beings, each with straight blonde hair and brilliant blue eyes, except for the king, who had bright red hair and deep black eyes, as did his eldest son and rightful heir, Prince Atrea. Around a grand white marble table In its center was an enormous red pentagram that covered the entire surface of the table. They were adorned in the most exquisite fabric that was made from pure golden thread. 9 Kings each representing great houses of the 9 realms of Agharta.

The Lords sat in order of rank, each having his number of power. Mim Lar of Lar, whose name is 1, Mim Ne of the land of Ne, whose number of power is 2, Mim Me of the land of Me, whose number of power is 3 Mim Mar of the land of Mar, whose number of power is 4, Mim Tu of the land of Tu, whose number of power is 5.

Mim Lamkhar of the land of Lamkhar, whose number of power is 6, Mim Tu Shar of the land of Tu Shar, whose number of power is 7, Mim Maat of the land of Maat, whose number of power is 8

"Sargon. I'm afraid his taste for blood has overtaken his senses. He would bring us all to the time of the war makers and weapons of terror once more," said Mim Me.

"They are in league with the Human magician and the Illuminati. They seek the lifespan of the gods on Nibiru. They would see all creation perish for the fulfillment of their desire to cheat death and escape their eternal oblivion."

"The time has come. We will call together the armies of Agharta."

"What do the Astrologers foresee?" said M Shar," his face covered and strained, his skin now glowing a pale green. His tattoos seemed to be moving and changing shape all over his entire body.

"The Grey's are rebelling on mars, and have cut off the supply of anatomic gold to Nibiru. The planet's atmosphere is failing again, and the people and the land are divided. Some of the people are calling for Enlil to return and pointing the blame to Enlil for sparing the humans and creating the races, with his experiments."

"The bloodline of Thoth is now in the hands of the Dark One." Said Mim- Lar, oldest and wisest of the 9.

"He desires the OmniPath, for the children will harvest the star fire, giving him the power he will use to open the gates on Earth and Mars to send armies to march on Nibiru."

"The process will more than likely cause loss of life to the children, ending all mankind forever, " said the female Mim Tu Shar. His eyes filled with sorrow as he spoke.

"What of Lord Thoth?" said M Shar as he looked in the direction of his son Atrea.

"The Brotherhood has set a circle of protection around the form of Thoth. I believe he will attempt to awaken the children of the light in the realm of dreams beyond the deep magic that binds his oath. We believe he means to face Enlil in the Akasha. So above, so below," said the prince, his eyes lowered as was customary when addressing the king, even if he was his father.

"The children carry the pure bloodlines. Their combined blood will give him the power of the old gods. We cannot allow powers of such magnitude to fall into the hands of that evil little troll. Enlil unleashed a fate upon us all to play this dangerous game," said Prince Atrea.

"What is your command my lord?" the members of the council asked the king in unison as if they were all at once of one mind.

The great king's heart was heavy. He feared for his son and the path that lay before him as the Royal Astrologers have seen. Death would visit the land of Agartha once more. No one had died in Agartha for over 12,000 years, not since the time of the great wars and the weapons of terror.

"Let the scribe write down my words now, true and without prejudice. Lords of Agharta we make ready for war. Prepare your armies in the North and in the East, the West and the South. The times of darkness have come upon us." Said the king as he smashed his fist violently on the grand white table. His face was stern but noble.

"My Lord, what of the children? Shall we not first find them safely here in Agharta?" said Prince Atrea.

"Their fate is not for us to decide, my son," the king said sadly. "I must protect the people of this realm. If fate decrees that the unnatural humankind must perish, it is for the Cosmic to decide. I must protect the realm and our way of life, as it has always been."

"But father, I swore an oath to Lord Thoth," Atrea exclaimed in a curious tone that stunned his father, the king, and the rest of the council. The king stood up so quickly it appeared as if he did not move at all.

"How dare you speak to your king that way," said Mim Mar, High Commander of the seven armies.

"Father, with all due respect, would you have me dishonor this house and not keep my word to protect the children of the light? This is not our way, my lord. You have taught me this since the time I was a boy." Said the crown prince, as calmly as he could muster. He knew he had nearly forgotten his place, which would be shameful for a royal of Agharta.

Thoth had been Atrea's teacher and mentor in the time before. He taught him many secret things as was his birthright, but the friendship and affection he had for Thoth grew beyond mentor and apprentice.

"I shall not break my oath, no matter what you decree next father," he thought to himself. Atrea sat back in his chair and folded his arms on the table, a gesture of submission.

"Three days from now, I order the seven gateways to be closed, and reptilians and their ambassadors to be expelled from the land of Agharta. We shall protect Agharta, and we will strike without a quarter. Send word to Nibiru that the children of

Agharta stand with them. As for the Children of the light, it is for this reason all has been said and done. Atrea, my son, you will take 10 of our best warriors, and if the gods are with you shall return with the children unharmed."

The king ended by making the mystical declaration, "So mote it be," which was then repeated one by one around the table by the rest of the war council.

Chapter Forty Eight

"*The wind blows where it wills, and you hear the sound of it, but you do not know whence it comes or whither it goes; so it is with everyone who is born of the Spirit," (John iii, 8).*

CHAMBER OF DEATH

"There!" said Professor Wilson. He pointed his pinky finger to an area on the computer screen. It was a thermal image of the Giza plateau taken from a US spy satellite using advanced military grade, ground-penetrating radar scanning technology, revealing what looked to be a clearing a series of tunnels, and large open rectangular spaces and circularly shaped rooms.

"I don't understand, how did these tunnels get there?" said Dr Mubarak, who seemed in much better spirits since being rescued from the near heat exhaustion three hours ago in the tombs.

"Look closer," said Mary.

Seth's father and Mubarak both reached into their shirt pockets and popped on their individual reading glasses. They leaned in closer, now getting a better look at the screen.

Garofalo was standing in the corner of the room whispering to two men dressed in plain grayish suits who had met them when they landed at the military base.

Mary found the behavior most irritating. Whispering in the presence of others was something she always felt was quite rude, to say the least.

Though she tried intensely to gather what exactly was being said, she was only able to make out a word or two.

"Can you see it now?" said the Professor.

"Yes, it looks like definite heat signatures are indicating organic material," said Seth's father.

"I count at least two or three dozen." Said professor Wilson.

"Maybe Garofalo is right and this is a fanatical religious terrorist organization after all," said Mary. She suddenly thought of the famous book by Dan Brown, but she could never remember the title.

"Damn, what is the name of that book?" she thought to herself.

Professor Wilson looked up over his shoulder, still keeping his eyes on the photograph.

"Agent Garofalo, I think you should see this," said Professor Wilson.

Garofalo excused himself from the two gentlemen and double-timed it over to the desk. He stood uncomfortably close to Mary. She took a step to the side in an attempt to relieve the immediate and visible tension she felt when he moved too close to her.

"What did you find?" ask Garofalo, trying not to let on his disappointment at Mary's reaction.

"A few years ago, teams using ground-penetrating radar discovered a network of tunnels and chambers running across the Giza complex, Particularly the large area beneath the Sphinx and the Great Pyramid. And here you see that under the surface complex. Now, in the thermal range, Those heat signatures can only be human beings. It appears the tunnels have expanded.

"My guess is the terrorists have the children somewhere right there under the Sphinx," said Professor Wilson.

"Under the Sphinx is where Thoth is said to have hidden a flying disc in the same location as the "weapons of terror," said Seth's father.

"That means the tablet is the last book of Enki. The myth says Enki poisoned his brother Enlil who had gone mad with lust for blood and his hatred of mankind. He allowed the weapons of terror to be used, causing the destruction of Sumer," said Dr Mubarak.

Seth's father was surprised by his nemesis's understanding of the very topic that got him removed from his position at the university he so loved. Authors like Zechariah Sitchin and other ancient alien theorists had uncovered mountains of data proving alien visitation, but without the University backing, he wasn't able to continue his important research.

The thought made him pause for a moment, then continued.

Thoth's tablet gave instructions on how to return the ship to Nibiru. The keys unlock its location, but it is protected by an invisibility spell," he said.

"The Ancient kings were mummified with their organs preserved, as well as their royal belongings, and in some cases, they had their slaves buried with them for one simple reason, they believe that God's number one had the technology to reanimate them. And number two, they believed the gods would someday return, and a new kingdom and new heaven would be ushered in by the return of the gods from the stars, and they would be reborn."

"So how do you see it once you find the location," said Garofalo, scratching the back of his neck.

"Something is missing!" said Mary.

"The ring of Thoth, It said it would be found by the chosen one," said Seth's father.

"My guess is the terrorists have the ring, right?" said Dr Mubarak, now looking over at Seth's father for the first time. He had not looked at him at all since they arrived.

"No, If you read my book you know the ancient text clearly describes the chosen one as a child of 13 from the bloodline of the gods." Said Seth's father, excitedly.

"Maybe they don't know about the ring," said Professor Wilson.

"OK, so we know where they are, but how do we get those children out of there safely?" said Mary.

Everyone looked around at one another as if expecting someone else to answer Mary's very urgent question.

"I know the tunnels like the back of my hand, and there's a hidden way in, a small tunnel that runs from the worker's village. The tunnel connects with this passage here." Dr Mubarak drew an imaginary line from point to point.

"Which is well away from this area, where they seem to be occupying," said Seth's father.

"We need a distraction to get the kids out. I'm sure they are being guarded."

"That's easy enough, I guess we are the distraction," Seth's father said.

"What do you mean?" said Dr Mubarak.

"We tell them we have the ring and will bring it to Giza. While they're dealing with us, Garofalo and his boys over there will get the kids out safely. Then the strike team goes in and finishes the job!" Said Seth's father. "Pretty simple!"

Garofalo raised his eyebrow and lifted his hands, clapping soundly 3 times.

Mary gave a faint, unconvincing smile.

"Couldn't have said it better if I tried," said Garofalo. "Perfect." His look was quite a bit more serious now.

"Let's stop wasting time and get my son out of there!" Said Seth's father.

Chapter Forty Nine

"L*ist ye, O man, to my voice,*
     telling of pathways to Light,
showing the way of attainment
when ye shall be One with the Light."

WHAT IS DONE IN THE DARK

The room fell away and was replaced by a great city of stone, marble and gold. Wondrous gardens were in every direction. The people were dressed in all sorts of finery. He could see feasting and sport and merrymaking with wine and beer.

IN AN INSTANT, A BLACK wind came from the North. It bore down carrying a face of evil as it came closer and closer. The people panicked and were sorely afraid. They cried out and looked to the gods to save them to form the black wind.

But, the gods were silent, and the gods abandoned the people who had for 450,000 years worshiped and loved the gods.

The people watched in horror and despair as the gods abandoned the temples, and cities fleeing into their sky boats to leave the Earth.

He looked to the East, and the sky had been blotted out by a tremendous black storm, an evil wind with the odor of death that made his stomach turn. Instinctively, Seth turned and ran.

He ran as fast as his legs could take him, but it wasn't enough. His eyes burned and his skin crawled as the evil wind drew closer.

Vomit rushed from his throat and out his nostrils, pain gripping his abdomen as he buckled over. He fell to his knees. The great cloud was upon him. He closed his eyes.

"You're not dreaming, boy," Seth heard a voice say. It sounded to him like it was in the cell itself, The same feeling he got on the plane flight to Cairo.

He felt something was watching him, and he was sure of it this time.

"They will come for you soon. I am here to work the deep magic. The magician desires your heart most of all, choose one!"

"Chosen one? I'm not a chosen one. What the heck is going on?" Seth looked around frantically, trying to pinpoint where the disturbingly frightful

Oracle was coming from.

"This is not in my head," Seth said to himself. He thought of his father and mother and how much he wished they were here now. Suddenly, Seth's limbs went stiff. He couldn't move a muscle. His eyes were open, and he could see and hear, but it was as if he was suddenly paralyzed by some unseen force seizing control of his limbs.

He felt a massive weight crushing down on his chest. A figure, all black except its red eyes and long white fangs, could be seen. It was like looking at a black outline of an enormous and frightening beast.

It hissed and growled and mocked Seth. He wanted to scream, but nothing came out. He began to panic uncontrollably in his mind. His body wasn't responding no matter how hard he tried to move or speak.

The creature's black claws raised up and took him by the neck, coldly choking him slowly. It laughed a hideous laugh and dripped foal mucus on Seth's face as it laughed

The creature was sheer terror to look upon. Seth began shouting and crying for dear life. Fear gripped his heart and mind completely. He was ready to give up, but as suddenly as it came, the creature vanished.

Seth struggled to inhale and coughed and coughed, spitting up unpleasant things into his hand.

"Oh, my god," he sat up and cried for a moment, feeling overwhelmed by his experience. He'd never felt so helpless and afraid in his whole life. He steeled himself and wiped his eyes dry.

"Seth is that you?" said a voice.

"Adenesh, is that you?" said Seth. He listened very carefully this time.

"Seth, yes, it's me. Where are we? What is going on?" she shouted.

Seth realized the sound was coming from the food door. He went and sat in front of the door and opened the food tray slot.

"I don't know. Are you OK?" He could hear she was overwhelmed with fear. He knew he would have to be strong to make her feel better.

"Seth, I'm really scared!" she said, speaking louder this time, as she too had opened the food slot to speak. Her voice created a deep echo down the chamber.

"Seth, Adenesh, It's Elle. I'm down here. Can you hear me?" she shouted.

The voices of the children shouting and crying filled the chamber.

"Guys, guys, everyone shut up!" Seth shouted with all his strength through the food slot. He nearly strained his vocal cords.

He covered his mouth and coughed a bit, then carefully wiped his hands on his shirt.

The chamber was quiet.

He opened the slot again and looked around. He could see several cell doors on one side of the hallway, and from the direction he heard the shouting, he assumed there must be more cells on either side.

He moved closer and used one eye to spot a large wooden door at the end of the hall. He waited.

"Oh man, thank you, god!" he thought to himself. He expected guards to come rushing in to torture them for making too much noise.

"The last thing I remember was being in the tomb and hearing a hissing sound like riot gas canisters. I saw Adenesh fall. I don't remember anything after that," said Seth

"We've been kidnapped? What? Heck no!" Said Rhonda, trying to whisper best she could.

"But why?" Seth heard Elle say from across the hall from the cell next to Adenesh.

"I don't know, but whoever did is coming back, and we'd better find out what they want," he whispered, still keeping his eye on the wooden door.

"Dear Sweet, Mother of Jesus, what is happening!" said Elizabeth. She was in the cell closest to the main wooden door. Elizabeth's soft voice went unnoticed, and the children continued muttering different ideas of why they were being held captive and by whom.

Without warning, the heavy wooden door swung open, and the creature entered the room, still dressed in black robes. The black priest held a large decorative sword in one hand and a glowing glass crystal ball in the other hand, that lit the entire room. He stood in the middle of the hallway. Behind him, 12 men dressed in black robes entered, chanting sacred rites that Seth recognised from the key of Solomon.

"The Dark Brotherhood!" Seth thought to himself. Seth remembered his mother telling him of the power of the Dark Brotherhood, a secret shadow organization composed of dark magicians

From an early age, Seth felt the occult pull of magic, Freemasonry, the Golden Dawn, and the Illuminati, and other secret societies. Seth already knew a lot about the various magical systems and their practices.

The sound was louder now. Seth pushed his fingers deep into his ears, hoping to mute some of the sounds which were becoming completely unbearable. All at once, the chanting stopped, and the room fell silent once more.

There was a long pause.

Seth could no longer see around the room. One of the black-robed men was standing directly in front of his door, blocking his view.

They did not move or speak.

Without warning, the black-robed magicians lifted their wands with their left hands, pointing them directly toward the cell doors.

"Transfer my soul into this vessel. Let me not have to wrestle. Make it easy, make it fine. Let these bodies become mine."

"Transfer my soul into this vessel. Let me not have to wrestle. Make it easy, make it fine Let All body become mine."

"Transfer my soul into this vessel. Let me not have to wrestle. Make it easy, make it fine. Let this body become mine."

Without warning, Seth's body was violently seized by a frightening invisible force. He was suddenly compelled to stand up straight, hands down by his side.

The cell door opened before him. In the doorway stood the magician, and pointed directly at Seth.

He tried to move, but his body did not respond. The magician had taken control of his body.

Keeping the wand pointed at Seth, the magicians made a series of strange gestures, and Seth's body responded, leading him out of the cell.

He fell in line along with the other children, each led and controlled by one of the robed magicians.

Using their powerful magic wands, the magicians led the children out of the chamber and into a long tunnel shaft. Seth could see no torches, lanterns or candles. The light came from some unknown source.

Seth thought about his father. He wondered if he would ever see his father again. The professor and the police have to be looking for them.

"How will they find us? What if the bad men killed all the adults when they took us?" He thought to himself.

Surprisingly, Seth was able to move his eyes to look around. He wondered why his eyes remained unaffected by the spell.

"Think, Seth, think," he thought to himself. His father had always joked about his mother being a witch.

Seth had learned a great deal about magical arts from his mother. He had seen some success, experimenting with magical training his mother had shown him before she died.

She had promised Seth she would teach him many secrets once he reached the age of 13. She told him magic was in his blood, and he was special.

"The gods have a plan for you, Seth," she used to say all the time, especially whenever he was feeling down.

The creature Stern was strangely silent and seemed to glide across the smooth, luminous limestone floor as he led the procession through the tunnels toward the Great Pyramid, or Omni path as it was known in the old times before the great wars.

Seth could hear his own heart beating in his chest. He thought about Adenesh. He saw the terror in her eyes looking at him from the small slot in her door.

He heard a voice in the head.

"Remember your dreams. Everything you need is inside you. Fear not, and remember, same as above, so below," it said.

Then the voice was gone.

What exactly, Am I supposed to remember? Seth thought to himself.

He remembered his mother saying more than once during his lessons.

"All magic is limited; all magic can be broken,"

"Think Seth, think," he said to himself. "

The procession reached the end of the long passage. In front of them was a false door surrounded by magical writing along its borders, gold inlay covering the wooden door from floor to ceiling.

Stern knelt before the great door.

"Hail, O ye who make perfect souls enter into the House of Ra make ye the well-instructed soul of Ra the dwelling of thy servant, whose word is true, to enter in and to be with you in the House of Marduk."

There was a massive flash of blue light that engulfed the chamber. The false door transfigured and gave way to a broad, dark pathway.

The priest led the children forward, using their magic wands to guide them through the doorway and into the darkness.

Unfortunately for Seth, the last thing he saw was Adenesh, a fountain of tears pouring down her cheeks, just before everything went black again.

Chapter Fifty

"*L IGHT is thine ultimate end, O my brother.
Seek and find ever the Light on the way.*"
STARFIRE STARLIGHT

"I am Alpha & Omega, the beginning and the end, which is, and which was, and which is to come, the Almighty. I am the first and the last, who is living, and is dead, and behold I live forever and ever; and I have the keys of death and hell."

"Yes, of course, I understand completely," said Professor Wilson. He adjusted himself several times in his chair, tapping his foot over and over. He looked at Mary, who was sitting in his office recliner speaking to Asim's father, whom best he could tell, was giving a severe Mary a dress down.

He could see the expression on her face each time she was forced to move the phone away from her ear, to get a break from the extremely loud shouting, and sometimes vulgar language spewing from the other end of the line.

He and Mary had been on the phone speaking with the parents of each of the children for the past two hours. Understandably, their reactions were difficult to contend with.

Professor Wilson did his best to remain as sympathetic and hopeful as possible. After all, the children had been kidnapped on his watch.

"We are working with the authorities, who assure us the children will be returned unharmed," said Professor Wilson.

"I understand you want to come, but the police are telling us that would be unwise, as to compromise the safety of the children. We don't want to do anything to put the children in any further danger of reprisal from these vicious terrorists," he said as calmly as he possibly could to the panicked, sobbing mother crying and wailing uncontrollably into his earpiece.

"Miss, I assure you the police and the federal authorities have the situation under control," said Professor Wilson. "Yes, Yes," Again he adjusted himself in his chair.

"I'm ruined." He said to himself. "Yes, sir, he's right here," said the professor.

He handed the phone to Agent Garofalo, who had been sitting in front of him listening intently to the professor's conversation with the billionaire oil tycoon who threatened to have professor Wilson's head if anything happened to his only son and heir.

His throat was tightly clenched, and his breathing grew short. He looked up and then slightly turned away from everyone, trying to shield his adverse reactions.

The professor took a deep breath, offered a few more apologies and ended the call with a cordial smile and glimmer of his pearly white teeth.

Garofalo handed the professor his phone back, head down and deep in thought.

His phone buzzed in his pocket.

"Excuse me, I gotta take this," said agent Garofalo. He turned and stepped out of the room.

"I've finished reviewing the most recent satellite imaging we got from Garofalo's people." Said Seth's father.

He placed the photos on professor Wilson's drawing board in order.

"We have 12 signatures here, and then in these areas, we have signs of movement— and eight to 13 images."

"Those must be the children," said Mary.

"The heat signatures mean they are still alive, thank god," she thought to herself. She breathed a sigh of relief.

"Yes, we can assume this is where our children are being held," said Seth's father.

"There is an anti-chamber connection right here," he said. He pointed again to the right center of the thermal image.

"There doesn't seem to be any activity from the terrorists at this particular entrance point," said Garofalo. He hung up his cell phone as he re-entered the room and the discussion."My team is already in place." We will be going in as the bait, but no one is getting out unless those children are released unharmed. I assure you we will use full force without prejudice.

The room was utterly silent for a moment.

"I say, Ryan, do you have any of the good bourbon left?" asked Dr Mubarak, folding his hands in front of his chest.

"I do believe I do," said Professor Wilson.

"I'll take one of those too, bartender!" said Mary. She crossed her legs and folded her arms above her head.

"What is happening?" she thought to herself, and slowly rolled her eyes.

"Make mine a double!" said Garofalo.

"We just got the call from the terrorists. They are calling themselves the Order of brotherhood of the Dragon. They want the box delivered tonight. They are demanding professor Wilson bring it alone," said Garofalo. He rubbed his chin and continued.

"They say if they see anyone else they will kill all the children. There will be an unmarked van to take the professor and the box to the children where the exchange will take place."

"Doesn't that mean my father has to go in there, basically the lion's den alone," said Mary, her face full of displeasure, but still holding some sense of rationality. She stood up out of the comfortable chair and pulled her long black hair back over her head in absolute frustration.

"Look, my men will be everywhere, and we have full, long-range surveillance already on the entire area. Nothing can move in or out of that area without us seeing it," urged Agent Garofalo, hoping to reassure Mary of the plan.

Mary sat back down in the chair quickly grabbing her drink.

An iPhone on the table began to ring.

"That's mine!" said Dr Mubarak. He sat down, looked at his drink and picked up the cell phone to answer it.

"Excuse me for a moment," He said, looking around the room. He took a few steps back and stood in the corner of the room, watching as the others continued in conversations, discussing the children and addressing each parent's concerns.

"Hello, this is Dr Mubarak, he said

"Washington, DC tonight. Your flight is booked, a car is waiting downstairs." The caller hung up.

Mubarak very slowly placed his cell phone into his pocket. He looked around the room and smiled politely.

"I'm afraid I have another emergency I must attend to at once!" said Dr Mubarak, no longer smiling, but appearing confidently sober.

"Is everything all right, Dr Mubarak? You look troubled?" Said Mary.

"She's right. Who was that?" asked the professor. "What can be more important than what's going on here?" He asked.

"I'm afraid. It's extremely important and very personal. I wish I could say more," said Mubarak. He looked at his watch and then back at the professor.

"My car is waiting for me downstairs. I will contact you as soon as I can." And with that, he left the professor's study and headed to the Cairo airport.

As he got into the limo, He reached into his suit pocket and pulled out a small, shiny object. He stared at it for a few minutes as the limo sped down the road towards the airport. Clenching his fist around the object, he closed his eyes and began to pray in Arabic.

"A`ûdhi bi-kalimâti Llâhi tammat illati la yajawizuhunna barrun wa la fâjir

"min sharri ma yanzilu min as-samâ'i

"wa mâ ya`ruju fîhâ

"wa min sharri mâ dharâ'a fil-ardi

"wa mâ yakhruju minhâ

"wa min sharri fitan il-layli wa fitan in-nahâr

"wa min sharri tawâriq il-layli wan-nahâri

"illâ târiqan yatruqu bi-khayr

"ya rahmân

"Driver, how long before the airport?" Asked Dr Mubarak, looking down at his watch.

"Should be able to get you there in about 25 minutes more or less, sir. Are you in a hurry? I know a shortcut, if possible, no?" said the very neatly dressed and quite well-mannered driver.

"No, please, take your time," said Dr Mubarak.

"I'm not in any rush," he thought to himself.

Chapter Fifty One

S ERVING TWO MASTERS
"The Secret Doctrine (Ancient Wisdom) teaches the progressive development of everything, worlds as well as atoms."

G-10 EMERGENCY SUMMIT, Geneva Switzerland

The night was quite cold but mildly pleasant for the season, General John Smitherson thought to himself as he entered the orate 5-star restaurant known as Le Chat- Botte, famous for its excellent French cuisine and outstanding Diamond service. He was promptly greeted by a smiling, and somewhat pleasant to look at young hostess.

"I'm meeting Mr Dottington. We should have a private table reversed," he said dryly to the smiling, pretty hostess.

"She's a piece of ass," he thought to himself. "I Bet she's a lot of fun, in the right situation!"

"Yes, please follow me," she said with a thick French accent. —The hostess had on a tight black dress and long black heels. A real looker, he thought to himself.

She led him into a small room where a table for two had been set off to the corner of the room.

Lord Dottington was already seated and having a glass of wine. There was a smell of fresh baked warm bread coming from a covered basket at the center of the table.

The hostess pulled out a seat for the general, who was dressed in civilian clothes— A simple blue suit and a red tie. His short buzz cut was freshly cut, and he was newly shaved.

He felt more comfortable in uniform, but he wanted to blend in as best he could, he didn't wish to draw too much attention to himself.

"May I suggest you try the Sommelier Vincent Debergé, John? It's quite brilliant," said Lord Dottington. He too was wearing a suit, but Lord Dottington's outfit was clearly handmade and tailored to fit, cut from the most beautiful fabrics. But if one didn't know the difference, what did it matter?

"This one definitely could see the forest for the trees," Dottington thought to himself as he stood up and shook the personality-challenged general's hand.

The two men shook hands for a few moments longer casually passing cordial greetings.

"Have a seat," said Lord Dottington.

They both sat down at the same time. They both adjusted themselves as if to settle in for a long journey.

"Dottington looked at the hostess, making eye contact.

"Send us another bottle of the Sommelier Vincent Debergé, and tell the waiter we will let him know when we are ready to order," he said.

"Oui, mousier," said the hostess, still smiling blankly as she turned to walk away from the table. She closed the white, wooden, double glass-paned doors as she made her exit.

"So, generally what was so urgent that you called me for an unscheduled meeting of our two, shall we say, departments, my old friend," said Dottington as he took a long sniff of the elegant glass of wine he was enjoying. "Divine," he whispered to himself.

"It's the Eagle. It has become a clear and certain danger to the G.A.N.A Treaty" said General Smitherson. He hadn't touched his glass, his hands resting in his lap. He was in his late 50's, with solid gray sideburns and jet black hair. He had thick, bushy eyebrows and a large scar on his left cheek caused by piece shrapnel he got during his time in the Gulf war.

"In what way exactly is it a danger, General?" Dottington slowly set his glass on the table and pushed it away from himself a few centimeters, then folded his hands on the table

"My informers are telling me the Eagle wants to give full disclosure in the morning at the press conference," said General Smithson.

"What are you going to do about it, General?" said Dottington.

"I'm going to have an agent take him out tonight. It will look like a terrorist plot. It is standard protocol."

"No, we can't have that. The Eagle still has a role to play just yet," said Dottington, staring the general straight in the eye, as if to bore straight through his head.

A minute went by as the general thought through his reply to Dottington's.

"I have a better idea," said Dottington. He unfolded his hands, picked up his glass of wine and took a long, smooth sip.

"Just lovely," He said. He rolled his eyes back in his head, overcome by the pleasure of a great-tasting wine.

"Tell your men to stand down. They can observe but not interfere or take any action."

"Understood?" he said.

"Loud and clear, said the general." He offered a hint of a smile, which for the hardened military officer was a feat in itself.

" Shall we eat then? I hear the steak is quite remarkable this time of the season!"

Chapter Fifty Two

T HE PAWN'S BREAK
"The river needs to take the risk
of entering the ocean
because only then will fear disappear,
because that's where the river will know
it's not about disappearing into the ocean,
but of becoming the ocean."
-Khalil Gibran

GIZA UNDERGROUND COMPLEX

It was just before 11 p.m. when the professor was picked up outside his office by the unmarked car with no visible license plate or registration tags of any kind. The driver wore a dark green military jacket, cargo pants and a pair of desert commando boots. Not a big fellow, his eyes told a gruesome story that the professor's eyes did not care to view.

Without warning, the professor was pushed into the back of the van by two oddly dressed terrorists dressed in mix-matched military uniforms. They covered their faces with traditional Egyptian headdresses, noses and mouths covered up. The professor realized his assailants had been hiding out of sight near the bushes along the building itself.

"Where are you taking me," he said, trying to maintain his balance getting off the floor of the empty van. He reached over to the small bench running along either side of the van.

The men who had just kidnapped him were already seated on the other side of the van. They didn't answer.

Professor Wilson recognised the Russian-made AK-47's with extra clips strapped to the shoulder harnesses each of the men carried.

"Not a very believable terrorist," he thought to himself. He was careful to maintain eye contact with the armed men. "More likely paid mercenaries." He held the box tightly to his chest as tightly as he could.

"You can let your employer know I have the box containing the missing ring. All we want are the children out safely." He gave a gentle smile and tapped the lid of the box with his fingers a few times.

He ignored the impulse to scratch the persistent itch he was feeling for the last 20 mins. It was his right shoulder where Garofalo's people injected him with a microscopic tracking device. "I told them I had sensitive skin." He thought to himself before giving in, and just for a second, he reached across his chest to scratch his shoulder vigorously.

The van reached its destination after what seemed like an eternity. Finally, the professor could feel the van slowing down. "Definitely in the sand," he thought to himself.

One of the gunmen spoke.

"Put this on now," He held out a black hood and gestured to take it and put it over his head.

The other guard pointed his weapon toward the professor's chest.

"Hold on, I'm putting it on, can't I take my hat off first," the professor said quickly. His hands were shaking.

One he had the hood on completely, the men opened the door from the inside. They helped the now-blind professor out of the back of the van and led him down a long hallway for about 200 meters, he estimated.

When they reached the bottom of the slope, they stopped, and he was then led forward to an area where the ground levelled out.

The air was thick and hot. He could hear the sounds of the city faintly in the distance. He could feel the natural sand under his boots.

One of the gunmen had taken the box from him while getting out of the van and was now carrying it, as he followed them close behind.

"Welcome professor Ryan Wilson."

The gunman that had been guiding the professor reached up and removed the professors' hood.

Professor Wilson looked up as he put on his glasses. His hair was all over the place from wearing the hood.

"The man speaking was older than he expected, with blond hair and hazel eyes. He was an average build and dark complexion.

The robed man gestured to the gunman holding the box.

"Are my students unharmed?" ask the professor, his eyes now adjusting to the dimly lit room.

"What is my task now, Lord Therin?" said professor Wilson as he bowed and gave the secret sign of the Brotherhood of Darkness.

"You shall be rewarded, welcome new apprentice. You shall have dark wealth and lustful desires of all matter, long life and power— a dark gift for your service, and loyalty to the brotherhood.

"Therin gave a dark and sinister smile to the professor. " How delicious! He betrays his only daughter," Therin thought to himself.

Two black-robed brothers entered the room. Therin handed them the box and gave them instructions.

"Begin the invocation." He handed a black robe to professor Wilson, his eyes now glowing bright red.

"Welcome home, brother!" he said as he grinned and put his hand on the professor's now hooded shoulder.

Chapter Fifty Three

L IARS OF TRUTH
    "Let them be as dust before the face of the wind. And let the Angel of the Lord scatter them. Let all their ways be darkness and uncertain. And let the Angel of the Lord persecute them."

CIA CENTER

Mary sat in a reception area overlooking the control room floor of the CIA field operations center.

"I Never thought there was a place like this lurking underground outside of Cairo," she said, speaking to Scth's father and Agent Garofalo, who had just re-entered the reception area.

"That's why we're the CIA Black Ops, Ms Wilson," said Garofalo.

She smiled back. "What a wise guy," Mary thought to herself.

"Mr Strange," she said.

"Call me Abraham," said Seth's dad.

"I was just thinking, really." She adjusted her blouse. "In all the confusion, you didn't tell us what you are doing in Cairo," She smiled just slightly. "And why were you at the dig site? Your son never mentioned you were in Egypt,``said Mary.

Garofalo noticed Mary's line of questioning was bordering on highly suspicious. He decided to listen carefully.

"That's interesting," Abraham thought to himself. He turned in his chair to face Mary squarely.

"I was asked to come here by your father. He said it was urgent."

Seth's father used his right thumb to scroll through his messages. "Here's the text," he said, handing her his cellphone.

Mary read the text and looked surprised.

"I don't understand." She paused and reread the message. "Why didn't he tell us about contacting you?" she said.

"I got a message from my son as well five days ago." She handed him his phone back. He quickly pulled up a string of photos; Seth had sent off the tablet and of the interior of the tomb.

Mary was utterly shocked and tried her best to hide the sudden eruption of anger she felt boiling in her stomach. She didn't like liars and she especially didn't like being betrayed.

"We told them no cameras and no texts," she whispered angrily.

"How did they get pictures of the tomb in the dark?" Mary thought silently to herself, throwing her hands on both of her womanly hips. She could see Seth's father was just as surprised as she was about what exactly was going on here.

" Well, I didn't believe it at the start. I figured he was a wise guy— and if you met my son, that's pretty understandable. But when I got the urgent text from your father, I took the next flight out here soon as I could," he said.

"A lot is going on, it sounds like to me," said Agent Garofalo. "And some of it sinks." He looked them both up and down.

"What do you think it means?" said Seth's father.

"I got a few ideas, but right now we got movement inside the chambers." He pointed to the monitor mounted on the wall. "The infrared is showing moments everywhere. We think we located the children!" Said Garofalo.

Chapter Fifty Four

"In all space, there is only ONE wisdom.
Through seeming decided, it is ONE in the ONE.
All that exists comes forth from the LIGHT,
and the LIGHT comes forth from the ALL."
BLACK INVOCATION

Professor Wilson looked at his watch, 11:45. He grinned and wiggled his flat round nose as he put on his black robe.

"I've waited a long time to wear this robe," he thought to himself. He felt a sense of triumph different from anything he ever felt before. He liked this feeling and wanted more. For him knowledge was power. Finally he would have access to unlimited knowledge and power.

He took off his glasses, raised his hood and entered the room. He followed the white circle on the floor and took his place next to Therin, the Heartless.

Professor Wilson, headed into the main chamber. "The Creation Chamber," he said quietly under his breath. Professor Wilson never shared his passions of the dark arts with anyone, not even his beloved daughter.

"Welcome, dark and worthy apprentice. Take your place behind me. I, Therin the Great, Master magician of The Brotherhood of Darkness and keeper of the sacred fire, come proudly before the inner circle. I accept this brother as his keeper, his life and his death." Therin raised his arms over his head and made many signs in the air. And then, out of nowhere came a frightening blade, red and glowing but not of any metal he recognised.

The room went silent and dark. Therin raised the sword and made the shape of a pentagram in the air in all four directions, and suddenly, the 12 children appeared in the chamber all lost in a deep sleep.

Though they could hear everything, they could not move. The children lay in crystal caskets covered in magical writing and Zodiac symbols. They were arranged in a circle in the middle of the vast chamber.

"Brother's So shall it be,

"DUGGA.DUGGA, DUGGA

"ZI KIA KANPA

"ZI ANNA KANPA

"ZI DINGIR ANNA KANPA

"Hear me, O Thou DUGGA

"Come to us by the powers of his Word and Will of Truest Darkness oh Great and powerful Dugga

"Open thy chest and show us the knowledge for Entering the Halls of Amenti,

"ZI KIA KANPA

"ZI ANNA KANPA

"UGGA.DUGGA, DUGGA MERCFUL DESTROYER

The rest of the brothers began to chant in unison. As the chanting very slowly became louder Seth and a few of the other children woke up.

"I can't move," Seth thought to himself. "We're still being controlled by the leader with the wand in his hand. Seth watched the black robes moving around him. They had begun slowly walking a circle around the children.

"DUGGA.DUGGA, DUGGA

"ZI KIA KANPA

"ZI ANNA KANPA

"ZI DINGIR ANNA KANPA

"Hear me, O Thou DUGGA

"Come to us by the powers of the Word and Will of Truest Darkness oh Great and powerful Dugga

"Open thy chest and show us the knowledge for Entering the Halls of Amenti,

"ZI KIA KANPA

"ZI ANNA KANPA

"UGGA.DUGGA, DUGGA MERCIFUL DESTROYER!

The black robes chanted until they were shouting out loud a horrible wailing noise that filled the chamber from end to end.

Then without warning, everything went silent , and the room went pitch black.

Seth was engrossed in panic, still locked deep in his mind. "What's that smell?" he thought to himself. "We're sitting ducks." A bright red and orange light formed outside the circle.

"We have come before you with the gift of the sulfur of the 12. Your majesty, DUGGA, master of space and time. In return, you promised the secret passage to travel through the Halls of Amenti that we may free our master and have our revenge on the usurpers!"

"The orange and red fire had taken the shape of an old man. You must take the chosen one to the Creation Chamber. His life force will reactivate the OmniPath and allow you to travel through the portal of Amenti in the galaxy of Sirius, where your master is exiled to." The old man said.

"Now give me the blood of the children, as we agreed. I hunger, and my patience is no more. Give me the children, or I will feed on you, magician."

All at once the black robes pulled out flaming red blades.

"No!" Seth screamed in his head as loud as he could and closed his eyes.

Suddenly, the floor beneath the room began to shake and rumble wildly. The black robes were thrown off balance. Before they were able to recover, a colossal tunnel began to open up in the middle of the Creation Chamber.

"What is happening?" Seth thought, still unable to move. The magician still held their powerful wands.

Seth watched the magician turn toward the opening to see the Knights of Agharta coming rushing into the chamber, swords in hand. Another tunnel opened, and then another. The black robes were surrounded.

"I am Prince Atrea, crown prince of Agharta. In the name of the EA, you will surrender the seed of our lord Enki, or you shall all face death this very hour." He pointed a strange-looking, crystalline-like device at the magician.

None of your magic tricks will work with the nulling crystal present. You will hand over Enki's seed at once.

Therin said nothing. He knew his fate was already sealed. Desperately the other magicians

began furiously waving their magic wand in the air, speaking death formulas, but to no effect.

All at once, the children were released from the dark spell that bound them to the altar tables.

The red demon shaped like and the old man began to howl violently in every direction.

"Save the children, my knights!" shouted Prince Atrea!

Seth was in a terrible state of panic and confusion. He could not believe what was happening around him.

"This has to be a dream, he thought." This can't be real, he said out loud to himself this time.

He saw the one called Atrea running toward him. The black robes now had swords and were attacking the knights in white. There was slashing and blood tossing onto the floor.

"Seth!" screamed Klaus, who was jumping toward him. Instantly he saw the creature Stern, who had been watching from the shadows, heading directly for Seth, holding a long red and white dagger. It was too late for Seth to react. He waited for the blade flying toward his heart.

"Seth!" he heard Klaus cry out again as the poisonous blade was stopped by the sizeable muscular frame of Klaus

The force knocked both Seth and Klaus to the ground.

"Klaus!" Seth screamed. He saw the blood flowing from his chest. Seth didn't know what to do.

He looked around. The black robes were in fierce hand-to-hand combat with their rescuers.

The other children were screaming. Some were not moving; he could not tell if they were dead or alive, but there was blood everywhere. "What's this?" He looked down and noticed all the blood in the room was flowing toward the red old man. He was on all fours, licking wildly at the floor, howling and drooling, his eyes black as midnight.

A hand reached down. "Come with me, the seed of Enki. Today is not your day to die. You will live to fight another day."

Seth said nothing, he was in shock. Atrea picked up the small boy and quickly handed him off to one of his brave knights.

"Get as many of them to safety quickly. I'll hold them off."

The tunnels the knights entered through began to close as they were making their escapes.

"Stern, I should have finished you a long time ago. Atrea removed his royal crown and white cloak.

"Yes, you should have, White Prince of Thieves." Stern removed his red rope to reveal shining black armor underneath. He held grip tightly around the hilt of the glowing sword. It was forged of the indestructible black steel of Nibiru's fire mountains.

"Abducting innocent children for your insane dream of releasing your master. "You and your kind are but the bastards that should have been exterminated long ago."

"I shall have the privilege of finishing you personally, prince of fools." He raised his sword and smiled fearlessly, before lowering his eyes and focusing his strength for battle.

The room was in sheer chaos, Atrea could see his knights escaping through the rapidly closing magic tunnels they used to enter the Creation Chamber.

"Only one of us will walk away from this night, monster," Atrea said forcefully.

The two demi-gods circled each other near the edge of the gaping hole in the floor. The old man in red crouched and watched as it drank from the blood still flowing into its mouth.

Around them, many knights had fallen, and a third of the priests were left dead on the floor.

He could see at least 3 of the children still and lifeless on the floor, "Which meant at least more than half were safely on their way to his father.

"With honor, I gladly taste death," He thought to himself. He was surrounded with no way out. He gripped his sword tightly, and with a roar, he charged forward.

Chapter Fifty Five

"*Forth were WE formed after our order: THREE, FOUR, FIVE, SIX, SEVEN, EIGHT—NINE.*"

CODE BLACK

CIA BLACK OPS HEADQUARTERS, CAIRO

"Sir, we should send in the strike team. There's a massive amount of movement on my screens. There appears to be another unit of could-be soldiers entering the chambers," Garofalo pleaded with the director.

"Sir? What are your orders?" said the assault team sergeant, who was watching the monitors light up all over the place.

"Send in the strike team now. Get those kids out of there right now, sergeant!"

"Yes, Sir!"

"All positions, you have the green light. I repeat you have the green light, operation Desert Pike. Go, go, go!" said the sergeant.

Mary and Seth's father watched the viewing monitors in complete disbelief. The screen was littered with red bleeps running all over the room.

"My god, what is happening in there?" said Mary, holding her hand over her mouth and trying not to bite her nails anymore than she already had, surprised and a bit confused at the site.

"Something bigger than all of us is happening," Seth's dad thought to himself.

Seth's father grabbed Garofalo by the arm. "You gotta get my son out of there!" He shouted.

"We are, Mr Strange. The strike team is three minutes away from the main chamber."

Mary started to cry. She grabbed Abraham's hand, and he pulled her close to comfort her.

"He's going to be OK, They'll get them all out of there."

Chapter Forty Six

"Whatever thou resolvest to do, do it quickly. Defer not till the evening what the morning may accomplish."—Unto Thee I Grant

THE ANGELS OF DEATH

Smoke and fire were exploding all around them.

The last of the priests were gathering around Prince At Rea.

"The demon will offer a sweet reward for your blood, prince," said Stern.

Before another word was spoken, they lunged at one another, swords flying, crashing metal to metal. Huge sparks of emerald green and blood red lighting exploded with each strike.

"He's much stronger than I remember," the prince thought to himself.

"You are weak, prince. I have grown more powerful than ever!" said Stern.

"You are a fool not to believe the human magician will turn on you soon enough Stern."

"Soon no power will be able to stop me, prince. I will be like the gods, and you will be dead!"

"Stern charged at the prince again, this time cutting deep into the prince's side with his blade.

"AGGHG" The prince cried out in pain, holding his side. His blue blood splashed to the floor with a thump.

The prince fell to one knee. He looked up and saw the smile on the demon's face.

The blow came in one clean cut. Stern separated the prince's head from his shoulders with one strike. The blood poured like a fountain.

The old man jerked and moaned, growled and licked and rolled around like a pig in mud. The demon transformed into a snarling beast, an indescribable, disgusting creature covered in blood.

Stern looked down at the now lifeless body of Prince Atrea. He took his sword and staked the now dead prince's head on the end of it.

"Disappointing," he said, looking into the dead eyes of the once-great prince. "A pity, not what I expected at all," Stern said, disappointed with the ease of such a long-awaited victory.

Just then Stern heard explosions going off, and the central chamber entrance was blown to pieces. Gas canisters were tossed in from every direction.

"Three squads of Black Ops special forces stormed the chamber.

"United States CIA. Get down, don't move."

The soldiers circled the room, but as the smoke cleared, they could find nothing. The Hostiles were all gone.

"Commander, this is Eagle Rescue 1," one of the soldiers spoke into his communication device. The area is secure, but there is no sign of an enemy."

"What of the hostages?" Garofalo asked.

"Looks like we have 3 children down, No sign of the other children."

What about my father, Mary shouted into Garofalo's phone.

"We have the professor." He seems to be a little shaken, but he's alive."

"Can I speak to him?" Mary wiped her mascara trying not to smear it too much.

"Mary, I'm OK," Said the professor on the phone. "They took the children. I tried to stop them but I couldn't."

"Are they still alive?" said Garofalo.

"I believe they were unharmed," said Professor Wilson.

"I'm so glad you're OK. I was so worried,``said Mary.

"Let's not worry about me. We have to save those children!"

"You are fortunate to be alive, professor," said Garofalo.

"Sergeant!" said Garofalo, speaking to the strike team leader.

"Yes, sir!"

"Secure the area. No one in or out, and I want a forensic team in there ASAP!" said Garofalo. "I want to know how they got out of there right in front of our noses."

"They must have had a backup escape route in play" replied the sergeant. "No one got past us, sir. My guess is they were gone when we entered, sir!"

"Search the entire area, sergeant, and clean up the mess. No traces, understand?" said Garofalo.

"Roger that!" said the sergeant.

"I'm on my way," said Agent Garofalo.

Chapter Fifty Seven

*"*I *am Sama Veda among the Vedas; I am Indra among the Devas; I am the mind among the senses; I am the consciousness in living beings."*

CLOAK AND DAGGER

"I think I can speak for all the gentlemen here: The situation could cause a financial crisis of the worst sort. We may be looking at serious consequences to the general public on a global scale," said the US president, Donald T. Johnson.

He was speaking to the G-10 emergency summit taking place in Geneva, Switzerland, which included the heads of the world bank institutions. Security surrounding the event was on high alert.

Lord Dottington loved hearing those words. Everything was just as the master had foretold. The world was nearly ripe for the pickings. He tried not to smile with a devilish grin.

We believe the central bank has been hacked. Billions of dollars are lost, backup files erased, systems going haywire. All trading and transactions have come to a halt. Lord Dottington couldn't help himself, so he released a faint glimmer of a smile; The room remained silent.

"These fools, thinking they were masters of the world? They are nothing, but pigs for slaughter, " Lord Dottington thought to himself. This time he couldn't hide his smile, the joy was too exquisite, and it also went utterly unnoticed.

One after the other, the elected officials, CEOs and bankers took the podium. There were cries of anger, accusations were levied at the Russian government as the suspected source of the massive security breach. Which Included thousands of personal emails from among high-level IMF and central bank officials.

Lord Dottington felt a buzz in his pocket and discreetly pulled his cellphone just enough to look at the incoming text.

"Fools!" He said to himself under his breath. He quickly wrote a reply to the disappointing text he just received. He cursed some more as he continued to type the message. He was turning red in the face as he responded.

"Is everything OK, sir?" Dottington looked up at the floor attendant staring at him. "Can I get you some water? You look quite red in the face sir.

"No!" He snapped, hastily putting his phone back in his pocket.

"Wait, yes, Bring me bottled water." He regained his composure and even smiled at the attendant.

"Of course, sir."

The attendant returned a moment later with a cold bottle of Evian and a glass, and he sat them both down next to Lord Dottington.

The US president was speaking to the global delegation.

"Gentlemen, freedom is our God-given right. But in times of chaos, we, the elected representatives of the people, must act on the people's behalf and restore order. The recent market global financial crisis has unleashed unprecedented looting and violence on a scale we have not seen before." Said the president.

"I know what I am suggesting is frightening for all of us, but we have all known this day could come. I don't believe now is the time to be timid. We must not hesitate to respond properly to this potential impending danger. I am firmly urging for martial law and a joint declaration of war against the Eastern Alliance."

Just then an aide stepped up to the podium and whispered in the president's ear. The president immediately left the podium without making the announcement concerning the alien alliance, which didn't surprise Lord Dotttington.

The British prime minister stood and announced his second to the president's motion. It was quickly followed by a round of cheers from the remaining delegates.

Lord Dottingham was the last to give his enthusiastic "aye." He reached back into his pocket to type out a short message. After sending his text, Dottington took a few steps away from the room and dialled an old friend.

The phone rang twice, and the gentleman answered.

Dottington whispered a spell under his breath, hung up and placed the iPhone back in his pocket, returning his attention to reviewing the speech he was scheduled to make in front of the world press corp and the heads of states of the EU, United States and international banking community.

Chapter Fifty Eight

"*From the centre where the Will of God is known Let purpose guide the little wills of men, the purpose which the Masters know and serve." -Arcane School*

THE REVENGE

WASHINGTON DULLES, AIRPORT, WASHINGTON D.C.

Dr Mubarak sat quietly at the concourse of Dulles International Airport. He felt unclean surrounded by Zionist snakes and mindless Americans devils. He was trying to remember why he was there. Part of him kept saying he was supposed to be somewhere else. And at that moment, his phone rang.

"Hello, this Dr Mubarak," he said into the earpiece he was wearing.

A voice spoke to him through the phone then hung up.

"Thank you, and goodbye," said Dr Mubarak. He hung up the phone and sat it down in the empty chair beside him. He was having tea and biscuits as he appeared to watch CNN on the overhead monitor—typical businessman prose— a custom he acquired during his years as a professor at Oxford.

He started thinking of his family and friends, the things he discovered throughout his career. He remembered the day he met his wife, how beautiful she was on that particular day. He looked into her eyes and saw the love of Allah. He thought of his children, and how they had changed the sort of man he thought he was. He thought about the unconditional love he felt for them, the kind of love he didn't know could exist.

Dr Mubarak took another sip of hot tea and finished his biscuit. He looked down at his suit, and remembered it was his best suit. He had it especially tailored in Italy during a visit to meet with the Pope. He was disgusted with the Vatican. He could feel the homosexuals all around him and the Idol worshiping infidels bowing their heads to pray to their false god sickened him the most. He never let it show

After returning to his hotel, he nearly vomited. He was a servant of Allah and did what must be done. He was comforted by that thought.

He finished his cup of tea and placed it in the trashcan nearest him.

That is when he stood up, adjusted his clothing and took off his glasses. His plane had just arrived, and the attendant was calling passengers for boarding.

He casually walked over to the flight customer service desk. The pretty Asian woman looked up at him and smiled. He smiled back but said nothing. He felt a feeling of peace come over himself and all the noise around him seemed to fall away in a waterfall of silence. He took a long, deep breath, and with both hands, he suddenly reached across the desk and grabbed her microphone, but before anyone could react, he put the microphone to his mouth and with a terrifying voice he shouted, "Allah Akbar, death to the whore of Babylon! I am death!"

It would be the last thing thousands of travelers on that day would ever hear.

He quickly dropped the microphone to the floor to free his left hand. The crowd of travelers stood by, curiously watching as Mubarak calmly pressed a small pin on his watch. Three-seconds later everything was engulfed by a flash of blinding white light and a thrust of tremendous force like a giant tidal wave.

Concrete, steel, plastic, and flesh, all at once melted like butter on a hot skillet.

There was no time for prayer or regret or even tears for the matter. 10 seconds later, everything had been obliterated by a compact undetectable nuclear device that was hidden in his pocket. Everything within a half-mile radius was turned to a pile of rubble and ash.

Chapter Fifty Nine

"L*ife and death, joy and sorrow, gain and loss; These dualities cannot be avoided. Learn to accept what you cannot change."*

IT ENDS IT BEGINS

CNN, Atlanta, Georgia

"For those of you heading to the Northeast, look for a beautiful weekend along the Atlantic shores!" said Steven Rivera, a CNN weather forecaster. He was about to continue when his producer suddenly shouted in his earpiece,

"There has been a terrorist attack of catastrophic proportions at Washington, D.C. Airport we're switching over to Bob Costa," said the segment producer.

"Ladies and gentlemen, this is a national emergency. A massive bomb has just gone off at Dulles airport. We will be switching to the president in Geneva as soon as we can.

"We have a team of reports on the ground in Washington. We have no idea of the death toll at this time, but we are getting reports it was a massive explosion, felt as far away as Williamsburg!"

"I think we have a live feed now. Let's go to Tara Jones, who is as close as we can get to the airport,``said the anchorman. "Tara, can you give us any information?" Are you close enough to see the extent of the damage to the airport?"

"Bob, we are about a good mile and a half from the airport. The police and armored vehicles have shut off all access to roads and aircraft from landing. From where I am, all we can see is a massive cloud of smoke and fire. It looks as if a nuclear bomb went off. Trees and buildings have been completely leveled, and everything is gone. There's a huge pile of rubble and smoke in the air. There's an intense level of heat coming from the direction of where the airport once stood. It's total devastation, Steven. In all my years of reporting in the Middle East, I have never seen nor imagined anything like this could happen. The loss of life must be in the thousands." Said Tara Jones. "I can see an emergency team coming toward us. I can't quite make out what they are saying."

"Everyone, please leave the area immediately. If you remain in this area, you will be exposed to lethal levels of radiation. Please do not panic. Return to your vehicles and your homes for further instructions, said the head of the emergency team.

"There is no need to panic. We are taking every step to ensure public safety. I repeat, please leave this area immediately and return to your homes, for your own safety. This is an emergency situation. Be advised the longer you stay in this location, the higher your risk of fatal exposure to deadly radiation."

This time, Tara and her camera crew could hear the men in the hazmat suits clearly. Tara's face suddenly went white. Her expression changed to one of concern, to fear and panic. Her instinct was to run as fast as she could and get as far away as quickly as possible. She closed her eyes and started taking deep breaths. She counted to 10 out loud, and let out a long deep breath, allowing herself to find the courage to remain professional.

To her surprise, her cameraman was still rolling live feed, with the camera again focused on her. She took another deep breath and continued reporting.

"Bob, we are being told the area is contaminated with lethal radiation. Several men in yellow radiation suits have arrived on the scene, and people who were standing by looking at the devastation are now being told to clear the area as calmly and quickly as they can. Clearly, this attack was on a nuclear scale. What this means to the US will be difficult to imagine. This could be the start of World War III."

"Thank you, Tara. We are all shocked, to say the least. Get to a safe area as soon as you can." Said Bob Costa. I have just been told we are going to switch to the G-10 Summit, where the president just finished speaking to enter an emergency session which had just been called in response to the World Bank Hack job.

"Let's go to the president now," said the news anchor.

"Today at 6:12 pm what we believe to be a small nuclear device was detonated at Washington Dulles Airport. Reports of the extent of the devastation are still coming in at this time. However, we have confirmation from satellite images, aerial photographs and eyewitness accounts on the ground that the airport has been completely destroyed.

This tragedy is on a magnitude incomprehensible to the civilized world. We express our most profound shock and abhorrence of this act of sheer terror and complete evil. We have received a videotape from the group calling itself the Brotherhood, claiming responsibility for this unholy act of evil and senseless mass murder of thousands of innocent American citizens.

"As a nation, our hearts go out to all the people of Washington DC.

The United States military is prepared to take immediate action against the perpetrators of this monstrous and senseless act of violence!

"I am now calling for a state of emergency and ask Congress to officially declare war and to take immediate action to retaliate against this unholy threat. We will hunt down every last one of these monsters and bring them to justice!" The President said as the entire conventions stood and applauded!

.

Chapter Sixty

" 'My father, the king of heaven and earth, made me famous in heaven and earth. My elder brother, the king of all the lands, gathered up all the divine powers and placed them in my hand."

THE COUNCIL OF SOULS

"The Nine will see you now Lord Thoth", said Thogoth, Thogoth The Mighty. Thogoth was tall as a tree and thick as a rhino. He had Golden eyes that could see in every direction all at once, nothing in his sight. He wore a long black beard over his thick, strong jaw. His arms were like tree trunks. Thogoth was a rightfully fearsome site standing before the entrance way in his golden armor.

Thogoth had one purpose and one destiny. He was the Keeper of the Council and Guardian of the Nine. Thogoth, The Mighty, has stood watch over the great hall leading to the Council of the Nine, since the beginning of creation. He was unchangeable and as fixed as the stars.

Thoth stepped forward and entered the great hall. The walls were luminesced light shown from every direction. The floor also glows and translucent emerald green. There were five on each side and two on the other side of the nine.

The Nine have no real shapes. They are more like looking at an outline of angel-like shape. The Nine were being of pure light. They have existed outside this reality from the beginning. The Nine were with the All from the foundation of the universe. They guided the will and the ways of the races of beings.

Thoth knew why he had been summoned by The Nine, but what he would do afterward he did not know. For the first time, in 100,000 years he did not know what to do. Thoth's normally stoic face uncharacteristically turned to a look of sadness. the normally stoic face uncharacteristically turned to a look of sadness.

Thoth entered the main hall slowly with his eyes looking downward as was the custom, until he reached the glowing circle of light that was before The Nine.

As the door behind him began to close The Nine began to speak silently without words; their forms vibrated and hummed as the thought energy filled the room like a cloud. The primary audience room was made of a luminescence crystal from floor to ceiling. The walls and everything within the chamber vibrated with the sound of the universe.

HE SAID NOT A WORD, as they continued to speak to him in the vibrating silence. After some time the vibrating stopped. Thoth stood silent for a moment staring at the nine, then he bowed his head and reluctantly uttered "So mote it be' in a faint whisper. As he turned the great door had already started to open. Thoth walked out, his heart heavy now filled with a deep sorrow he had not felt since he was human.

He had seen the passages of time and the unfolding of many wonders, and terrifying disasters. He had followed the progress of the race for thousands of years. He was there when the humans were given a gift of knowledge from the gods. Knowledge his father passed down to him. He recalled when the gods first devised "man" in their image. A little lower than the angels and just above a slave. Had he made the right decision?

Could he now find the will to do what must be done?

Thoth hurried down the grand hallway his mind now fixed on what he knew he would have to do. From the beginning of time, the watchers of the worlds were given the task of observing and recording the progress of the races of beings throughout the universe.

They were not to interfere at any cost lest they forfeit their existence. Thoth had kept this one great law for more than 25 thousand years. His mind and emotions are still for he knew he must conceal his intentions from his Masters.

As reached his chamber and closed the door behind him, and began to meditate on emptiness, until his mind was blank. With a way of his hand, he opened the great portable between the worlds to earth. The portal grew more substantial, and he stepped through.

He knew what he was about to do there could be no turning back, but he knew it was the only way. He must break his sacred vow, and make contact. How he would do so was another matter altogether. Thoth was a Guardian Watcher; he had taken the holy pledge to never directly interfere in the lawful evolution of the children of men.

To break his vow would mean his soul would be handed over to the Lord of Darkness where he would be a trap in the cycle of death and rebirth for a thousand years. He needed counsel from someone he could trust, and he knew precisely where he now must go.

Before stepping through, Lord Thoth called his faithful apprentice Amuth and told him of his dire concerns. Amuth wasn't sure how he should react to his master confession.

"Master, what does this mean?"

I do not know, but I know where to find the answers.

Epilogue

THY KINGDOM COME
    "The Secret Doctrine (Ancient Wisdom) teaches the progressive development of everything, worlds as well as atoms."

ONE HYDE PARK, LONDON England

Today had not gone as well as Lord Dottington had expected. He no longer had the children or their precious Starfire. But the blood of the prince satisfied the demon to work the deep magic, so for Dottington and the dark brotherhood, all was not lost.

The Omni-Path was operational and war was inevitable, but he still needed the boy to guide him through the Halls of Amenti.

He knew now the boy was the key to Enlil's weapons of terror and the Halls of Amenti. Eternal life was now within his reach, and with that thought, he was more than satisfied.

He took off his clothes and neatly placed them on his bed for his butler, slipping into his grand oak bed and making himself comfortable. Dottington laid there thinking for a few minutes more, then he reached over and cut off his Tiffany night lamp and went peacefully to sleep. In the darkness, something stirred in the corner of his room.

A black figure crawled from his magic mirror. It slithered across the room to the edge of Dottington's bed. It quietly climbed atop one of the four posts that adorned the beautiful king-sized bed. It sat there on the end of the magician's bed, silently watching the magician sleep and smiled with a hate filled devilish grin.

CHILDREN OF THE STARS SERIES:
　　Book Two: THE RED TOWER
　　Book Three: WAR MARKER
　　Book Four: THE MAGICIANS GAME
　　Book Five: ISIS RISING
　　Book Six: A RETURN TO EDEN

Don't miss out!

Visit the website below and you can sign up to receive emails whenever Houston Lee Andrews Jr publishes a new book. There's no charge and no obligation.

https://books2read.com/r/B-A-RRWBB-PJTRC

BOOKS 2 READ

Connecting independent readers to independent writers.

Also by Houston Lee Andrews Jr

Children Of The Stars
Children Of The Stars

Watch for more at https://www.facebook.com/cotsbooks.

About the Author

Houston Lee AndJr aka Saint Andrews, is a US Army military veteran, self-proclaimed die-hard punk rocker, and dance music producer... His creative genius and LBGTQ business entrepreneurship made him an insider of the American Rap, Dance, and Hip-Hop Music Industry. He spent over 20 years in the American music industry working with legendary promoters and music executives at tier-one music labels including multiple major chart-topping artists.

In 2008 he founded GLAM (gay and lesbian alternative magazine) which was the #1 LGBTQ music sic magazine in the US. The success of GLAM allowed him to interview and work with some of the biggest names in the LGBTQ world.

After leaving the music business Saint Andrews retired to London where he spent 5 years writing his memoirs, and his passion Children of the Stars. The idea for the book series came from 20-plus years of studying the history of religion and its esoteric and mystical origins. His journey led him to the tales of the Sumerian tablets and the Annuaki gods.

In this epic series, he attempts to tell the story of the Annunaki and how a race of alien beings came to earth in search of gold and created man as a slave race to serve and worship them as gods.

The book is written as a historical fiction action-adventure in the style of Harry Potter meets the Davinci Code.

Read more at https://www.facebook.com/cotsbooks.